The Straight Six

John Pasquarelli

The Straight Six

John Pasquarelli

National Library of Australia Cataloguing-in-Publication entry

Creator: Pasquarelli, John, author.

Title: The Straight Six / John Pasquarelli.

ISBN: 9780994367808 (paperback)

Subjects: Private investigators--Australia--Fiction.

Horse racing--Australia--Fiction.

Doping in horse racing--Australia--Fiction.

Corruption--Australia--Fiction.

Extortion--Australia--Fiction.

Detective and mystery stories.

Dewey Number: A823.4

Acknowledgements

Luigi and Raimonda
Guiseppe and Marie
Palmo
Leon
Leonard and Maud Nelson
'Dusty' Rhodes
Ray Guy
Jack Read
Michael Toby
BAS
John Tuson Bennett
Alan Jones
Ian Downs
Johnny Young
Martin Kerr
Bruce Ruxton
Honest Bernie
Keith McGowan
Tim Burstall

Prologue

The young bull elephant was uneasy and his senses were trying to assess if man was nearby. He stood in the clearing, the tip of his trunk moving back and forth like a metal detector while his ears oscillated like a satellite dish. The rest of the herd, mainly cows and calves, were waiting for a lead from their protector, in the shade of some light scrub. Then the bull gave an angry trumpet blast as he tried to shift part of his 4.5 tonne weight off his nearside front leg. Half-buried in his right shoulder an ivory poacher's spearhead had been there for a week. It had missed a major artery. The wound was was proud and scabby. A partly congealed track of pus and blood serum ran from the wound to his foot, feeding a clientele of frantic ants and ecstatic flies. The spearhead, made by an ivory poacher from the leaf of an old truck spring, had just missed a major artery. The huge muscles now filled a rifle's telescopic sight. Tim Gill took a deep breath, holding it and in a steady, easy movement squeezed the trigger. Like a mini-scud missile, the gas-propelled dart zeroed in on its target, delivering its warhead of almost four milligrams of etorphine hydrochloride. Suddenly the pachyderm didn't feel angry anymore. Curtseying as if on centre stage, he went down on his knees, He held there for a while until his weight forced his back legs to give way and with a wheezing sigh, slowly rolled onto his side.

'Thank Christ he's fallen on his good side,' Gill yelled into his walkie-talkie. 'Bring up the truck and Land Rover.'

Half a dozen native helpers came leaping and whooping through the scrub.

1

Setting up an awning over the downed beast, Dr Tim Gill, Veterinary Director of the Zimbabwean National Game Reserve, got to work on his patient. In no time the spearhead, honed from the leaf of an old truck spring, was out and the wound irrigated and closed.

One of Gill's assistants discharged three king-sized syringes of antibiotics into the elephant's hindquarters. The job was done.

'Christ, that elephant juice packs a punch,' the vet said to nobody in particular, as he bundled up his gear.

1985 was a successful year for him. Although he was looking forward to spending Christmas with his family in Edinburgh, he had a nagging feeling that someone somewhere would be up to no good with such a powerful drug.

***

Fast forward to New Year's Day 1987, and a big crowd of enthusiastic racegoers had gathered at the Ascot racetrack in Perth, Western Australia, to watch the centenary running of the feature race, the Perth Cup.

Rocket Racer, a four-year-old chestnut stallion by the New Zealand sire Balmerino, broke the hearts of his opposition by running like an automaton, winning the 3200 metre race by nine lengths, one of the most impressive and decisive performances in the history of the race.

Coming back to scale, Rocket Racer almost collapsed and had to be held up on his feet by attendants. Tachycardia had pushed his heart to race at 180 beats p er minute instead of the 110 beats a horse normally registers after a race. The normally red vessels of his eyes now matched his purple tongue.

The on-course vets worked furiously to save the horse's life by pumping twelve litres of saline drip into him and injecting drugs to slow his machine-gun pulse rate. A tiny, illegally administered dose of etorphine hydrochloride had transformed a better than average galloper into a flying machine that almost flew apart.

Millionaire property developer, race fixer and friend of premiers and prime ministers, Laurie Connell had brought off a coup. The big businessman boasted that six weeks before the race, he had bet $200,000 to $4000.

On the day of the race, he took $700,000 out of the betting ring. In true Connell style he shouted drinks for 1500 grateful sycophants in the member's bar to celebrate his win.

Rocket Racer was not subjected to any post-race blood or urine tests. The medication given the horse to save him would have rendered any subsequent drug testing useless, open to legal challenge.

According to the stewards, the horse's life was the first priority. Rocket Racer did not go on to equine glory in the eastern states. He returned to one of Laurie Connell's properties where he died under mysterious circumstances and was cremated – a strange funeral for a horse.

Australians have been going to the races for a long time. Seven horses from South Africa arrived on the First Fleet in 1788, most of them Arabs. In 1799, Rockingham, Australia's first known thoroughbred stallion, arrived in the colony from England. In October 1810, the first registered horse race was organised by officers of the 73rd Regiment and conducted on what is now Hyde Park, Sydney.

Down in Melbourne, Flemington was first raced on in 1840, the Victoria Racing Club was founded in 1853 and staged the first Melbourne Cup in 1861, the same year that the Australian Jockey Club and Randwick racetrack came of age. Bookmakers, the traditional villains on the horseracing stage, had a haphazard history before they were organised and regulated by state governments and the racing clubs.

Early colonial bookies wandered through race crowds, spruiking the odds and taking bets as they went. Welshing and taking the knock – not paying – was the order of the day. The pedigree of the quintessential Australian bookmaker can be traced back to three Englishmen: Joe Thompson, Robert Sievier and Sol Green.

These men brought drama and big betting onto the racetracks and glamourised the duel between the punters and the bookmakers.

Sievier pioneered the practice of hiring clerks and placing bags of pound notes around their necks, while he stood on one spot instead of moving around. In the 1920s, the showman, all-year-round surfer and bookie, Andy Kerr had the words 'Coogee Bunyip' emblazoned on his clerk's bag. Imagine the politically correct outrage in the committee rooms of today's race clubs if some wag turned back the clock and used the words 'Footscray Ferret' or 'Parramatta Perve.'

The tote (or totalisator) has been around since 1931. The equipment used in Australia was invented by George Julius, a New Zealander who was the head of the CSIR before it became the CSIRO. The early totes were operated by private concerns who paid their respective dues to the racing clubs and the government.

In 1958, Sydney Turf Club Chairman H.E. Tancred declared outright war on bookmakers by announcing a trial whereby all bookmakers would be banned at the inner-city Canterbury racetrack for seven midweek meetings, giving punters no choice but to bet with the tote. Tancred promoted the concept of spreading the increased wealth from turnover tax among owners and racegoers, which was good politics but he appeared to have had definite personal reasons for hating bookmakers. The trial was a glorious flop and the triumphant licensed bookies were granted a reprieve.

These days the racing industry is a huge employer, from those who grow horsefeed and breed horses to those who serve meals in the clubs and work the computers in the TAB. The allied jobs from the top of the pyramid to the bottom are myriad. The chief protagonists are the punters on one side and the bookies and the TAB on the other. Governments and their treasurers stand smugly back as they look forward to spending the huge rake-off in betting taxes.

If horseracing was outlawed tomorrow, a section of the Australian economy would plunge into chaos. It is part of the backbone of Australia's culture, defying the efforts of the chattering classes and animal rights groups to make it vulnerable to the cultural cringe and political correctness. The racetrack embraces all – whether they be black, white or tinted, baseball-capped or fezzed.

The ready access to cash money is the overpowering bait that attracts those with baser motives to the races. Betting rings have always been laundries for dirty money. Drug bosses and other criminals have given certain bookies cash and received in return a winning betting ticket for a ten percent or higher fee.

The TAB, which was created primarily to destroy SP (starting price) bookmakers who were considered a blight on the sport of kings and to fund the racing clubs, has ironically from the day of its creation been a de facto bank for drug dealers, prostitutes, big time tax cheats and all those who live out there on the fringe. Some of its branches are in places where no conventional bank has ever ventured.

When the TAB first established telephone betting accounts in 1961, there were no ID procedures for opening one, likewise for deposits over $10,000. When the banks instituted these controls and checks in 1988, the TAB followed suit but clever people with computers and the latest high resolution printers can create false ID for a price. Criminals and others seeking the security of anonymity have always been able to find sanctuary in bodgie bank and TAB accounts.

As long as the person depositing knows the TAB account number and the PIN number, no other details have to be given. What better way to bribe a politician, policeman or a sportsman than to anonymously deposit cash to his or her TAB account? What better place to hide black money? What better place to safely stash the proceeds from a bank hold-up? Debtors protecting cash reserves from exasperated creditors and spouses involved in family law conflict doing the same thing are all part of the TAB's varied clientele. Many of them have never bet on a horse. Life goes on.

*****

1

Driving on the Hume Highway from Sydney to Melbourne these days is just a little better than it was in the 1960s. Car drivers have to be very careful now of the trucks, more so when they are travelling in packs. The monsters of today, with their huge turbo diesel engines and finger-tip auto shifters, are like extraterrestrial transporters, especially at night, when they are lit up like Christmas trees and thundering along at 120 km/h plus.

The big convoys usually start running after midnight when most drivers have called it a day and have left the road clear for the big boys. When driving on the Hume, Jack Read usually called it quits at about 1 am and camped at a roadside rest area or made it to the nearest motel.

The other thing to be careful of on the Hume is the food. Meal stops are now at huge 24-hour service stations that make more money from food than they do from their fuel pumps. But in the good old days when the 'Spot Café' ruled the roost in country towns along the way, you could enjoy a good steak, eggs and chips with bread and butter and tea. The steak had a rind of good yellow fat and was properly seared, and the black sauce was genuine Lea and Perrin. The bread was fresh and white with a hard, charcoaled crust. The butter came as curled balls and the tea was brewed in a pot. Today, you get margarine shrouded in silver foil, likely to be rancid, and the teacup has a sodden bag drifting just below the surface like a turd off Bondi Beach.

With food like that, Read was sure that Bonzo, his five-year-old bull terrier, would think twice about having a go at it. The menus read like instruction manuals for growing stomach ulcers. Discerning restaurant critics are unlikely to venture into the culinary wastelands that flank the Hume.

Read was making good time and pulled in at a service station to top up the Range Rover and to call Peter Welsh and let him know that he was on time. Welsh had been in Papua New Guinea but he was now working for the Victorian Attorney-General's Department. Welsh was divorced, he could put up with Read and he lived in Carlton so it was a handy arrangement.

Read had started up Sterling Investigations in the mid-1980s in Sydney with another New Guinea hand, John Steele. Post-Independent PNG had been more than the two men could handle and they found themselves in Sydney at a loose end. A barrister mate suggested they speak to an insurance executive friend of his.

Read and Steele met with Brian Hogarth for lunch at the Golden Sheaf Hotel in Double Bay, Sydney on a clear sunny day. Hogarth was easy to get on with. He was a good talker and knew his way around the racetrack and, more importantly, he paid for the lunch. Read would never forget that meeting. They were well into the second bottle of a just-so red when Hogarth said, 'Do you think you could do some insurance investigating work for me – household burglaries, arson and all that sort of stuff?' Read and Steele looked at each other for a moment, shrugged and nodded in the affirmative.

'Look, Brian,' Read replied, 'I reckon that to do what you're talking about just needs common sense, a basic knowledge of the law and how to handle people. Let's come up to your office when it suits and you can show us exactly what you want done.'

Hogarth went on, 'There's an opening in my company because of the Chick Affair last Christmas.' Read and Steele knew exactly what Hogarth was on about as he told them what they already knew. All of Australia knew.

'There was this investigator, Phil Chick,' Hogarth said. 'He was a little extroverted and believed in self-promotion. He did quite a bit of work for us and despite his eccentricity he got results. He drove around Sydney in a black Porsche with 007 plates. During his Christmas office party he blew his brains out all over his secretary when he lost a game of Russian roulette with his Smith & Wesson .357 Magnum revolver. The poor girl sat there, covered in her boss's blood and grey matter, frozen and gibbering until an ambulance officer jabbed a needle into her arm. It was a bloody mess all round, in more ways than one, believe me, and we got the sort of publicity that we really could have done without, if you know what I mean. The media loved it.'

It turns out that Read and Steele had been in the right place at the right time. They did a lot of hack work to begin with but it was bread and butter money and kept them out of the pub. Steele handled any jobs north of the Harbour Bridge and Read looked after the rest. Read lived in Balmain in a place he had bought in the late 1960s when he was down in Sydney from PNG for a spot of leave. It was only a small terrace but it suited him and it had a good view of the harbour from his upstairs bedroom. He was always renovating but liked the pottering around. Read had never married so the house would be finished when it suited him.

Read felt guilty about having a dog in the city. He took Bonzo for plenty of exercise around Balmain and always had him along on hunting and fishing trips. In PNG, Read had always used bull terriers to hunt wild pigs and as guard dogs. He was used to the furtive looks when he ran with Bonzo, what with all the publicity about dog attacks but Bonzo was great mates with the local kids. He was almost a vegetarian so maybe that explained things.

Since they had started up, Read and Steele had covered all the areas of insurance and private investigation. They were licensed in New South Wales and Victoria and had a network of good contacts. They knew plenty of police, some bad but most good. The bad ones had proved to be very bad and a lot of them had been given the flick.

A few of them had even become private investigators. Read had the odd drink here and there with his police contacts but met most of them at the racetrack where they were more than happy to do business.

Whether it's outback Birdsville, or big city Randwick or Flemington, the racetrack is the great Australian melting pot, where even a non-gambler can be entertained. Many women love going to the races. They dress up and in their minds, attract admiring and sometimes vengeful glances from men and women alike.

Then there are the colours. The jockeys' silks, the carefully tended flower gardens and shrubs against the backdrop of the almost too-green grass. One Australian Jockey Club publication asserts that 'Horseracing is one of the colourful threads in Australia's cultural tapestry.' A bit over the top but true.

Read finally got onto Peter Welsh.

'Jack, good to hear from you,' Welsh said. 'There's a bed here for you as usual. Looking forward to picking up on all the gossip.'

Read rang off and walked back to his car. He had brought the Range Rover down from PNG and although a little battered from the corrugated roads and half-cleared tracks, it still ran well but was in need of a cut and polish.

He headed back onto the highway and set off for Melbourne. A big Kenworth truck blasted past him, rocking his car in its wake. He wasn't in a hurry and the closer he got to Melbourne, the more likely he was to run foul of a speed trap.

It was just on dark as Read drove past Pentridge Prison. For a Thursday the traffic was bearable. He had last been in Melbourne the previous March for the running of the Newmarket Handicap down the Straight Six at Flemington.

Welsh opened the door. Just like his house, he was in original condition, about five feet ten, wiry, lean and no fat. He practically lived on fish and vegetables and swam twenty kilometres a week in the Frank Beaurepaire Pool. He used to be an awful drunk but didn't touch the stuff now. Like Read he was a non-smoker. Welsh bought most of his clothes at op shops and was just a few years behind the latest fashions.

'Hello, Jack,' he said.

'G'day Peter, how are things in Melbourne Town?' Read replied.

'Well, Jack, it's all right if you're a dutiful and obedient public servant like me, or better still, a caring and compassionate social worker. If things get too hard, you can always put in a stress claim and look forward to a redundancy package.'

Read knew what Welsh was on about. The new economic policies of the major political parties were having mixed results. Big business was getting stronger and fatter at the expense of its weaker cousin, small business. Workers were finding themselves on the dole queues, 'downsized,' not sacked. Once comfortable and prosperous country towns shrivelled as drought and the exodus of their young people gripped them tighter. Soaring unemployment led to more crime, with heroin being sold at bargain basement prices on the streets and at railway stations by migrant teenagers, a lot of them Asian. Packs of feral youths savaged old people in their homes and on the streets. Rape figures were sky high and child abuse stories clogged the media. Socialite lawyers and shrinks donned the cloak of victimhood and fearlessly went on talk-back radio to explain away why they were cocaine addicts. Rorting politicians with skins as thick as a rhino's shamelessly defended their positions. Against this backdrop of decadence and social disintegration, down-to-earth, ordinary Australians fumed as they saw badly needed police playing the role of revenue collectors for their political masters. Read and Welsh discussed these things well into the night, as well as politics and the good old days in New Guinea.

Read was up early next day and walked down to the Fitzroy Post Office. Passing the council flats, he nimbly negotiated his way through a cluster of knotted and loaded condoms. *Just the right way to start the day,* Read thought.

There was nothing for him at the post office. He was waiting on documents that Brenda, his secretary in Sydney, was going to send down. He walked over to the newsagents, got the papers and dropped in for a cappuccino at the cafe where a tall German girl with big tits worked. Read bypassed the flats on the way back to Welsh's place and then called Brenda.

'Hi Jack,' she said. 'How are things in Melbourne?'

'All right, Brenda, has John Steele got that stuff on Ahmet Terkel yet?'

'Posted it late yesterday,' Brenda said. 'John was waiting on some extra information from someone at Fedpol.'

Read and Steele often got valuable assistance from the Federal Police, especially in cases where drugs were involved. It was simply a case of quid pro quo at a time when undermanned police forces needed all the help that they could get.

Ahmet Terkel was an interesting character. When he first came to Australia in 1980 on a family reunion program, he was Yimil Yirkis on a Turkish passport. In his second week in Sydney he got a job as a labourer in a tyre warehouse. Three weeks later, Terkel suffered an 'alleged' back injury when he 'allegedly' slipped and 'allegedly' fell off a ladder onto the concrete floor. The 'alleged' accident was not witnessed. Soft-tissue injuries are almost impossible to deny by today's justifiably cautious doctors, what with all the medical negligence writs flying around.

Terkel went off on a worker's compensation claim and shopped around until he found a Greek doctor and a Greek solicitor in Marrickville to pursue his common law claim for 'pain and suffering.' The only 'pain and suffering' was endured by Read's partner, John Steele, who was cooped up in a Kombi van during the middle of a bad Sydney winter, taking surveillance film of Terkel and his Mauritian girlfriend, who were grossing $1000 per day, tax free, selling sausages in a roll at Paddy's Market.

Sterling built up a library of twenty-four video cassettes showing Terkel performing a variety of strenuous tasks, including lifting the mobile kitchen tow bar onto the ball joint of his Falcon car. Other footage showed the lad lifting and carrying cartons of groceries and bread rolls from his car to the food van. Sterling even had video film of Terkel vigorously playing with his two savage Alsatian dogs and playing soccer at Merrylands.

Read reckoned it said a lot about the Australian legal system that Terkel was still able to receive a substantial out-of-court settlement, despite the fact that Sterling's damning videos and supporting evidence were presented to his lawyers. As with most workers' compensation cases, the insurance company didn't want to risk going before a jury. The common perception was that insurance companies were corporate monsters with plantations of money trees.

It was no coincidence that Terkel's legal and medical advisers had an army of clients just like him. Read chuckled to himself as he remembered what Steele had facetiously called Terkel's lawyers – 'Sue, Grabbit and Run.'

After his efforts in Sydney, Terkel popped up in the ACT using the alias of Sam Suleiman. He became involved in a well-organised motor vehicle accident scam in which claimants suffered a variety of neck and back injuries and milked the Third Party personal injury compensation system. Such injuries were easy to fake and the rorters had a field day.

Terkel came undone when one of the cars used in the bodgie accidents was traced back to a Sydney address he used. He had minor convictions for trafficking in cannabis and the NSW police had little trouble unravelling his aliases and exposing his past fraudulent behaviour. He was charged over the ACT car accident fraud but was bailed on six months adjournment. He promptly moved to Melbourne still using the alias of Suleiman but worker's compo and car accident fraud had become too tame so he graduated to joining a heroin-dealing ring that specialised in supplying the street dealers in St Kilda. Terkel finally fell foul of the Victorian Drug Squad but was amazingly granted bail. He made the most of his reprieve and fled to Turkey on a false passport. The squalor and poverty of his home turf was too much even for Terkel, so with little difficulty he came back to Australia using his real name. That was why Read was back in Melbourne.

Terkel was dobbed in by one of his fellow conspirators in the car accident fraud deal. He had failed to pay his helpers properly and one of them had opened up to one of the detectives who had arrested him when he was known as Yirkis. The informant was paid to inform and continued to supply information about the involvement of Middle Eastern migrants with insurance and other fraud. Read had heard that things were so bad that underground newsletters are regularly sent overseas, advising the best way to rort the system in Australia. Ironically, some of the authors of these documents had obtained their degrees at Australian universities.

When Terkel arrived back in Australia, he flew into Melbourne. His ex-accomplice advised his police contacts and the word was passed down the line. The Federal Police decided not to arrest Terkel there and then because they wanted to see if he resumed contact with his Melbourne drug links. That was where Read came in.

Because the police forces were so strapped for cash they often couldn't pay the overtime for surveillance, particularly when it wasn't urgent. Sterling Investigations had an arrangement whereby it carried out surveillance in certain cases in return for assistance when required.

Terkel, who was driving a green Mazda 323 sedan, had set up camp in a scungy flat in Richmond. Because Read was staying with Welsh in nearby Carlton it made surveillance of Terkel fairly easy. After talking with Brenda, Read sorted out some paperwork then walked up to North Melbourne to hire a Rent-a-Bomb. The Range Rover, dirty as it was, was hardly a surveillance vehicle so he always rented a common Japanese sedan, white or cream, to make it look just like one of the mob.

As Read walked across Carlton, he passed the Lemon Tree Hotel and promised himself a drink there in the afternoon. Over in the Exhibition Gardens a group of people were setting up for a party.

Read picked up a white Corolla, squeezed himself in and drove to Terkel's Richmond address, just to check out the locality. In the busy, nondescript street, Terkel's flat was in a block of ten, 1960s vintage, orange brick, flat roof and dark stairwells. Read, who had been born and raised in Richmond, lamented the fact that some quaint little period cottages would have been bulldozed to make way for the architectural atrocity that now stood on their grave. Among the assortment of rubbish bins outside the place a couple of street-smart cats were eyeing off some equally smart sparrows scavenging for scraps. As a sign of the gentrification swamping Richmond and its proud Catholic working-class history, there was a row of single-fronted cottages opposite the flats. Some had been renovated but a couple looked just too trendy. The street's through traffic enabled.

Read to take up a reasonable position without exciting too much interest. The block ran at right angles to the street so Terkel's flat, No. 5, was on the first level at the rear. Among the ten car spaces under the flats, there was no sign of the green Mazda. It was getting close to 4 pm so Read called it a day. On the way back to Welsh's house, Read decided to keep his promise about that drink and he walked up to the Lemon Tree to save the parking hassle.

2

The Lemon Tree had changed a bit over the years. Read had first drunk there as a young man when it was an original drab and dingy Carlton hotel and six o'clock closing was a national sport. Unless you were in the publican's good books, you were thrown out at 6 pm along with all the other drunks. The SP bookies and the standover men who did their bidding used the place as an office and settling house.

The Lemon Tree was no stranger to violence. In the 1920s Squizzy Taylor used to drink there in the bad old days and plenty of blood had been spilt on the much-patched lino. A long simmering feud had been settled in the men's lavatory. The victim was almost blown in half when a sawn-off shotgun barked its fatal message. Read remembered gazing with morbid fascination, weeks after the murder, at the pellet-scarred, brown earthenware urinal.

Read smiled to himself as he entered the bistro bar. The place had been gutted and completely renovated in the early 1970s and had been given the treatment again in the 1980s. During the boom of the late 80s the Lemon Tree became a hangout for the Porsche and new mobile phone crowd. On Friday nights, packs of young men, straight out of Vogue magazine with their gelled hair and padded shoulders, paraded before the beautiful young women who gathered there. The old Lemon Tree mob would have not been able to cope. Read pulled up a stool to the bar and ordered a pot of Carlton Draught.

He couldn't take his eyes of the barmaid – clearly European, mid-thirties, tall, long black hair and quite pale skin. Her full, prominent breasts had, over the years, made her shoulders slightly rounded. She was slim and that only accentuated her breasts. But today she didn't look too happy.

'A beautiful day,' Read said, in a pathetic attempt to start up a conversation.

'If you say so,' was the reply. Read could see that he was not getting very far so changed tack.

'Look, tell me to get lost but you look sad and a beautiful girl like you shouldn't be sad on a day like today.' The girl looked at Read as she pulled a beer for a customer. Her bottom lip trembled and just for a moment Read thought that she was going to cry. His routine wasn't working and he felt a prick.

The bar wasn't that busy. Read finished his beer and pushed his glass forward. The barmaid took a fresh pot and filled it expertly, giving the beer just the right amount of head. She handled the tap correctly, without flicking it on and off with a noisy flourish. Read was always annoyed when bartenders did that. It looks gung-ho but it just stuffs up the working parts and soon the tap starts dribbling like a leaky dick and a lot of the profit ends up in the drip tray. The girl put Read's beer down, took his money and looked at him. She saw a tall man, a bit on the heavy side but with the weight well spread out. He wasn't good looking but had something about him. He looked old enough to be her father, maybe.

'You know how to cheer people up, don't you,' she said, with more than a hint of sarcasm. Read leant forward and looked straight at her.

'I'm sorry, I really am,' he replied. Read was feeling a real arsehole. 'I was just trying to make conversation and it looks as if I've failed bigtime, anyway, I'm Jack Read and I used to drink here a long time ago, which is certainly well before you were born.' Read thought he would give her plenty of leeway with her age.

'Sylvia Scarrone and flattery will get you everywhere,' she said, putting out her hand. Her handshake was firm and she had long fingers. Read, who always picked up on the little things, noticed a small flat mole on the web between her index and second fingers as he let go her hand.

'I was just a little girl when you were here, no doubt trying to crack onto the barmaids.' She smiled for the first time and looked a lot better.

Read spared her his memories about the barmaids all those years ago. One had bright hennaed hair and make-up so thick it would have fallen off in chunks if she had smiled. She had run off with one of the lesser SP bookies who drank at the Lemon Tree. The SP's wife had come to the hotel and stacked on quite a turn, a few glasses flying through the air and lots of swearing and spitting.

Read felt that he was getting on with Sylvia after a false start, so he decided to push his luck. She had worked her way back to his end of the bar and was picking up some empty glasses.

'Sylvia,' he said, 'when do you finish work?'

'Why?' she replied almost cheekily. She was not looking sad any more.

'Well, I'd like to take you out for dinner when it suits you, provided your weightlifter boyfriend doesn't mind,' he added, facetiously.

'I could beat my last boyfriend at arm wrestling, but you don't have to worry, I left him behind in Sydney. I've only been here in Melbourne for three weeks and yes, I'll come out with you but leave it until next week when I'll be on day shift. 'I finish at 6.30 pm.'

Read decided to call it a day. The bar was getting busy and he didn't want to make a nuisance of himself. He had to be up early next morning to start work on Terkel.

'See you later, Sylvia,' Read said as he walked outside and headed back to Canning Street.

'Goodbye, Mr Read.' Sylvia's voice followed him out into the street.

Read picked up a small napoletana pizza on the way. He thought of Bonzo, his dog, who loved the stuff. When Read got home, Welsh was sitting in the lounge listening to Mozart. Read didn't want to disturb him by saying goodnight. He left a slice of pizza for breakfast, showered and hit his bed. He had a busy day ahead.

When Read rose early Welsh was in the shower making lots of noise. Read pulled on a plain shirt and jeans and put binoculars, mini-recorder, video camera and mobile in a blue sports bag. He was ready to go and look at Mr Terkel. At 7 am, there was not much traffic around so Read took off in the Corolla and headed for Richmond. He would check his mail later.

He entered Terkel's street and pulled into the kerb diagonally opposite the block of flats. From this point he could just see the front entrance of Terkel's flat but was unable to get a good look at the car spaces under the building. Read skimmed through a *Bulletin* magazine and waited a while. Scanning the street he saw that he had a good excuse to go for a walk. One of the houses on his side of the street displayed a 'For Sale' sign.

He strolled along to look at the house and was able to have a good view of the car park. There was no sign of Terkel's Mazda. He could be anywhere, doing a drug deal or shacked up with some whore. Read had been told that Terkel's current de facto had stayed behind in Sydney with three kids all under the age of five. He could have even shifted out and moved on. Read walked back to the Corolla and drove across Abbotsford and Collingwood back to Fitzroy.

The file on Terkel was waiting for Read at the Fitzroy Post Office. He picked up some newspapers and drove back to Welsh's place. Read opened the large postpak and slid the contents out onto the kitchen table. There were lots of blown up still shots of Terkel taken by John Steele. There were the original reports to the insurance company relating to Terkel's compo claim shortly after he first arrived in Australia. There was a copy of his criminal record, giving all his details along with his aliases. A video cassette with surveillance footage of Terkel could be interesting so Read went into the front room and loaded the video into the VCR.

Watching Terkel made Read cranky. Steele had taken most of

the film apart from the odd times Read had relieved him. Steele had become bored from watching Terkel deal out sausages in a roll and had zoomed in on the inflow of cash. That was when Steele estimated the spiv was taking $1000 plus per day. Read skimmed through the video with the remote control, focusing on Terkel's face and his body language. He was about five feet nine and of nondescript build. He had a hawkish, acne-pocked face with a perpetual scowl, one of those *'Don't hassle me'* looks that is supposed to intimidate. Read got fed up looking at the video and decided to run back to Richmond for a quick look.

He went the same route but pulled in further up the street to get a clear look at the carpark. Again, there was no sign of Terkel's Mazda. He decided to prop for about thirty minutes to give his man a chance to show up.

After about fifteen minutes he saw movement in the rear vision mirror. A police van was moving up slowly behind him. He could see the constable in the passenger seat using the radio and knew exactly what had happened. In one of the little cottages some budding Miss Marple or Hercule Poirot would have noticed Read's earlier visit, and his return had convinced them that Read was up to no good. People with a lot of time on their hands notice little things and then assume they'll be targeted for a break and enter or home invasion. The police van stopped behind Read. The driver got out, put on his cap and walked up to him.

'Good afternoon, sir,' the senior constable said, politely and correctly, just as he had been trained to do at the Police Academy.

Before he could go on, Read cut in. 'Look, mate, I'm an insurance investigator on a job and this is a hire car. Can we pull out of here into the next street and sort this out? I don't want to get sprung here.'

The policeman looked hard at Read for just a moment, sizing him up. He looked back at his partner and gestured that they would be leaving. By this time Read was showing his Victorian Inquiry Agent's licence.

'All right, you go ahead and we'll follow,' the policeman said, as he headed back to the van.

Read breathed a sigh of relief and slowly moved off. All he needed was Terkel turning up and witnessing the debacle. He turned out of the street and across the next one, turning left into a street flanked by warehouses. The police van pulled in behind him and this time both policemen got out. Read walked back, introduced himself and they got on fine.

He knew that most police were fairly cooperative with people in Read's line of work. Maybe they could see themselves in his shoes one day. What had happened was all Read's fault and he was mentally kicking himself. What he should have done was to alert the Richmond Police Station that he would be conducting surveillance in the area and given them all his details along with the rego of his car. Read had paid the price for being a slack-arse.

He farewelled the policemen and told them he would ring in the details when he changed over his hire car. He headed back to North Melbourne and swapped the white Corolla for a blue Holden. The girl doing the paperwork looked at Read quizzically for just a moment, then returned to her task. Read wasn't going to satisfy her curiosity. He thanked her and walked out to the car. Read decided to check out Terkel's place at 3 o'clock the next morning. If he wasn't at home then, Read would have to start thinking about what to do next. He decided to go back to Canning Street via the Lemon Tree.

On the way he passed a perfectly restored British Racing Green 1968 Series 2 Jaguar E-Type roadster parked outside what used to be Poynton's Hotel. The old Carlton pub had been one of Read's watering holes when he was young and silly but a massive renovation had completely changed the place. It just didn't look like it belonged in Carlton anymore. Halted at the lights, Read could see that the place was empty. Memories of the packed bars and bistro when Peter Poynton owned the place told Read he was right.

The sleek and glossy Jag made Read smile as he remembered his hefty trifecta win at Randwick that had made it possible for him to import a 1964 E-Type coupe from California. The car was a basket case when he brought it in but the numbers on the body, chassis and mechanicals all matched up and being a Californian car, the dreaded rust was not much in evidence. Read had done a fair bit of work on it but it helped to keep him poor. He kept the Jag garaged at a mate's place in Sydney.

Geoff Maggs had a smash repair shop at Ultimo in inner Sydney and had met Read through the insurance business. Maggsie was a genius with a hammer and dolly and knew how to treat metal and he rarely used body filler or bog when he was working on collector vehicles. He was one of the few panel beaters that Read knew who could use lead to smooth out body imperfections. Read knew that one day he would proudly drive the car out of Maggsie's workshop, its reworked engine making that great Jag burble. The actual day of that event was the subject of much chiacking from Maggsie and the boys at the panel shop when Read and others were there after work on Fridays, during the weekly piss-up. Maggsie's mates were a motley bunch, a couple of detectives from the Stolen Motor Squad, insurance loss assessors, a horse trainer who restored old cars, and assorted petrolheads who were old enough to know better.

Read came back to reality as he parked the Holden just around the corner from the Lemon Tree. The bar was reasonably busy and Sylvia smiled when she saw Read. She looked a lot more relaxed.

'A pot of Carlton Draught, Mr Read?' she said very professionally.

'Yes, thanks and all my friends call me Jack.'

Sylvia wiped the bar in front of Read and put the beer down on a fresh Toohey's coaster.

Read thought CUB was getting slack, letting things like that happen on their home turf.

'Familiarity breeds contempt, don't they say?' Sylvia replied, again with a smile. She went on. 'I trust that you've had a good day.'

Read smiled back at her. 'No, it's been a bugger of a day, as a matter of fact, mainly due to my own stupidity but things will improve, I'm sure.'

'You know what I do, Jack, but what do you do for a living?' Sylvia asked as she moved off to serve another customer. Read waited for her to come back.

'I'll give you all the details of my pedigree and what I do when we go out next week. Can you stand the suspense?'

'Ah, hah, a mystery man, eh? I can hardly wait,' Sylvia replied.

Read finished his beer and stood up. 'Well, Sylvia, I'm going to love you and leave you.'

'You wish!' she said as Read walked out of the bar, smiling, throwing her a wave over his shoulder.

Read changed his mind and decided to walk down to Lygon Street for a quick look. He came to Melbourne a couple of times a year and tried not to miss the Cup and he wanted to see which restaurants had closed and opened since the last time he was in town.

Lygon Street had become a tourist trap with more pasta places and women's fashion boutiques than you could poke a stick at. They even had spruikers outside the eating places touting for business. As Read walked past a laneway, a young woman's voice searched him out.

'Good evening, sir, this way, sir. Come to the Gentlemen of Verona and enjoy the best of Lygon Street.'

Read propped as a young woman in a long dress emerged from the shadows. She looked like someone down at the Arts Centre handing out programs for the theatre. As she approached, Read could see that she was holding menus but decided to give her a hard time.

'How long has Lygon Street had a red light zone?' he said. The girl looked flustered.

'Excuse me, sir, what did you say? I don't understand.'

'It's alright, love,' Read said, 'I'm just pulling your leg. How long has all this been going on?'

He took one of the menus and looked at it.

'What's your real job?'

'I'm at Melbourne Uni, sir,' the girl said, wondering where all this was going to end. Read wasn't going to give up.

'I never bloody well thought that I'd see this happening in Lygon Street, this is Third World stuff. Look, don't take this personally. I should be having a go at your boss. It's not your fault. My bark's worse than my bite.' Read patted the girl's shoulder and went on his way. She shook her head and waited for the next target.

Read wandered further up the street and cut across to window shop at the gelato and cake place. *Just the place for someone on a Jenny Craig course to test their resolve,* he thought. He took a deep breath and inhaled as he slowed his pace outside Grinder's coffee shop. Giancarlo had defended his patch for as long as Read could remember. Tiamo was doing good business. It was one of the few places on the strip that had kept its character. Read put his head inside Jimmy Watson's and saw that nothing had changed. The same sort of crowd, a different generation was doing its thing. He almost headed over to Percy's Bar, which used to be the Astor Hotel, but changed his mind and went back to his car. Another time.

Back at Canning Street he decided to call Alan Sedgwick at Federal Police headquarters in Sydney to bring him up to date. He was another New Guinea contact. Sedgwick had been a District Officer up there but had taken a golden handshake and joined Fedpol. Sedgwick came on the line.

'Hello, Jack, how's things? Where are you?'

'I'm in Melbourne, Alan, I've got a few bits and pieces to sort out here so I'm having a look at our greasy mate, Terkel. I haven't actually sighted him yet but when I do I'll let you know what gives. You can bet anything that he's up to no good whatever it is. It pisses me off that we let bastards like that into the country in the first place.'

Sedgwick tut-tutted. 'Don't let it get you down, Jack. If there were no Terkels around, you and I would run out of work.'

'Yeah, Alan, you're right but it fucking well shits me to think that he has bloodsucked on Australia ever since he got here and to add insult to injury because he has kids who were born here, he's now an

Australian citizen, for Christssake. Anyway, sorry for blowing down your ear. Where are you working at present?'

'At the moment I'm working out at Mascot with the immigration people. There's quite a few Pacific Islander illegals coming in at present. Believe me, there's plenty to do. Look, I've got to go. Catch up with you later, Jack. Cheers.'

'Cheers, Alan.' Read hung up, feeling a bit pissed off. Australia's immigration policy was stuffed up. Gutless politicians on both sides were to blame. Just watch them knock at the knees when you mention the ethnic vote. What about the Australian vote?

His mobile squawked. It would be Brenda or John Steele.

'Jack, how's things?' It was Steele.

'Okay, John, where are you? Manly?'

'Yes, and shortly I'll be at the Steyne having a nice cold schooner, so think about that.'

The Steyne Hotel right on the beachfront at Manly was the hangout for Steele and his surfie mates – old surfie mates who used to surf on those huge Hawaiian boards that weighed a ton. Nowadays they did their surfing in the gym and the back bar of the Steyne. Steele went on. 'I'm calling to let you know that there might be a job coming up for you in Melbourne. Les Trist from Centaur Livestock said that it could be interesting and quite a lot of money is involved.'

At that stage, Read had absolutely no idea what he was in for and if he'd known, he would have certainly thought twice. Later, he would reflect and wish that he'd never taken on this racehorse claim in Melbourne.

3

Les Trist ran a thoroughbred livestock agency. He handled transport and insurance for gallopers and trotters in and out of Australia. He had a big book of clients. Read often met him at the racetrack in Sydney and always bumped into him at the Melbourne Cup. The member's bar was his office. The last job Read had done for him was an amateurish fraud involving the alleged death of an expensive trotting stallion. On a scorching day in the middle of a withering drought, Read found himself in a paddock outside Parkes in western NSW, looking at a jumble of hide and bones that had once been a horse. Even the flies were looking for shade. Read had asked the owner the usual questions and managed to separate most of the hide from the skeleton, wrapping it in plastic and dumping the mess in the back of his car. The Range Rover smelt like a glue factory for weeks.

Mike Rowlands, a lecturer in anatomy and animal pathology at the Sydney University Veterinary Faculty, had used the latest technology to decipher the brands and establish that a clumsy attempt had been made to superimpose the stallion's brand over the existing one on the remains Read had brought in from the bush. He subsequently found the stallion alive and well at Cowra. After Read had snooped for a few days, the owner's spurned mistress blew the whistle. It had been, as they say, an open and shut case.

This memory was going through his mind as Read set the alarm for 2 am. Despite that, he was up before the alarm sounded. A quick cup of tea and Read was ready. Outside, the sky was clear and there was the whiff of a breeze. He stowed his gear in the car and set off for

Richmond again. He came into the street from the other end and drove slowly past the flats. Bingo! There was the green Mazda.

The flats were in darkness. Read pulled up, and doused his lights. He walked quickly and quietly into the driveway of the carpark and went straight to Terkel's car. The bonnet and exhaust were cold so Terkel had been home for a while. Read returned to his car without glancing back. At least he knew that his man was back in town.

After spot-checking for most of the weekend, Read caught Terkel on the move late on Sunday afternoon and followed him to South Melbourne and St Kilda where Terkel made calls at five brothels. So much for the brothel industry's bullshit about prohibiting addicts from working. Because Terkel was carrying an airlines bag, Read guessed he was on a delivery run. Keeping a discrete distance behind, Read followed Terkel to a grotty little coffee shop in Sydney Road, Brunswick, one of those places where Greeks sit around all day smoking, drinking black coffee and playing cards. Read sat off the place and settled in to observe.

After a while, Terkel came outside with two men and sat in a Ford. From what Read could see, Terkel and his two companions were arguing and there was plenty of aggro body language. Terkel got out and slammed the door so hard the car rocked. He stormed back into the coffee shop. The Ford moved off and Read went with it, first for a petrol stop at a BP service station then onto the Tullamarine Freeway. When Read suddenly noticed streaks of red dirt on the Ford, it dawned on him that Terkel's mates were most probably out-of-towners. They set sail for the Calder Highway and could have ended up anywhere. Read noted the car's registration number, dropped off and headed back to the city.

Read was looking forward to his date with Sylvia and could hardly wait for the week to end. He was into younger women – known to his mates as cross-generational fucking – and he had always been able to score now and again. The only downside was meeting the parents, which he avoided at all costs as many had firm views about men like Read.

Back at the Lemon Tree, Read killed time over a glass of Carlton Draught while Sylvia handed over to the barmaid coming on for the night shift.

'Come on, Mr Read, see you later, Rachael.' Sylvia offered Read her arm. He put his through hers, walked out onto the street and helped her into his car.

'What's that thing?' she said, looking at the cushioned handle of a baton sticking out from under the passenger seat.

'You won't believe it, Sylvia, but that is called a Magic Wand. If you look closely, you'll see that name branded on it.' The baton was one of those long, high-tensile steel tubes made by the American firm, Bianchi. Read had got it from a member of the New South Wales Riot Squad and had once used it to slow down a very unfit bikie who had kept on trying to kick him in his one ball.

'Sylvia, let's go for a drink and then down to Ho Chi Minh City for some roast duck, if that's okay with you.'

'Sounds great, Jack, and then you can tell me about yourself.' In Fitzroy, Read pulled up outside the Rainbow Hotel. Since his last visit it had been extensively renovated. The bar was bright and airy, a far cry from the dingy dump it had been. A few dykes in the bar eyed Sylvia off. Read had a beer and Sylvia settled for a Bacardi and Coke. Read thought about the first time he had spoken to Sylvia at the Lemon Tree.

'Sylvia, what did I say to upset you when I was busy being stupid last week?' She suddenly looked sad again.

'Look, everything has just been happening at once. I had this boyfriend for a few years and I've just found out he's on heroin – incredible! I just can't believe it. We used to smoke dope and that was cool but the other stuff's different. I was living with him and didn't even realise it. He wasn't injecting into his arms so he was an expert in getting a needle into the least noticeable parts of his body.'

Read said, 'A doctor mate once told me about cunning addicts who injected into their penises.' As he said this, Read's single ball tightened up and he broke out into a sweat just thinking about it. In

PNG, Read had fallen into a native pig trap, which was a camouflaged hole in the ground with upright sharpened bamboo stakes, one of which had neatly skewered and excised his left ball, resulting in an agonising day's hike to a native aid post where Read had himself pumped full of penicillin.

Sylvia stopped, looked down at her drink then went on.

'I just had to get away so I packed up and left Sydney, came to Melbourne and then I found out last week that my mother is dying of leukaemia. So there, that's why I'm not too happy and not bubbling out all over. Anyway, what's going on, Jack? You're supposed to tell me all about yourself.' Sylvia looked relieved at having unburdened herself.

Read told Sylvia as much as he thought he should about what he did for a living. 'I prefer to be called an insurance investigator rather than a private eye or PI. It doesn't sound so wanky.'

'Jack, do you have a gun or anything exciting like that?' By the tone of her voice, he thought Sylvia was trying to take the mickey out of him.

'Sylvia, I think you're having a lend of me and I'd like to tell you that I was armed like Dirty Harry but no, I'm not that exciting. No, I don't have a licence to carry a gun.' He didn't tell her about his illegal handguns. One was a Colt Woodsman, a .22 automatic pistol with interchangeable long and short barrels used mainly for recreational target shooting. The other was a Colt Python .357 magnum revolver that could break up a V8 engine block with metal-piercing rounds. It was given to him by a mate who was wiped out by cancer. It was a real Clint Eastwood piece and Read thought that he should hand it in when the next firearms amnesty was declared. Despite his good intentions, he had held on to the weapon. There were a lot of nutters out there and he wanted to be in with a chance if some lunatic ran amok one day with an AK47.

Sylvia shouted the next round and changed the conversation.

'Are you married, Jack?'

'Never, and not likely to be. I just wander around preying on

28

attractive young barmaids.'

'Attendants,' Sylvia cut in. 'Bar attendants, not barmaids.'

'Well, well,' Read said. 'A feminist as well, one of Germaine Greer's disciples, no doubt.' Sylvia smiled.

'I know who Greer is, Mr Smarty-Pants, but I've never read any of her books.'

'Don't bother,' Read said, as he stood up and ushered Sylvia out to the car. They were hitting it off okay.

As they drove towards Victoria Street in Richmond, Read reminisced about growing up in Richmond, telling her with a hint of sentimentality in his voice that his father had been a highly skilled fitter and turner at the Rosella factory in Cremorne, a small suburb right next door to Richmond bounded by the Yarra River, Punt Road, Swan and Church Streets.

'Almost all the real estate and businesses are now owned and operated by Vietnamese but back then Greeks and ocker Australians owned everything. It started to change after the Vietnam War when Malcolm Fraser purged his guilt. So now it's an Asian enclave, testimony to their enterprise and hard work.' He paused and changed this tone. 'You can't help but wonder though, how some people who came here, claiming to be destitute refugees, on the bones of their arses, can make it to the top so quickly. It's no secret that plenty of enterprising Vietnamese peddled prostitutes and drugs in Saigon. Anyway, that's history now, just like the Italians in Griffith with their grass palaces and the murder of that good Australian, Donald Mackay.'

They went to one of those restaurants where the ducks, chickens and roast pork hang in the window, the ducks and pork with their red glaze and the chickens polished with soy sauce. They had a plate of sliced roast duck with steamed rice and a big bowl of fish ball soup to wash it all down. Read smacked his lips. He loved coriander. Sylvia handled her chopsticks well.

Sylvia was renting a small, two-bedroom, single-storey, semi-detached brick cottage in Keele Street, Collingwood. She was looking for another girl to share with her because the weekly rent ate up a lot of her wages. Read helped Sylvia out of the car. As she stood up, they were very close. It just seemed natural for Read to kiss her. She pushed into him and Read could taste coriander again.

'Jack, come inside and have a look at my humble abode.' She took her keys out of her bag as she spoke. Read wasn't going to argue with her. Her place had been given a cosmetic renovation a while back. There were a few patches of rising damp but nothing that a good paint job wouldn't hide. Sylvia put the kettle on and started rattling cups and saucers around. She looked good in her working gear, white blouse and medium-length black skirt. Her long hair was up. Read wasn't interested in the coffee. He followed Sylvia into the small lounge room where they sat facing each other. He could not disguise his pleasure when gazing at her.

'God, have a good look why don't you,' Sylvia chided him gently. She got up and put her hands out to him. 'Come into the front room where it's more comfortable.' Read felt flushed as he stood up and followed her, putting his hands lightly on her waist.

Her bedroom was basic, with a large double futon bed and not much more. Sylvia stood in front of Read, let her hair down and unbuttoned her blouse. Read couldn't help staring at her huge breasts. He came to with a start but was still not quite with it.

'Jack,' Sylvia said softly. 'I'll leave my bra on.' She unzipped her skirt and let it fall to the floor. Her white, shorty briefs framed her large, soft pubic triangle. Trespassing curls of hair told Read that she wasn't into waxed bikini lines. Her legs were white and long. The buzzing in Read's head grew louder and his mouth was full of cottonwool. Sylvia goaded him.

'Come on, Jack, isn't this what you want?' She slid her panties down her legs, kicking them off. She slowly lowered herself onto the bed, raised her knees and spread her legs. Read fumbled as he undressed. He had lost control. Sylvia was running the show. He could hear himself saying her name. His voice was husky and detached and he was breathing like a chain-smoker. As he knelt down to meet Sylvia, she guided his head between her legs. In a detached, almost clinical way, Read noticed that Sylvia had a small mole at the bottom left side of her labia majora, just like the one between her fingers on her right hand. He started to do what Sylvia wanted him to do. He had no fight left in him. He was gone.

At a café next morning, Read was on his third cup of tea after ploughing through the Centaur brief. Steele had sent it down by certified mail. On the first page was a handwritten note: 'Hope you can sort this one out for us, Jack. Good punting. Les Trist.' Read's mind wasn't on the job. He was still thinking about Sylvia. He left the café and walked back to Welsh's place. Read was wondering what to do next about Terkel. It was obvious that he was running drugs around the brothels and Read would bet good money that Terkel's out-of-town mates in the dusty Ford would be nurturing a crop of cannabis somewhere out in the boondocks. Read decided to bring Sedgwick up to date and then call it quits. He would be able to get his Victorian contacts to keep tabs on Terkel and his cronies.

The Channel 9 evening news changed that idea. Read wasn't paying attention until he heard Terkel's name. There he was, splattered all over the car park outside the Baghdad nightclub in St Kilda. What was left of him had been found early in the morning by a security guard. The announcer's tone was professional and matter of fact. 'Ahmet Terkel, well known to police in New South Wales and Victoria … used several aliases … blasted at close range with a shotgun … drug dealer … police believe Terkel was the victim of a gang feud over drugs territory.' Read thought about Terkel arguing with the two men in the Ford. Well, that was that.

The small-time compo conman and pusher had finally made the big time, a fleeting spot on the national news. From a nondescript village in Turkey to the coroner's slab in Melbourne. Read wondered if anyone would mourn him, apart from his soon-to-be single mother's pension-drawing de facto in Sydney. Most probably some panicky whore wondering where her next fix was coming from until she found another Terkel. Read made a note in his diary and then started on a brief report for Alan Sedgwick. Now that Terkel was out of the way, he could concentrate on the Centaur job. Read was starting to feel keen. He went to bed with Sylvia still on his mind.

4

Clyde Trueman was a trainer based at Flemington, specialising in sprinters and milers, and over the years he had been consistently successful. He often took his horses interstate and had won his fair share of the big sprints in Brisbane and Sydney. Read had met Trueman at the track a couple of times when he had been with Les Trist of Centaur Livestock. A lot of Trueman's owners were insured with Centaur. Trist was an aggressive salesman and had offered attractive insurance rates to most of the top trainers in Australia for passing on to their clients.

Two horses in Trueman's care had recently died. The first was a three-year-old colt by Sir Dapper, insured for $300,000 and the second horse had died the weekend before Read took Sylvia out. He was a four-year-old gelding by Atlantic Flyer, insured for $100,000. Everything had been done by the book. Acting as agent for the owners, Trueman had immediately notified Centaur in Sydney and with their approval, called in his vet to conduct and report the post-mortems. Centaur had paid out promptly on the first claim but decided to fully investigate the second one, mainly to keep the underwriters happy and to make sure everything was as it should be.

On the face of it, the paperwork gave the all clear. The colt involved in the first claim was put down after he had smashed his nearside front leg when he went through the running rail during an early morning gallop, and the gelding had died in his stall at Trueman's stables during the night. The post-mortem revealed heart failure.

Read rang Trueman's stables and spoke to a girl who sounded like a strapper. He could hear her calling for Trueman. When Trueman came on the line he was out of breath.

'Clyde Trueman here, what can I do for you?'

'Clyde, it's Jack Read here, acting for Centaur Livestock Insurance. It's about that claim on the Atlantic Flyer gelding that died in his stall.' Read gave Trueman time to respond before he went on.

'That's good,' Trueman replied. 'I was talking to the owner last night. He said that he's sent all the paperwork off. Do you need any other information?'

'Well, as a matter of fact I do, Clyde. It shouldn't take long but Centaur want me to come out and see you and get the full story in more detail. I'll have to speak to the vet as well. Give me a time that suits and I'll come out and sort things out. I'll need to speak to your security people and the person who last saw the horse alive, as well as the person who found it dead in the stall.' There was a pause and then Trueman spoke.

'Yeah, okay, no problem. I'm the first person you need to see. Can you make it to my office tomorrow morning at eight?' Trueman paused again. 'No one came to see us about the Sir Dapper colt. There's no problem, is there? I don't want the owners on my back, they're good clients.'

'No, no, Clyde, no problem at all,' Read said. 'It's just to keep the underwriters happy. I should be able to wrap it all up tomorrow morning. Looking forward to meeting you again. You might remember me when you see me. Les Trist and I had a drink with you when Be Careful won the Challenge Stakes at Randwick. See you tomorrow morning. Cheers.' Trueman thanked Read and hung up. Read skimmed through the file again. The same vet from the practice that serviced Trueman's stables had performed both post-mortems.

Read pulled up in front of Trueman's house in Ascot Vale. It was basically a 1970s brick veneer, substantially added on to over the years, attesting to Trueman's climb up the trainer's premiership ladder. The house had been given an art deco facade, rendered and finished in the latest Mediterranean pastel colours. *Post-modern with a twitch,* Read thought. A Mercedes with personalised plates CT-111 was parked in the driveway that ran alongside the house out to the stables at the rear of the premises. Parked in front of it was a BMW convertible with sister plates ET-111.

Read walked down the drive towards a gate set in a sturdy security fence that separated the house block from the stables. A couple of chained-up, solid-looking blue heeler dogs stiffened up and silently eyed Read off as he opened the gate. A horse was being walked into the stables from a rear laneway. Clyde Trueman walked into view out of a horse stall. He was a big man, bluff and with a solid paunch. He looked relaxed and prosperous.

'Good morning, Clyde,' Read said, as he walked towards Trueman, hand outstretched. Read could see that Trueman recognised him. He had the sort of head that stands out in a crowd. They shook hands.

'Yes, good day, I do remember you. That was a great day at Randwick. I recall you telling me that you had a good win on Be Careful.'

Read remembered the day well. A lot of the smart, big money followed Trueman's stable and Les Trist and he had taken the 8 to 1 offered at the opening of betting before a flood of commissions drove the price down to 7 to 2. The win was quickly extinguished when Geoff Maggs gave Read his bill for the bodywork on the Jag.

'It was indeed a pleasant day, Clyde,' Read replied, then went on. 'How is Be Careful? I hope he's got a few more wins in him.'

'You can have a look at him before you leave,' the trainer replied. 'He's just come back from a spell and I reckon he'll win his second Newmarket.'

Read followed Trueman to the rear of the stable area.

'That fence runs right around the perimeter of the stables,' Trueman said, pointing it out. 'It's ten feet high with razor wire on top.' Read thought that it was illegal to use razor wire to protect private premises but so what, it wasn't his problem. Trueman continued with the tour of inspection. 'The gates have double padbolts and locks and are locked at night. The dogs are off the leash at lock-up time and they do bite, believe me. There's an alarm system that goes off in my house and the local police station as well, if someone tries to climb the fence or has a go at the gates. Floodlights come on automatically. It's a good system and it works.' *It would make a prison governor jealous,* Read thought.

They walked back through the stables where a couple of stablehands were mucking out soiled bedding straw. Read liked the smell of fresh, healthy horse manure and chopped, fresh hay. Trueman stopped at a stall with a golden horseshoe fixed to the door.

'Here he is,' Trueman said, pointing inside. Read looked and there was Be Careful, one of Australia's best sprinters, standing quietly at the rear of his box. A big, black, beautiful four-year-old stallion by Bletchingly, he was over-conditioned and burly after his time in the spelling paddocks but Trueman would soon have him honed down to racing trim. Be Careful whinnied and shook his head. He came forward snorting and nudged Trueman firmly but playfully on the shoulder. That horse was all man. Trueman pointed back to his house.

'Let's go up to my office and you can start on the paperwork. We'll have a cup of tea first.' They walked back past the two dogs who wagged their tails in recognition of Trueman, determined to impress their master, but continued to give Read the silent eye.

Clyde Trueman's spacious, well-appointed office at the rear of his house had all the mod cons, a photocopier, fax and word processor. A quick glance told Read that Trueman's office was his shrine, proclaiming its owner's position as one of the high priests of the Australian horse racing industry. The walls were covered with race photos and framed press cuttings that told the story of a successful career. Photos of beaming owners were everywhere.

A large glass display case had numerous trophies and other racing paraphernalia. Taking pride of place behind Trueman's antique cedar and tooled leather-topped desk was a big glossy photograph of

Trueman, a prominent politician, and an owner named Eric Ferber. It had been taken at Doomben after the running of the 1984 Ten Thousand. Trueman had trained Flourish, the winner, for Ferber who had later gone to jail for his role in the notorious bottom-of-the-harbour tax schemes.

Trueman walked in followed by a woman carrying cups and saucers on a tray.

'Jack, I'd like you to meet my wife, Edith.' Edith Trueman put the tray down and shook Read's hand.

'Pleased to meet you, Mr Read.' For a woman she had a firm handshake and Read reckoned that the money she spent on manicures in a year would put new rubber on his Jag. 'Coffee or tea?'

'Tea please, Mrs Trueman, white with one sugar.'

Edith was about ten years younger than her husband. She was wearing expensive, tailored slacks and a long-sleeved shirt. Her glossy, bottle-blond hair was perfectly coiffed. Those fingernails were works of art. It was still not 9 am but Read reckoned that her make-up had taken her a good hour to put on. He also thought she would resent being caught unawares by visitors. *I'll bet she's never had children*, he mused, noting her firm figure and mother-earth mammaries protruding through her shirt. Trying not to leer, Read deduced that they were indeed the real thing.

Read had left his briefcase and portable word processor in his car so Edith took him through the house to the front door. There were lots of parquetry and floor tiles covered with expensive-looking rugs. The Truemans liked leather lounge suites and expensive glass, crystal and porcelain objet d'art, a clear sign that Edith had spent a lot of time at Georges and Hardy Brothers.

Trueman was on the phone when Read walked back into his office. He hung up and Read gained the impression that Trueman didn't wish to continue the conversation in his presence.

'Well, Jack, you've seen the basic security we have here. The premises are also patrolled by Wormalds and most times there are a couple of stablehands or strappers sleeping in the flat out back.'

While Trueman was speaking, Read had been reading again the details given on the claim form.

'It says here, Clyde, that you were the last person to see the gelding alive.' Trueman nodded. Read went on. 'In which case, I'll take a formal statement from you, getting all the relevant details and then I can talk to …' Read looked back at the claim form. Trueman beat him to it.

'Joylene, Joylene Mills,' Trueman said. 'She's my best strapper. Joylene was the first person to find the dead horse. She's still over at Flemington with the horses. She's running late but will be back here shortly. I told her that you were coming.' Trueman went on. 'Jack, I've got to keep going. I'll give you that statement and then I'll have to be off. My secretary, Elizabeth Wilson, will be in soon and she'll help you out with any other queries. You can interview Joylene in here when she turns up.'

Read plugged the word processor in and started taking Trueman's statement. It was simple and straightforward. Trueman was signing his statement when an efficient-looking middle-aged woman walked in. Trueman introduced Read to Elizabeth Wilson, who without further ado, started operating her PC. Trueman got up from his desk.

'See you later, Jack. Get back to me if you need anything else. Keep following Be Careful. I reckon that this will be his best preparation, for sure.' Read heard Trueman talking to his wife and then the Mercedes starting up. The trainer ran a tight ship.

Read didn't want to annoy Trueman's secretary, so he walked back outside to the stables. The dogs had decided to studiously ignore him. The clip clop, clip clop sound of a horse being led on the trot came from the back lane and then a young woman appeared through the rear gateway, leading a brown horse and a grey which she ushered into their boxes, closing the lower half of the door. She took off the animals' headstalls and hung them on their hooks just to the side of the doors. She wiped her hands on the seat of her jeans and acknowledged Read with a wave.

'I'm Joylene. I'll be with you in a minute.' Her voice was firm and husky with plenty of twang. Joylene called out to a stablehand and then walked up to Read. She dresses like a real horsewoman: tight jeans and RM Williams elastic-sided boots. Her windcheater, damp with perspiration, was clinging to her body. A golden, lucky horseshoe charm dangled from a chain around her neck. She was barely five feet tall and wore her thick, black hair in a ponytail. Joylene knew what Read was there for and she walked back with him to Trueman's office. On the way, she stopped outside a stall, two past that occupied by Be Careful.

'That's where I found Bert dead,' she said. 'Bert was his stable name. He raced as Gold Crest.' Read knew what Joylene Mills was on about. Most racehorses are known in their stables by their nicknames, which tends to confuse some owners when they turn up to visit their investment in the bloodstock dream time, only to hear a strapper yell, 'Bring Charlie out.' All becomes clear when Silver Arrow is paraded.

Read took Joylene's statement under the watchful eye of Elizabeth Wilson. Joylene was twenty-three and had worked with racehorses since she was sixteen. She had that worldly-wise look about her. She usually slept in one of the strappers' flats and on the day in question, she had risen as usual at 4 am and started to get the stables ready for the day's work. She had disarmed the alarm system and unlocked the rear gate after chaining up Read's friends, the two cattle dogs. It was when she was switching on the lights in the horse boxes that she found Gold Crest dead.

'He was lying on the floor, all sort of stretched out and there was a lot of bloodstained foam all over his nose and mouth. I ran back to my flat and rang up the boss's house. He came straight out and looked at Gold Crest and wasn't too happy. Later in the morning, about 9 am I think it was, the vet Jim Griffiths turned up and cut the horse open to find out how he had died. Later in the day, the knacker's truck came and took him away and that was that.' Read got Joylene to read through her statement a couple of times before signing it. He gave her a copy and his business card as they walked out to the entrance to the stables. As Read was getting ready to leave, he couldn't help himself.

'Joylene,' he said. 'has Clyde any family?' Joylene nodded.

'Yes, but Edith is his second wife. She's spent all her life looking after herself. I shouldn't say this but we call her 'The Body' around here. There, I'm being bitchy. But really, could you imagine her with kids?' Read was right about Edith and sensed that there was more to hear about Clyde and his matrimonial affairs but he wasn't a gossip columnist. He told Joylene that he would get back to her if he had to.

5

Because Read was running all right for time he decided to call in at the Ascot Vale Veterinary Clinic unannounced. The receptionist called Jim Griffiths, one of the vets, on his car phone on his way back from a job. One look at the occupants of the waiting room and their feline and canine companions told Read that this busy clinic had a flourishing small animal practice as well as looking after horses. After a closer look, Read had to stop grinning like a fool. *Why do a lot of people look like their pets?*

'Mr Read?' The query came from a man in a white boiler suit who had suddenly appeared in the doorway which led to the clinic's surgery area. Jim Griffiths was in his mid-forties, about five feet ten, skinny and with stringy, sandy hair that flopped over his forehead. He looked at Read through thick-lensed glasses. He didn't do much for Read who got quickly to the point.

'I'm here, Jim, on behalf of Centaur Livestock Insurance in Sydney, to assess the claim on Gold Crest, that gelding that died at Clyde Trueman's stables. I need to take a statement from you, just to get more detail about the post-mortem you performed. It's routine stuff, on the basis that two horses have died within a short period of time in Clyde's care. I'll be as quick as I can and get out of your hair. I can see that you're a very busy man.'

Read followed Griffiths into an office at the rear of the clinic.

'Yes, I'd appreciate that,' Griffiths said. 'I've got some urgent calls to do and we're pretty flat out at the moment.' Griffiths was

41

very cooperative and couched his statement in simple language. Gold Crest had died from heart failure. Griffiths gave Read a layman's lesson in equine pathology. 'When I looked at his heart, I found a cardiac aneurism that had burst.'

From a shelf nearby, Griffiths picked up a large, colourful, cutaway plastic replica of a horse's heart. 'That's a bulge caused by the thinning of the wall of the lower left ventricle,' Griffiths said, pointing to the relevant part of the plastic heart. 'That's the part of the heart that pumps blood out of the heart into the body. In Gold Crest's case, it could have been hereditary, a genetic flaw passed on. With all the in-breeding that goes on these days with the thoroughbred, a lot of inherent defects pop up to haunt future generations. It's a pity but the racing game has too many misfits in it – I mean the horses. There needs to be a good flushing out of all the inferior stock to stop them passing the weak genes on down the line.' Read decided to get what he could out of Griffiths while he was in the mood.

'What was the story about that colt that smashed himself up, Jim? That was bad luck.' Griffiths looked at Read, still holding the heart.

'Yes, that was very bad luck indeed,' he said. 'The colt could have been spooked by a bird or something else. He just bolted and the jockey couldn't hold him. He smashed straight through the running rail and went down. He was in a very bad way when I got out to Flemington. I shot him with the .22 rifle I carry in my Range Rover. Well, I'll have to keep on going, so if that's all, I'll be off. Glad to have been of help.' Griffiths signed his statement and kept a copy.

As Read was about to drive away from the veterinary clinic, his mobile phone burbled. It was Alan Sedgwick from Sydney. 'Jack, how are you? I thought that you'd be back in Sydney by now. I rang your office and Brenda filled me in. I'll be down in Melbourne tomorrow, staying at the Downtowner Motel in Carlton. Let's get together.' Read was pleased. It would be good to see Sedgwick and catch up on things.

On his way back to Carlton, Read drove past the Zoo. On impulse he kept going down Elgin Street to Johnston Street and into Collingwood. With a bit of luck, Sylvia would be home. He felt like a chat and a cup of tea. Sylvia's front door was open but the security screen door was locked. Read made like a delivery man.

'Hello there. Anyone home?'

'Well, well, look who's here.' Sylvia came into view at the end of the hallway. She was dressed in a white tee shirt and jeans and was bare footed. 'No hawkers or peddlers of religion welcome,' she said as she unsnipped the door. She was smiling and smelt of soap and face cream. Read held her and kissed her. She pressed into Read and it felt good. She wasn't wearing a bra. Read started to get hard.

'Just thought I'd drop in to see how you were and catch up on all the gossip,' Read said, as he followed Sylvia down the hall. The house was a bit better organised and it was already starting to look lived in. Sylvia picked up on Read right away.

'Do you approve, Jack? Remember that I've only been here a few weeks. A little more time and I'll be ready for *Home Beautiful* magazine.'

'You're doing great. How are things going about getting someone to share?' Read replied. Sylvia wrinkled her nose just a bit.

'Jack, I haven't really tried. I've spoken to a couple of girls at work but that's all. I suppose I will have to advertise. I just don't want to get someone in and then find out that I don't like her. It's really difficult but I've got to get someone as I can't really afford to pay the full rent.' She smiled. 'Would you like to help out a poor working girl?'

Read smiled back. 'Sylvia, I'll buy you a lotto ticket, no, seriously, just organise yourself and go for it. Advertise and then really try to screen the applicants. You might just be lucky.' Sylvia nodded in agreement and handed Read a cup of tea.

'Anyway, forget my problems for the moment. How has your day been?'

When Read told her about the Centaur job, she was obviously interested.

'Jesus,' she said. 'Those horses are worth an absolute fortune, Jack. The insurance company wouldn't be too happy about that, would it?'

'No way, definitely not but nine times out of ten, good racehorses manage to last the distance. Because they're worth a lot of money, they do get really looked after in all respects. Everything is done to keep them fit and a lot of money goes into security and veterinary care. Clyde Trueman has a horse called Be Careful. He's worth 1.5 million and he'll be worth more if he has a good season and because he's still got his balls, he has a stud career ahead of him, lucky bastard.' Sylvia laughed at Read's joke, pursed her lips and made a low whistle. Read went on. 'You should come to the races with me, Sylvia, before I go back to Sydney. I think that you'd enjoy it.'

'Yes, Jack, I'd like that. I'd like that a lot. Just give me some notice so that I can swap shifts at the Lemon Tree if I have to.' She looked at her watch. 'Can you give me a lift into the city? I've got to do a bit of shopping before I start work. Give me a few minutes to get ready.'

As she walked to her bedroom, she started undoing her jeans. It was all too much for Read. She was sitting on a chair pulling her jeans off when he came into the room. No words were needed to tell Sylvia what Read wanted.

'God, you want it, don't you?' she said with a wanton, half smile. In no time she was breathing hard. Read choked up as he dropped his pants and boxer shorts to the floor. Sylvia finished taking her jeans and panties off and went down on the floor on all fours, her arse cocked up at Read. 'Fuck me hard and quick, Jack. I haven't got all day.' Read was down at her and slid into her quickly and easily. She was warm and wet and that told him he was wanted. He felt powerful. He parted her buttocks and found himself staring in fascination at her mushroom pink anus which puckered up and winked at him as Sylvia pushed back hard against him, grunting. 'Cum, Jack, cum quick.' Sylvia turned her head back towards him and her luring eyes urged him on. It was all too much for Read and he blew. At that moment of wild lust, he loved her.

His knees were shaking as he stood up, pulling up his pants. Sylvia flopped into the chair, her face flushed.

'Shit, I need to shower now because of you, the least you can do is give me a lift into the city,' she said, wiping herself with a wad of Kleenex. Read sheepishly retreated to the lounge room and sat down to regain his composure while Sylvia showered and made herself presentable. When she reappeared she was all business.

'Come on, come on, let's go, Jack. You and your cock have made me late.' She was wearing a mid-leg length skirt. Read thought that she looked great without make up. He dropped Sylvia off in Bourke Street and watched her stride off. She was tall and it took her a while to be swallowed up by the throng. The last he saw of her was her right hand waving to him, sticking up out of the crowd like a periscope. Read drew a slow breath and headed back to Canning Street.

At the Downtowner Motel, Alan Sedgwick opened the door of room 36. Read thought his casual attire made him look more like an investment adviser or a middle-level public servant than a cop. He lacked that naturally authoritative and sometimes aggressive aura that gives so many undercover policemen away. His time as a patrol officer, then as a district officer in the highlands of New Guinea had laid the foundations for a fit and rangy body. Though in his late forties, he still had most of his hair, and today was his usual happy self.

'Jack, good to see you and how are things? Come in. I've just got a couple of calls to make and then I'll be with you.' Read followed him into the room and while Sedgwick was on the phone, he marked time reading the predictable room service menu. *Club sandwiches have been around for a long, long time,* Read thought.

Sedgwick looked at his watch. 'Well, Jack, I've got to meet a couple of lads from the Victoria Police at the Corner Bar at the Windsor. Come on down, you could make some handy contacts. Let's walk, the exercise will do us good.'

Sedgwick and Read walked down Russell Street, past the old police complex sporting a For Sale sign.

'Jeez, Alan, isn't that a sign of the times! The government flogging everything off to reduce debts that the next generation will still be paying off,' Read complained. They turned left into Bourke Street and walked up the hill towards the best-looking parliament house in Australia. The Corner Bar was right opposite the parliament. On the other corner was the Imperial Hotel, made famous in the 1950s and 60s by the Molina brothers, Lou and Joe. In a previous life the Corner Bar had been a long-established and popular Italian restaurant.

They found Sedgwick's mates drinking pots of beer though one of them was sitting on an orange juice. Sedgwick introduced Read. 'Larry Hill, Neil Ryan, this is a mate of mine, Jack Read. Larry is Noddy and Neil's Shorty, if you get what I mean. He's called Noddy because he's always falling asleep on the job.' Read nodded and the men laughed. 'Jack's down from Sydney on a job. He's one of those private eyes that you read about, you know, fast cars, fast women and all the top cops in his pocket.' Hill and Ryan grinned approvingly and enjoyed Read's obvious discomfort. All Read could do was grin as well.

'You'll keep, Sedgwick,' he said. 'When you get drummed out of the job, don't bother looking for a job with me. Now just for being a lousy comedian, Alan, it's your shout.'

It turned out that Hill was a detective sergeant with Major Crime and Ryan was a chief inspector in charge of the Racing Squad. Hill had the sort of physique that comes with plenty of roadwork coupled with workouts in the gym. He was of medium height and had prematurely grey hair. Ryan was outgoing, tall and very big but not sloppy. He had neatly trimmed ginger hair. His weight had stayed in the correct places. It was obvious that he was in the right job. He knew what he was talking about and spoke with authority about the horseracing industry. He had done his homework. It didn't take long for Read to tune into his wavelength. Read had a good memory for people and faces and felt sure he had seen Ryan at Randwick.

'Neil,' he said. 'Didn't I see you in the member's enclosure at Randwick, on Doncaster day last year?'

'Spot on,' Ryan replied with a degree of respect that Read hoped would erase any doubts about him. 'Jeez, Jack, you've got a bloody good memory.' Ryan looked over at Hill. 'This bloke should be in the Shadows.' Hill looked at Read and grinned.

'Look, Shorty, Jack might have a good memory but who could forget a big, ugly bastard like you?' As they all burst out laughing, the ice had been broken.

Hill described how the Shadows, a police surveillance unit used for observing criminals and their activities, had members with razor-sharp memories. Some of the anecdotes were amazing. Arrests, years after the event despite dramatic changes in appearance such as loss of hair and the sprouting of beards. Escapees sitting in a football crowd, being recognised by an alert detective watching the evening TV sports news. Talking with Hill and Ryan reminded Read of the particular Australian trait of tagging people with nicknames. When Read was in New Guinea, the Bank of New South Wales employees were known only by their nicknames. It was only when one of them was transferred that you realised you had never known their proper name.

Sedgwick was talking earnestly with Hill, and as the school was on its third pot, Hill was still sipping carefully at his orange juice. Ryan and Read tested each other out on racing trivia.

'Jack, I'm going out to Moonee Valley on Saturday,' Ryan said. 'If you like, you can meet me there. I might have a couple of good tips. I take it that you have the odd punt?'

'Is the Pope Polish?' Read replied. 'Yes, I'd like to come, Neil. Moonee Valley is a great little track, just the place for well-drawn front runners. Where do we meet?'

'I'll pick you up, Jack, it'll be the easiest way.' Read gave Ryan his address. The men had one for the road and then went their separate ways. Sedgwick and Read decided to walk back to the motel via Pellegrinis where they had a slice of pizza and a cappuccino.

'Bit of luck for you, Jack, meeting Ryan,' Sedgwick said. 'Him being with the Racing Squad and all that. You might need his help on this job you have at the moment.'

'No, I don't think so, Alan,' Read replied. 'It's one of those straightforward claims that go through the system. I just have to submit my report and then the insurers will pay out, and then I'll pick up my fees and get back to the rat race in Sydney.' They parted company at the entrance to the motel. 'See you later, Alan,' Read said as he walked away.

'See you in Sydney, Jack,' replied Sedgwick as he passed through the self-opening doors.

6

The high-pitched bleep, bleep of a car horn told Read that Neil Ryan had arrived at Welsh's house. Read was dressed for the member's enclosure – a reefer jacket and his Australian Jockey Club tie. He threaded his AJC membership badge through his lapel, picked up his Zeiss binoculars and walked outside. Ryan was double parked in a unmarked police car.

'G'day, Jack. Great day for the races,' Ryan said as Read slipped into the front seat. It was a clear, fine day with a bit of high cloud and just the whiff of a breeze.

'Well, Neil, I hope you have a couple of good things as I'm running short of drinking money.'

'Don't worry, mate,' Ryan replied. 'We'll get the quaddie up. Just you wait and see.'

The drive out to Moonee Valley from Carlton took no time at all. Down Nicholson Street, left into Brunswick Road and straight through and over the Tullamarine Freeway, right into Pattison Street and into the Moonee Valley Racecourse carpark. Ryan flashed his 'Freddy,' his police ID, and was directed into the members car park. A short walk, and Ryan and Read were at the secretary's office where Read was issued with a guest pass on the strength of his AJC membership.

'You could have come in on my pass, Jack,' Ryan said. Read good naturedly waved the offer away as they walked into the betting ring.

Moonee Valley racecourse has changed a lot since it was just a couple of paddocks purchased in 1882. All seating and betting facilities are totally under cover and the track surface has been upgraded. A track surface, which used to become a bog if a dog cocked his leg on it, now sheds water like the proverbial. Almost amphitheatre-shaped, Moonee Valley is renowned locally and overseas as the venue for the WS Cox Plate, a blue ribbon, 2040 metre (or ten furlong) weight-for-age dash. Just like in a grand prix car race, the pace is a cracker from the moment the starting gates clang open, and only those horses and riders with big hearts and cool heads stand a chance on the turning, tight track. Many champions, used to the wide open stretches of Flemington and Randwick, have been made to look pretty ordinary at Moonee Valley.

'There's the quaddie, Jack,' Ryan said, pointing to the ringed numbers on his Best Bets form guide. 'Horses 9, 3, 4 and 10 in races 4, 5, 6 and 7 will bring home the bacon, just you wait and see.' Read looked at the form and saw that it favoured horses 3 and 10 but the other two were good double figures in the prepost betting. If it got up, the quadrella would pay big dollars. Ryan had that look about him of a man in the know. 'Give me $50, Jack, and we'll have $100 on it.' Ryan took Read's stake and headed off to a tote window. He moved through the crowd easily as people intimidated by his size made way for him.

Read walked past the rails bookmakers, sussing out the prices. Years of government-sponsored and protected TAB betting had thinned bookmaking ranks and wiped out most of the off-course SP bookies. A lot of the big, on-course bookmakers had gone broke in the past few years, almost unheard a couple of decades ago. Their courage had gone too. The prices they bet now would make a Jewish pawnbroker look generous. The traditional enemy of the bookmaker, the cashed up, big time punter in the know, had also disappeared. Now the huge plunges, when they came, depended on whether Kerry Packer was in the mood or not or whether the big drug dealers had a pile of dirty money ready to launder. Read looked approvingly at the real redhead in the tartan jacket pencilling for bookmaker Michael Faulkner.

Read backed the favourite in the second race, a 1200 metre sprint but the horse couldn't go the early pace and was never in the hunt. It looked like being a leader's day. He was crumpling up his losing ticket when he felt Ryan's hand on his shoulder.

'Let's go for a drink and see who's who and what's what, Jack.'

The member's bar at Moonee Valley fronts on to the saddling enclosure. It is still a place where deals are done that may not have anything to do with horse racing and there are plenty of know-it-all, out-of-the-side- of-mouth whispers into eager ears. Meeting after meeting, you'll see the same faces protecting their territory in the member's bar. Read and Ryan sat on light beers and took in the crowd. The girls and women were there, some well dressed, some overdressed. A lot of them tended to group in small cliques while their male companions laid claim to the bar.

Read found himself drooling over a gorgeous twenty-something-year-old within touching distance. She knew she was a stunner yet seemed modest and sensible. Read snapped out of it when her mother arrived on the scene and was straight on to him. The mother's leathery skin on her face, neck and arms told Read that she had spent too many unprotected days on the beach at Portsea and Lorne as a young girl, before the days of Le Tan and Blockout. Her hard eyes, glaring out of her trowelled on, made-up face, blazed at Read, *Piss off, you dirty old man!* Chastened, Read's gaze diverted to a group of people at the far end of the bar when a red flag immediately started signalling in his mental computer.

His eyes refocused and zoomed in on a face that was meant never to be forgotten. Millisecond flashbacks took Read to the Kangaroo Club in Manila years before where the man he was looking at had sat in the corner of the bar, loudmouthing and yobbish, accepting free drinks from fawning Aussie white trash.

What the fuck is he doing here? Read moaned to himself. While Ryan talked horses with the barman, Read's mind rattled up the facts about this man. Lou 'Ironbar' Miller was real bad news. Also known as 'Mad Dog,' he was heavily involved with the mob in Sydney and had been level pegging with that city's 'Mr Big,' Lennie McPherson. Miller was actually Milan Petricevic, an orphaned Yugoslav who had been brought to Australia by his aunt and uncle in the late 1950s. *Another multicultural misfit,* Read thought, as he started recovering from the shock of seeing Miller in the member's bar.

Hulking and overweight, crew cut, with a meaty, Slavic face, Miller was a killer and master of the 'king hit.' The name 'Ironbar' said it all. Miller's favourite trick was to walk up to his victim, preferably from behind, and belt the target with a rolled up newspaper. Tame stuff, except that hidden inside the paper was a length of industrial electrical flex coated in thick, orange plastic. The flex was stranded copper wire, almost an inch thick, heavy but flexible.

At the end of Ironbar's swinging forearm, the lethal cosh could crack skulls and cheekbones, splinter teeth out of jawbones and smash noses and lips into red mush. Now here he was, dressed like a pox doctor's clerk and in earnest conversation with a short, baldish respectable-looking man wearing glasses. Read noted that Ironbar was wearing a guest pass and his listener had a member's badge. Ironbar was doing all the talking.

Read couldn't contain himself any longer. He tapped Ryan's arm. 'Neil, look at that big bloke down at the end of the bar talking to the short, older guy. That's Ironbar Miller from Sydney. You should know all about him. He's a real bad bastard.' Ryan squinted a bit and looked intently in Miller's direction.

'So that's the shithead, is it? I've never had the pleasure of meeting him but I've heard all about him from the boys in major crime. Real bad news.' Read kept on.

'Who's that with him? He looks half respectable.' The other man's body language conveyed a need to disengage from listening to Miller.

Ryan looked back at the two men again. When he turned to Read he looked almost unhappy.

'I can't work this out, Jack,' he said. 'Your mate Ironbar Miller is talking to Reg Johnson, who is one of our senior magistrates.' Read pursed his lips and let out a low, subdued whistle. Ryan continued. 'Of course, we don't know what the score is. They most probably have just struck up a conversation coincidentally. You know, two blokes next to each other having a few drinks and filling in the time between races with small talk.' Read's curiosity was well and truly fuelled.

'I wonder who signed Ironbar in then,' he said. 'I don't think the committee would think too highly of having that bastard as one of their guests. He's done time for criminal assault and has starred in every Royal Commission for as long as I can remember. God knows how many people he has killed. He should spend the rest of his life in the slammer.'

Read looked back down the bar. The two men had split up but Ironbar had held his place at the bar and was looking at his form guide. Before Read could get back on track, he was knocked off balance again. From nowhere, Clyde Trueman had materialised, standing next to Miller and ordering a drink. Their body language told Read that they knew each other. He could see that Miller was talking, head lowered but looking straight ahead. Read wished that he was closer to the pair but dared not take the risk. Trueman had not spotted him. After draining his glass, Trueman moved off to join a group of noisy men who had the look of racehorse syndicate members stamped all over them.

The day passed quickly. Ryan had some official business with a few racecourse officials and arranged to meet Read up in the top stand just before race 7, the final leg of the quadrella. The first two legs were won easily but the third horse's effort had Read getting to his feet. Railing just behind the leading pack coming to the turn, the horse had nowhere to go, with a wall of horses in front of it. Like Moses parting the waters, the leaders rolled out rounding the turn, burnt out, legs flailing. Horse 4, Burning Bright, still had plenty of petrol in the tank and goaded on by his jockey's windmilling whip, went for the paint run, diving through the gap between the other horses and the rail, leaving some of his hair behind and winning by half a neck.

'You beauty,' roared Read to a mostly silent and sour crowd as he sat down. A 20/1 shot, the horse was roundly heckled as it trotted back to scale, the jockey smoothing down its sweat-frothed shoulder in congratulation. Read celebrated with a half scotch and mineral water, no ice.

'Well, Jack, can I tip or can't I?' It was Ryan as he took his seat next to Read. He was holding the quadrella tote ticket up for Read's benefit, then he kissed it. 'If Teetotaller gets up, you and I will be in the money. It's 15/1 in the ring and a touch longer on the tote. It could start at tens.'

'It's been a great day already, Neil,' Read said. 'Thanks for bringing me along. Win or lose, I'm in front though seeing that ape Ironbar has given me plenty to think about,' he replied.

As the horses came out onto the track for race 7, Read put the glasses on Teetotaller and liked what he saw. The horse was a gelding by Noalcoholic and was lining up for his third race after a spell. His form showed that he had finished eighth and sixth at his last two starts at the provincials and at his last city start he had finished on well over 1200 metres. He looked fit and athletic and his ribs showed out the way they should. The 1600 metres at the Valley would suit him.

The race was never in dispute. Teetotaller jumped out from barrier 6 and was leading by the time the field had reached the sweeping turn that led to the back stretch of the track. He had picked up the bit and was doing everything right. A length in front nearing the turn into the straight and he had the others beaten. His jockey could hear the rasping and groaning of labouring horses, and the yelling and curses of frustrated jockeys chasing him into the turn. Whips slapping sweaty horsehide sounded like firecrackers going off at Chinese New Year. His jockey showed Teetotaller the persuader and that was encouragement enough. Eyes glowing, the horse flared his nostrils wider, taking in valuable extra oxygen, shifted into a higher gear and increased his lead to three lengths. It was all over.

High in the stand overlooking the winning post, Ryan and Read were ecstatic, pounding each other's shoulders.

'You little bloody beauty,' Read shouted.

'Ripper, ripper,' echoed Ryan. 'Winners are grinners, losers are wankers,' Read chimed back. The quaddie was going to be a big one. The crowd around the pair was cranky and starting to switch off. The tall poppy syndrome was starting to take effect.

'Jesus, Jack, look at the quaddie.' Ryan was pointing down at the results being lit up on the semaphore board near the winning post. The illuminated numbers were showing $550 for each dollar invested. Read couldn't believe his luck. The adrenaline was pumping him up and he felt powerful and jubilant. As soon as he got back to Sydney he would tell Maggsie to drop everything at the workshop and get the Jag finished. Read and Ryan decided to pick up their winnings on Monday at TAB headquarters at Queens Road.

'This calls for a drink, Shorty,' Read chuckled, as he steered Ryan back to the member's bar. On their way, Read laughed and nudged Ryan, pointing at a man picking up discarded betting tickets. 'There's an 'Emu' busy at work,' Read said. 'I've seen that bloke before at other tracks. He's been around for a long time. You'd have to think that he scores now and again, the time that he puts in. Imagine if you'd dropped our quaddie ticket and he'd come across that.' Read followed Ryan as the attendant opened the door for them. The first thing Read did was look for Ironbar Miller and there he was, this time blowing down the ear of a couple of pissed punters who had probably spent their whole day drinking, watching the races on the bar TV. *Why bother going to the races at all?* Read thought.

Despite all the euphoria of the great quaddie win, Read came back to the real world with a jolt. He nudged Ryan.

'Shorty, I want you to do me a very big favour. You've already been incredibly generous letting me in on this big win but I want to wait here until that shithead Miller leaves and then follow him and see where he goes.' Ryan screwed up his nose and his eyes slitted for an instant.

'Jeez, Jack, we could have a bloody long wait, picking our noses while that bastard gets pissed. He could be here until they pull stumps.' Read refused to be put off.

'Look,' he said, 'Miller is up to something and that something surely involves racehorses, doping and money. This cunt – I shouldn't call him that, a cunt is friendly and useful – was up to his eyeballs in all the Sydney race rigging with George Freeman and his Jewboy sidekick, Joe Silver. In your position with the Racing Squad, you should be really interested. At least give it a go. If it becomes too difficult, we'll rack off.'

'Alright, Jack,' Ryan said with a half-laugh, half-sneer. 'We'll sit here like clowns and see how long it takes to get pissed on light beer.'

The crowd in the member's bar started to thin out after about an hour. Ironbar Miller glanced at his watch more than once and that told Read that he was getting ready to move. Downing his drink, Miller walked out of the bar and through the members betting ring to the exit.

'Come on, Shorty, let's go.' Read and Ryan followed their target, at some distance, to the members carpark where Miller got in a nondescript Holden Commodore with NSW registration. Keeping a couple of cars between his and Miller's, Ryan tracked out of the carpark up to Ormond Road where Miller turned right and headed up to Moonee Ponds. 'I'd like to see the prick pulled over and breath tested,' Read said. But the chase was over before it had even started. Miller drove to a large two-storey house in Ascot Vale Road and parked in the side driveway alongside a double garage under the house. Read wrote down the house number as Ryan turned the car and headed back to the city.

'Well, I wonder who owns that house, Shorty?' Ryan didn't seem to hear so Read let it go. In no time they were back at Welsh's house.

'See you at the TAB on Monday, Shorty. You're a friend for life after today.'

'All part of the service, Jack,' Ryan said as he expertly spun the wheel and drove off.

7

Read and Ryan stood back and chatted while the TAB cashier processed their pay-out. Both had opted for cheques. The young woman motioned to them to come to the counter.

'There you are, Mr Read and Mr Ryan, your cheques for $27,500 each. Congratulations and have a wonderful day.' She flashed a smile that, coupled with her body language said, *ask me out for dinner and I'll say yes.* The two men walked out into the street, shook hands and departed. The first thing that Read was going to do was search the title of the house that he and Ryan had followed Ironbar to.

Read opened the letter from the Titles Office that had taken three days to get to him after he had lodged a $7.50 search fee.

'Well, well, well,' Read said aloud as he read the details on the single page. That house was in the name of Edtru Holdings, a company Read surmised would have to be operated by Edith and Clyde Trueman. Now things were getting really interesting. He sat in the clutter of Welsh's study and recapped the events that had occurred since his arrival in Melbourne.

What had started as a routine claim for a couple of unlucky racehorses was starting to get involved and messy. The arrival of Ironbar Miller on the scene and his covert contact with Clyde Trueman at the Moonee Valley track had bamboozled Read and he had to know what was going on. Read took his teledex out of his briefcase and flicked it open at 'S.'

Read had met Bert Sadler years ago when he used to go out to the Rosehill racetrack in Sydney to watch the horses doing their early morning gallops. Sadler was part of the Sydney racing scene and had been a jumps jockey back in the days when those events had been on the Sydney racing calendar. He had gone on to make more than ends meet as a trainer of milers and middle distance horses. Now retired, he was a walking encyclopedia of racetrack gossip as well as the myths, facts and fictions of the racing industry. He and Read had hit it off well and the old man had found a ready listener in the younger man. He still went to the races and he still had all his marbles.

'Bert, it's Jack Read calling from Melbourne, can you hear me?'

'Jack, Jack Read, you young bugger! What are you up to down there? Behaving yourself I hope, and staying away from those dreadful bastards who wear bags around their necks.' Read warmed to the 'young bugger' remarks.

'Don't worry about the bookies, Bert,' Read replied. 'A mate and myself took the TAB for $55,000 on the quaddie last Saturday, so there.' Sadler's outback whistle coming down the line forced Read to take the phone away from his ear.

'Bert, I'm going to put your memory to the test. Tell me what you know about Clyde Trueman.' Read could see the old man sitting in his 1950s lounge room in Parramatta in Sydney's west, tugging his large left ear lobe with its sprout of white hair while he pondered Read's question. Sadler started talking.

'Jack, ask me to tell you what I don't know about Mr Clyde Trueman. Sit back and make yourself comfortable. After that win of yours this phone call won't break you.' After telling Sadler he was going to tape the call on his mini recorder, Read settled in.

Sadler was a good storyteller. He cleared his throat. 'Clyde Trueman was one of those fellas who was determined to get into the racing industry and was prepared to do what he had to do to get there. When he was young he was tall and lanky so he wasn't going to get there on the back of a horse. He had made a bit of quick money working on oil drill rigs in Queensland and over in the West so he had a bankroll. He bought himself a taxi and shared the driving. He was careful with his money and knew that punting was generally a mug's game. Are you taking all this in, young Jack?'

'Yeah, yeah, Bert. Keep on going. I'm all ears, just keep on calling me 'young Jack',' Read said. They laughed and Sadler went on.

'Clyde sort of insinuated himself into the Sydney scene. He had grown up on a farm and knew how to handle livestock. A mate of his owned a handy sprinter trained at Randwick and Clyde would go out to watch the horse work and then go back to the stables and help out for an hour or so. It wasn't long before the trainer was letting him do more and more and before you knew it, Clyde Trueman was a strapper. He kept his taxi and put another driver on and then I heard that he had gone off to be Ted Barnes' foreman and that's when the story gets interesting. Jack, just hang on, I'm going to get a glass of water.' Read could hear Sadler coming back to the phone and then a gurgling noise as Sadler swallowed. Read could visualise the man's onion-sized Adam's apple bobbing up and down in his neck.

'I'm still here, Bert, keep going,' Read said.

'Okay,' Sadler replied, taking another gulp of water. 'Jack, do you remember Ted Barnes, the trainer?' Read and anyone who had more than a passing interest in horse racing would remember the Ted Barnes case. A crushed and charred Ted Barnes was dug out of his incinerated Ford Falcon on the Sydney-Wollongong freeway in 1983. What was left of him was carried in a body bag to an ambulance by one not-so-large policeman. A post-mortem established that Barnes had suffered horrendous injuries before he had been placed in the vehicle. His cheekbones had been smashed, the scorched remnant of his upper right arm had been torn from its shoulder socket and both his femurs or upper leg bones had greenstick fractures, indicating the use of massive force. Despite an intensive investigation, no arrests were ever made.

Sadler muttered approvingly during Read's detailed appreciation of Barnes' murder. 'Spot on, Jack,' Sadler said. 'But did you know that Barnes was mixed up big time with George Freeman?'

'Shit,' exclaimed Read.

'Oh shit, yes,' said Sadler. 'Ted Barnes trained horses actually owned by Freeman but raced in the names of 'dummies.' It was a connection that never saw the light of day, even after Barnes was knocked off. It makes you wonder about some of these investigative media blokes, doesn't it, not to mention the police?'

'No, no, I didn't know anything about that at all but please tell me more,' Read urged.

'Well, Jack, after Barnes was fried in his Ford, Mrs Trueman's little boy Clyde got his big break. He got his trainer's licence and kept the stables going. After Freeman's death he closed the stables down and shifted to Melbourne to leave the past behind and make a fresh start and from what I hear, he's been pretty successful at that. Just hang on and listen while I give you the good oil on Freeman when he was around.'

'I'm still here, Bert, and reading you loud and clear,' Read said, as Sadler shifted into a higher gear.

'George Freeman made race fixing a fine art. He cut his teeth on the Sydney trots and for a time he controlled the whole kit and caboodle. He stood over those drivers that wouldn't go along with him and he had the stewards – the ones that counted – in his pocket. It was a bloody disgrace and even today, nobody wants to talk about it. He then took things another step. He started to specialise in Sydney mid-week races where the fields were small and by using standover tactics on the jockeys to make them team ride, he was able to get horses to finish one, two and three in the order he wanted.

That way he could set up the trifectas to get the best pay-outs from the tote. It was a joke, Jack – fair dinkum. Ironbar Miller was Freeman's enforcer and crooked and terrorised jockeys were his front line troops. During his time, Freeman turned Sydney racing into an absolute joke. Operating in an environment of crooked cops, bent racing officials and a media that treated criminals like celebrities, he was consistently able to engineer the best odds for the tote trifectas and quadrellas. He also made life miserable for those SP bookies who were still in business. Why would even a half-honest jockey or trainer have wanted to blow the whistle on Freeman when their only reward would have been, at the very best, a couple of broken legs? The punters never had a chance and that corrupt bag of shit, that NSW Chief Magistrate Murray Farquhar, was lured into the Freeman web by being given tips personally by the man himself. With the tips producing better than ninety per cent results, Farquhar pissed in the pockets of his very high up Labor Party mates by passing the mail on.

Payback time came when Farquhar conveniently looked the other way and perverted the course of justice whenever he sat on cases involving criminals in the Freeman mob. Imagine if you'd been sent to jail by Farquhar? How would you feel when you found out that he was a bigger crook than yourself, eh? Freeman went on to survive a hitman's bullet and defied all the odds by dying from an asthma attack. Going to get another glass of water, Jack.' Read waited for Sadler to come back to the phone. He was fascinated. The rest of the story had continued to bob up and down in the media over a period of time.

Freeman's death had rattled the Sydney mob and created a power vacuum. For a while it looked as if the criminal landscape would be blotted by a rash of old style, gangland slayings. Joe Silver, known as 'Jewboy Joe', had been a member of Freeman's inner sanctum and had always managed to stay on good terms with Ironbar Miller. He knew that keeping on side with a murderous brute like Miller would pay dividends one day. Silver would have made a good NSW politician. With support from Miller he reorganised the Freeman gang and upgraded the race rigging operation by using sophisticated drugs on the horses.

It was important that the race fixing remained successful as it helped launder a lot of the heroin and other drug money. Read recalled that Al Capone had gone to jail for tax offences, not murder. There was silence while Read took everything in. Bert Sadler sat in his chair tugging his ear and checking his memory to make sure that he had given Read the whole story. Read spoke first.

'Jesus, Bert, I'm bloody glad I got on to you. What you've told me has confirmed my worst fears. I've got the makings of a real problem on my hands down here and I think that I'm going to end up in deep shit the way things are heading. I'm not going to complicate things for you but I'll tell all when I get back to Sydney. I'll come and see you. Just to whet your appetite, Ironbar Miller is down here in Melbourne and tick-tacking with Clyde Trueman. I sprung them last Saturday at Moonee Valley. Thanks again, Bert, for all your help.'

'Jesus, Jack,' the old man said. 'Take it easy and look after yourself, son. Don't be a hero.'

Read hung up and switched off his tape recorder. He sat in his chair and after a while played back the tape. He removed it from the machine, dated and labelled it and placed it in a small plastic container. He was feeling depressed about what Sadler had told him and felt that he was losing control of the situation. He was now convinced that the death of the two horses in Clyde Trueman's care had to be treated as very suspicious. His initial unease about Griffiths the vet and Ironbar Miller's arrival in Melbourne had now been reinforced by what Sadler had told him. He was likely to get involved in something way outside his area of expertise. He didn't want to end up barbequed like Ted Barnes, all for a job that might bring him in a $3000 fee.

8

The Melbourne sky was a crisp, smogless blue and the sun had not long risen. The jangle of trams and the increasing hum of early morning traffic washed over Read as he briskly walked around the Exhibition Gardens. The female power walkers were out and about, almost goose-stepping, their swinging arms counterbalanced by the small weights they clutched tightly in their hands. One swept towards Read, ponytail flicking, her eyes rigidly fixed and looking straight ahead like one of the guards at the Shrine. Her military-like gait was not enough to suppress the sharp phut of a fart that sneaked out of her lycra tights. As Read roared with laughter, the woman almost broke into a run, terrified. He wasn't feeling as down as he had been the day before and he was starting to plan a strategy to deal with the Trueman claims.

'Chief Inspector Ryan, please.'

'I'll put you through, sir,' said the female constable at reception. 'Who shall I say is calling?'

'Mr Quadrella,' said Read, trying to be smart. 'Right, Mr Quadrella, putting you through now.' The receptionist was either being very cool or had never set foot on a racetrack. *She most probably thinks that I'm an Italian,* Read thought. A brief burst of police band muzak and Ryan came on the line. Read gained the impression that he was not amused.

'You fucking idiot, Jack.' Read felt a dill.

'Sorry, Shorty, I was being silly and it wasn't the time or place.' Ryan backed off.

'Now I've ticked you off, what can I do for you? I can't tip you into another quaddie, not for a while anyway.' Read got down to business.

'Shorty, it's about my mate, Ironbar Miller. I think you should put him under surveillance. He's obviously down here for no good reason. He's got a lousy track record, he's been up to his eyeballs in the race fixing game in Sydney and he seems to be on social terms with one of your senior magistrates. You're the boss of the Victorian Racing Squad so I imagine that all this should be of great interest to you and you should be really keen to know what Miller is up to.' Read decided not to tell Ryan about his conversation with Bert Sadler. Ryan took a while to respond.

'Yeah Jack, I can see what you're getting at but our overtime has been cut back and I'm a couple of men short. Things in the job are not what they used to be. The fucking bean counters rule supreme and the whole police culture here in Victoria is changing. Now the poofters are worming their way in, wanting the top jobs, so we're spending more time on internal politics than chasing crooks. I'd like to help you but I can't.' Read decided to press on regardless.

'Neil,' Read became more formal and decided to stroke Ryan. 'If this Miller thing produced results from your point of view, it would be a real bonus for you and it would look great on your record of service. You can delegate the job to Larry Hill, at least let him put in a couple of days on it.' Read sensed that Ryan was wavering.

'Look, here's my mobile number, give it to Hill and I'll liaise with him. I'll do a bit from my end and together we might get something firm for you. Come on, it gives me a chance to pay you back for the quaddie tip.' There was silence on the line while Read waited for Ryan's decision.

'Alright, Jack, you've convinced me but only for a couple of days. If something comes up, I might be able to take it a bit further. I'll brief Larry Hill and tell him to contact you.' Read eased his breath out.

'Thanks Neil, I really appreciate your help. Hopefully I can find out what really happened to those two racehorses. I'll catch up with you, cheers.'

Read was walking along Southbank when his mobile started heehawing. The Greensleeves ring tone was driving him mad and he promised to change it.

'Go ahead,' he said.

'Hello there, Jack, Larry Hill here. Where are you?'

'I'm at Southbank, Larry. The Yarra almost looks like a river again.' Read sensed an urgent note in Hill's voice.

'Jack, we've had a quick breakthrough with this shithead Miller. You'll find this hard to believe but he's at the Botanic Gardens right now.' Read was incredulous.

'What the bloody hell is he doing there, Larry? What do you want me to do?'

'Well, Jack, he's here with two young blokes and for my money they're jockey size. They look as if they've settled in for a while. You're very close to them so just walk across St Kilda Road and through the gardens. I'm sitting not far off them. I'm doing the boyfriend-girlfriend routine with a very nice connie who has just tried to hit me you know where!' Hill gave instructions as Read strode across the busy road into the park. It was a stroke of luck getting such a quick result but Read thought that he was due for a break.

Read moved easily through the gardens towards his target. Read grinned as he walked past a fully clothed couple who seemed oblivious of everything around them as they noisily approached what sounded like imminent orgasm. He wanted to come up from behind Miller's group. Suddenly, they came into view. Keeping cover behind some trees, Read took his mini-binoculars out of his jacket pocket. A present from a girlfriend, the glasses were invaluable and Read always carried them.

Read couldn't believe his eyes. There was Ironbar Miller, a feared standover man and thug, sitting on a bench in Melbourne's beautiful botanic gardens with two younger men feeding the wild black ducks cruising lazily around the pond. Miller was throwing the ducks what looked like potato crisps. There were more shocks for Read as he zoomed in on Miller's companions. *Christ, that's Ray*

'Dangles' Hicks, he said to himself as he identified Victoria's jockey of the year. Hicks had ridden Be Careful for Trueman on that great day at Randwick. It took Read a little longer to identify the younger of the two men but when he stood up and looked back in Read's direction, all was revealed. *Fuck me dead. Brent Adams!*

Read grunted to himself. Brent 'Pretty Boy' Adams with the Jason Donovan looks was Clyde Trueman's star apprentice and the darling of the racing writers. He looked to have a mortgage on the current apprentices' premiership.

Read traversed his glasses across the gardens and picked up Hill and his undercover policewoman companion. They were lying on the grass playing silly buggers, using the *Age* broadsheet newspaper as a screen. Hill had spotted Read and made rude gestures from behind his hide. *You'll keep, Hill,* Read said to himself as he walked away back towards the city. He didn't want to risk Miller and the others coming his way.

He had seen enough to convince himself beyond doubt that some serious criminality was taking place in the Trueman stables. It was mind-boggling stuff with Miller having the two top jocks in tow. Read made up his mind to upset the Trueman applecart as soon as possible. It was either stay on the case or crawl back to Sydney with his tail between his legs. His partner John Steele would never stop bagging him if he spat the dummy. He caught a tram back to Carlton to pick up his Range Rover. He knew exactly where he would be going.

The receptionist at the Ascot Vale Veterinary Clinic nodded in recognition at Read as he walked into the waiting room. The usual suspects were sitting there patiently with their charges. One woman had a sad and bedraggled cockatoo in a cage that looked like a candidate for that big, gilded cage in the sky.

'Is Jim in?' said Read. The woman put an incoming call on hold.

'Yes, he's busy out in the surgery. It's Mr, er…' Read helped the girl out.

'Read, Jack Read, on behalf of Centaur Livestock Insurance.

66

I just need some extra information but I'm in no great hurry. I'll sit here and wait until Mr Griffiths is finished. I've got some time to kill.' Read said 'no' to a cup of tea and flipped through the vintage magazines. Most of the covers had gone. Read passed the time reading a *1982 Australasian Post.*

'Mr Read.' Read looked up and there was Jim Griffiths standing in the doorway.

'Jack, just call me Jack,' Read said, walking towards Griffiths with his hand held out in the greeting position. The vet was slow in making the handshake, which told Read that he wasn't going to be invited home for dinner.

'Can I have a quick word with you in private, Jim? It's about that claim on Gold Crest.' Griffiths stood his ground in the doorway.

'What's the problem? I thought that we had finalised that matter the last time that you were here.'

'Yeah, but there's a few technical points to be clarified, you know,' Read said. 'Those little matters of fine print on the back of every insurance policy. You must know what it's like.'

'No, no, I don't know what it's like,' was Griffith's tart rejoinder. He could see that Read was not going to be fobbed off.

'Oh well, let's go into my office and get this thing fixed up once and for all. It really is a bloody nuisance.' Griffiths closed his office door and stood guard behind his desk. He was protecting his territory. 'Come on, Mr Read, what extra information do you need?'

Read stood on the other side of the desk and made a production of thumbing through a file that he had brought with him. He locked eyes with Griffiths as he spoke.

'Jim, was there any toxicology carried out on any of Gold Crest's organs? You know, for traces of any drugs or other substances?' The question forced Griffiths to look down at his desk before he looked up again. He didn't look happy.

'No, no, there was no need to. If you remember the first time that you came to see me, I told you that I had conducted a post-mortem on the horse and a physical examination of his heart revealed that he had died from an aneurism. Pure and simple.' Griffiths carefully clipped his words and put plenty of emphasis on 'Pure and simple.' He went on. 'If nothing had come to light after I had looked at all the organs, I would, as a matter of course, have then called for toxicology. I wanted to know why that horse died too, you know. Clyde Trueman is a good client and pays his bills on time.'

'I must say, Mr Read, that I think that all you have done is waste my time and yours, coming all the way out here to ask me that solitary question. You could have used the phone. Look, really, I've got to get back to work. No offence but I trust that this is the last time I will have to hear about this claim which should have been finalised and paid out a couple of weeks ago. Good afternoon.' Read didn't bother replying as he left the office and walked back to his car. The visit had paid off. His question had rattled Griffiths, confirming his suspicions that the vet was in it up to his eyeballs over the death of Gold Crest. Read had another call to make before he called it a day.

Lucy and Jim Prendergast lived in the right part of Toorak. Read sat in their drawing room and looked at a couple who had done very well in life. Jim Prendergast had everything going for him – Establishment stockbroker father, Geelong Grammarian, Trinity College at Melbourne University and an honours degree in Commerce leading to a rails run to a seat on the Melbourne Stock Exchange. Membership of the Melbourne Cricket Club and the Melbourne Club had been organised from the day of his birth. Members of the Melbourne establishment, Lucy and Jim Prendergast were blue ribbon Liberals and members of the Victoria Racing Club. To be invited to their marquee on Melbourne Cup Day was a very important step up the Melbourne social ladder.

'It was terribly bad luck about Gold Crest,' Read said, as he sipped his tea. It was his favourite, Prince of Wales.

'Damn bad luck, Mr Read,' said Jim Prendergast as his wife nodded in support. 'We had high hopes for that horse. Clyde Trueman was very confident that he would have gone on to win a good race but that's the luck of the game, I suppose. We've had success with some of the other horses we race and we intend putting the insurance money we get from Gold Crest back into another horse. Horseracing plays a big part in our life these days.' Read wasn't going to spoil the Prendergasts' day by telling them that the claim might end up being denied. Lawyers played a big part on both sides of the insurance fence and Read was sure that the Prendergasts would use only the best.

'I'm processing the claim as quickly as possible,' Read said, switching into PR mode. He was sure that the owners would not want to discuss the grubby subject of money though they appeared to be down-to-earth people, despite their obvious wealth. Their house, the older model Rolls and the original Olleys and Drysdales on the walls quietly proclaimed 'old money.' 'I'm sure that you are good at your job, Mr Read, and when all the paperwork has been completed, we will no doubt hear from Clyde Trueman.' Lucy Prendergast stood up. It was the signal for Read to go.

Driving down St Georges Rd away from the mansion, Read brought himself up to date. He should have visited the Prendergasts earlier as they were the actual policy holders but all the documentation was held by Trueman and anyway, at law he was the the Prendergasts' agent and Gold Crest had died in his care. The owners were gilt edged and obviously not involved in any illegality at any level. As Read assured himself of their innocence, his mind drifted elsewhere and soon he started to think of different ways to fuck Sylvia.

It was another perfect Melbourne morning and Read was sitting at the footpath table outside the café in Lygon Street enjoying his tea and raisin toast. He wondered what damage all those exhaust fumes in the atmosphere would be doing to his innards as he washed down the last slice of toast. It was a shame more people didn't use public transport. Violence and vandalism had driven a lot of commuters back to the motor car. Read had his day mapped out. It was time to go on the offensive over the Centaur claims.

***

9

Read stood on the footpath opposite Clyde Trueman's house. The big Merc had gone. It was a Wednesday and the races were at Ballarat. Trueman had a couple of promising young horses entered and was combining business with pleasure.

The owners were wealthy Hong Kong Chinese and Trueman wanted to make sure that they were given every encouragement to invest in his stable. Read wondered if Edith Trueman was at home. The double garage was closed and he couldn't see her car out in the street. He was there to have a stickybeak and a chance encounter with a stablehand might just produce results.

Read cautiously walked to the gate separating the main house from the stables. His mates, the two cattle dogs were nowhere in sight and he wondered why that was so. The thought of the two unchained dogs suddenly coming upon him gave him spasms in his groin. Prepared for a rapid retreat he quietly opened the gate.

He had nothing to fear. The two dogs were sitting in the locked and enclosed rear verandah, gnawing and slavering over some big, meaty beef bones given them by Edith Trueman. Any thought of their security duties had been extinguished by their discharging salivary glands.

Wearing his favourite synthetic-soled Rossi walking boots, Read moved silently and casually down past one row of boxes. A couple of inquisitive horses poked their heads out to see what was going on. From time to time, the silence was broken as a horse impatiently kicked out at the wall of its box. A swallow coming in out of the sunlight executed a split-arse turn and streaked through the stables, heading for its nest in the eaves. Read could hear muffled, indistinct sounds coming from the direction in which he was moving. He slowed his pace and relaxed, ready for a confrontation.

In horse stables, all the gear is kept in the tack room. Saddles, harness, headstalls, rugs and all the other racing paraphernalia are repaired, maintained and stored in the tack room. Most are a shambles but the Trueman tack room was a model of discipline and order. Everything was in its proper place and the leather was redolent of neatsfoot oil and leather soap. A lot of stable and racing gossip was exchanged in this workplace and a couple of old, three-seater club lounges provided just the place for it.

The outer door to the tack room was one of those old-fashioned, farm-style, vertically planked affairs but shrinkage between the timbers allowed Read to see through into the room beyond. Some coats hanging on the other side of the door still allowed a good field of view. He knew that he was taking a serious risk but the noise that he had first heard was close by and beyond the door.

As Read peered through the door, he jerked involuntarily and almost grunted aloud with surprise. Edith Trueman was standing, bent over the end of one of the lounges in the tack room with her hands on the seat cushions in front of her. Her bra was still on but her breasts were pushed out over the top of it, revealing her erect nipples. Read could see her slacks and panties at the other end of the lounge. He could also see that Edith Trueman had certainly looked after what God had given her.

The noise that had attracted Read was Edith's short, staccato grunts. The reason for it was Ray 'Dangles' Hicks, the champion jockey, thrusting into her, doggie style. He had gripped her firmly by her hips and was slapping her rear hard with his lower stomach and upper legs as he drove into her – thwack, thwack, thwack. Every so often she would lift her right hand to her left breast, twirling her nipple. Edith Trueman was being well fucked.

Read found himself fascinated by the performance on the

other side of the door and he wanted to swap places with Hicks. *Stop being fucking stupid,* he scolded himself. Edith and her jockey were approaching the end of their race. Read was jealous of Hicks' stamina and his performance. He was all ropey muscle and no fat, and was sweating up. *It certainly beats the fuck out of sweltering in a sauna,* Read thought to himself.

The mare under Hicks was pushing back and grinding her arse faster and faster. Her panting had deepened to an urgent groaning. Hicks had the whip out and was driving for the winning post. The muscles in his buttocks started twitching and his fuzz-coated balls contracted as he let go and pumped into his desperately receptive mount. Edith and Ray were speaking in strange tongues as they fell across the line.

Read suddenly snapped out of it and felt like a dill as he stepped back from the door. Now he knew how a Peeping Tom felt. He had a sudden urge to run but checked himself and walked away quickly, but as he was about to open the gate and leave the premises he decided to be a real bastard. He turned and walked loudly back towards the stables. He disguised his voice.

'Anyone home?' he yelled out. 'Hello there, anyone home?' He had a clear voice that travelled well. The dogs, aware of their dereliction of duty, started barking savagely, hurling themselves against the back door. Read grinned. He could imagine the absolute panic and chaos out in the tack room. He had done enough damage so turned and walked quickly back to his car. Checking his mirrors as he pulled away from the curb and catching a glimpse of himself, he couldn't but smile as his thoughts turned to Sylvia.

It had taken Read three early morning attendances at the Ascot Vale house to catch Ironbar Miller on the move. Being super-cautious and not wanting to be sprung, Read dropped back about three cars behind his target. It helped that Miller was not a fast driver. After a few kilometres it was obvious that he has heading for Tullamarine Airport.

Miller parked in the long-term car park and walked towards

the Qantas Domestic Terminal. Read watched him disappear inside the building and for a brief moment he thought about breaking into Miller's car to see if there was anything worthwhile looking at.

A security guard patrolling nearby was enough reason for him to give the idea a miss. He drove off back to the city, deciding to be cheeky and pay another visit to Clyde Trueman's stables.

Order had been restored. The two dogs were back on duty, chained near the entrance gate and Edith Trueman was watering some hanging plants at the rear of the house. She saw Read and told the dogs to behave themselves.

'Hello there, Mr Read,' she said brightly. She was perfectly groomed as always, confident in the role she played in her husband's business as hostess and companion for the wives and lovers of rich clients.

'Clyde's gone off to a stud to arrange a service for one of our broodmares. He won't be back until late. Can I be of any help?' Read thought about the servicing that Ray Hicks had given to Trueman's wife the day before and nearly cracked up.

'No, Mrs Trueman, is Joylene around? I just need to clear up a couple of points in her statement. You know, dot a few i's and cross a few t's.' Edith Trueman smiled, showing off her perfectly capped teeth.

'Yes, Joylene is here. She'll be out in the stables somewhere. After you've seen her, drop back in at the house and I'll make you a cup of tea.'

'I'll take you up on that, Mrs Trueman,' said Read, as he started to walk through to the stables.

'Call me Edith,' she said brightly. Read laughed.

'Alright, Edith, but remember my name's Jack.'

Read found Joylene in the tack room sorting out some harness. She knew what she was doing and kept working while acknowledging Read.

'Hello there, can't stay away from the place, eh?' Read couldn't resist the temptation. He sat on the end of the couch where Edith Trueman had been ridden the day before. He wrinkled his nose. It was there, barely perceptible, just a hint of perfumed fragrance, the only remaining forensic evidence of the previous day's feature race. All of a sudden, Read felt a fool. He had forgotten about the other evidence that may have been deposited on his end of the couch. He got up quickly, ignoring the temptation to closely inspect the area in question and reseated himself on the other lounge.

Joylene Mills took a break and sat down next to the cold potbelly stove.

'Well, what can I do to help you?' she said, fingering the good luck charm that hung from her neck. Read felt that he had established a rapport with Joylene despite their one brief meeting and hoped that she might want to open up to him.

'Joylene, I just thought that you might be able to help me with a bit of information. I can see that you really like your job and the horses and you're the sort of person who wouldn't want to see them hurt in any way. Anything that you might tell me will be strictly off the record, that means it's between you and me and nobody else.'

By trying to win Joylene's confidence, he was taking a big risk asking her questions about Ironbar Miller but he was sure that she was a straight shooter. Joylene looked at Read, still toying with her good luck charm.

Read went on and described Ironbar Miller. 'Have you seen this bloke talking to Clyde or hanging around the stables? He's got a bad reputation up in Sydney for being involved in a bit of dodgy business with horses and there's got to be a reason for him being down here in Melbourne.' Read held his breath while waiting for a response. He had shown his hand and it could backfire on him, big time. He was playing in the big league now but he wasn't going to tell Joylene the whole story. That would be tempting fate. Joylene bit her bottom lip and looked uncomfortable.

'Gee, Jack, I just want to do a good job here and not get involved in any trouble. Do you appreciate that? If anything bad was happening, I would certainly say something about it.' Joylene looked uncomfortable. 'Don't you think I would?'

Read had the feeling that he had gone too early with her about Miller. He backed off.

'Joylene, I don't think that at all. Come on, don't be silly. You're a good kid. I'm just a bit worried about some aspects of the Gold Crest claim and I have to do my job or else I'll end up on the dole queue. You can understand that, can't you?' Read could see Joylene relax a little.

He stood up. 'I'll give you another of my cards. If something crops up, please give me a call. Remember, I'm not a dobber and you're a good sort doing a bloody good job.' *A little flattery could pay results,* Read thought as they shook hands.

'I'm off to have morning tea with The Body,' he said with a grin. Joylene laughed.

'Would you like a piece of cake or a biscuit, Jack? I've got some fresh Anzac biscuits here.' Edith Trueman poured Read's tea from a silver, Robur, seven-cup teapot. These teapots were collectors' pieces but still regularly popped up at auction houses.

'I'll settle for an Anzac, thanks Edith.' Now on first-names basis, Read and Edith swapped small talk and chatted about horses. Read wasn't going to ask any curly questions. Now that he was up to date on Trueman's past association with the murdered trainer Ted Barnes and Barnes' links with George Freeman, he was not going to say anything that would get Edith off side. She was cheating on her husband but she depended on his success to maintain her lifestyle and she would defend him to the bitter end.

Read decided to find out more about the woman pouring him a second cup of tea.

'How did you and Clyde meet, Edith?' She giggled coquettishly as though ashamed,

'I'm not pulling your leg, Jack, but I was in charge of one of the cosmetics outlets at Georges, and Clyde was there buying perfume for his first wife. He came back a few weeks after that and we started talking. You know, one thing led to another and here I am.'

She flirted, smoothing down the upper front of her slacks. Read could visualise her at work, dabbing perfume on her svelte wrist, getting Trueman to sample the scent and ensnaring her prey.

'Wasn't I a naughty girl?' she added. Read finished his tea and made ready to leave. As they walked to the front door, she made body contact with him. It was a pat on his left forearm from her right hand but it told Read a lot. Driving away, he reckoned that he had worked Edith out. Her body language and her general manner told him that she liked men and that she liked fucking. *What's so wrong with that?* he thought, as he headed back to the city.

Read was browsing through the kitchen and cooking ware section at Myer when his mobile went off. As though answering a phone for the very first time, Read said, 'Go ahead.' His phone manners were a hangover from his PNG days of using two-way radios.

'Jack, it's Joylene here. I'm ringing you from a public phone box.' She hesitated. Read helped her take the next step.

'Joylene, great to hear from you. I'm glad that you called. What's up?' Joylene tugged at the front of her sweatshirt.

'Jack, I'd like to see you somewhere well away from the stables.' Read cut in quickly, taking advantage of the moment.

'Look, Joylene, no problems. Let's have a cup of coffee somewhere, it's up to you, you pick the place and the time.' Joylene paused.

'All right, do you know Kensington? You do! Well, there's a coffee shop called Coffee Break on the right side of the main street as you go up the hill away from the city. Let's meet there at four.' Read could sense that he was getting close to a breakthrough.

'Four at the Coffee Break. See you then, Joylene, and thanks again for calling.' He was out in the street and heading for the closest tram stop to take him to Kensington.

Joylene Mills was sitting at a table at the rear of the shop when Read walked in. She wore her usual uniform of jeans and windcheater. Her damp hair sticking to her scalp showed she had just showered. She smiled as Read sat down. After checking with Joylene, he ordered two cappuccinos. Read made small talk to give her the chance to get settled. She cracked her knuckles as she started to speak.

'How did morning tea go with The Body the other day?' Joylene was feeling her way.

'Edith's an interesting woman,' replied Read.

'I'm sure that she's an asset to the stables, good for Clyde's PR too, especially when he's out to impress Asians.' 'Yes, our Edith can charm them. I don't like her much but she's a good operator.' Joylene changed tack.

'Jack, I didn't want to say anything when you and I were talking back at the stables. I can trust you, can't I?' Read put his hand reassuringly on Joylene's and fixed his eyes on hers.

'You have to make your own decision about that, Joylene.' She decided in Read's favour.

'Jack, I think that Griffiths, the vet, is up to something. During the last few months he's been turning up at the stables at odd times. He was there very early on the morning Dapper Dan crashed into the rail at Flemington. Now, if a horse is crook or has a problem, I report it to Barry Hunt, the stable foreman. You haven't met him yet, he's on leave. He then arranges for the vet to come. For things like drenching and regular checkups, Griffiths or one of the other vets turn up at regular times and we have the horses all ready for them. We have a special calendar on the wall of the tack room showing all the dates for that.'

Joylene paused and pulled out a set of rosary beads. *A Catholic girl with a confession to make? Father Jack is all ears.*

'That Miller bloke you were talking about has been at the stables. He arrived early one morning and had breakfast with Clyde. He was there for quite a while. Your description was spot on. He's an ugly bugger, isn't he?' Read noticed what looked like an engagement ring.

'That's a nice ring, Joylene. Who's the lucky fella?' Joylene looked down.

'Yes, a gift from a great bloke. Pat Byrnes. We were going to get married, I don't know why I keep wearing it. He was a jockey on his way to the top but he was killed in a race crash at Rosehill up in Sydney. Them's the breaks, I guess.' She looked a little forlorn.

'That's very sad, Joylene,' Read never knew what to say at times like this. 'You never know in life when something is going to pop up and knock you for six just when everything is going okay.' He paused, he hoped for long enough, before saying 'Yeah, you're right about Miller. He's no oil painting, that's for sure. Very interesting that he came to see Clyde. I'll tell you what. You just keep your eyes open from now on and if you want to talk to me, keep on using a public phone. I don't want to get you into trouble. You've got a good job and you don't want to lose it. You're going to do alright out of life, believe me. Well, unless you want another cup of coffee, I must be off.' Joylene shook her head and they stood up. Read got to the street ahead of her. He waved goodbye and headed for the tram.

Joylene is a good kid, Read thought, as he drove past the Victoria Markets. He hadn't liked Jim Griffiths from the moment he had met him. Now he had to find out what he was giving to Clyde Trueman's horses. Read bet that whatever it was, it would be a little more complicated than a dose of vitamins. The first thing to do would be to report progress to Les Trist of Centaur.

Sylvia was swabbing down a table and replenishing the coasters when Read walked into the Lemon Tree. She was wearing her hair up, fixed by some combs and it softened her face. Her smile of recognition told Read that everything was okay and that made him feel good and possessive all at the same time.

'Hello, Mr Read,' she said brightly as Read breasted the bar. 'The usual?' she put a pot of Carlton Draught on the bar.

'What if I had wanted a rum and Coke?' Read asked.

'Stop being a dickhead, Jack,' said Sylvia as she went to the other end of the bar. As she stood in profile, Read undressed her with his eyes. He was getting hooked, and he didn't mind.

'Sylvia, when you've got a moment please.' Sylvia waved him away haughtily as she served other customers. She was being cheeky. After a while she returned to where Read was standing, leaning forward she whispered '

'Stop being a dickhead Jack' before walking to the other end of the bar. She enjoyed being a tease and it had the desired effect – Read felt a tingle in his cock.

Read turned his glass upside down, indicating that he didn't want another drink.

'Cracked the shits and leaving are you, Jack?'

'No way,' Read said, 'but I've got to go and do some work or else I won't be able to take you to the races at Flemington on Saturday.'

'First I've heard about it,' replied Sylvia.

'How do you know I don't already have a date with a real spunk?' Read knew she was revving him up but despite that, he felt a niggle of jealousy.

'Well, you've heard about it now, Sylvia. I'm not in the spunk league, so I'm at your mercy. Go on, knock me back and destroy me.' Sylvia smiled.

'Just kidding, can't you take it? You know I want to come to the races with you as long as you treat me like a lady and don't leave me sitting around on my own.' Read felt back in control again.

'I'll pick you up at eleven, that'll give us time to get there for the first race. We'll be going into the members section. I'll be wearing a jacket and tie so you can put on your glad rags. I'd better get going. Take it easy and be good.'

'That last part might be hard,' Sylvia parried back as Read departed. *I wonder if she's sharing it around?* he thought.

Les Trist was on the phone. 'Jesus, Jack, what's going on down there? Sounds as if you've got some real problems.'

'Well, what do you suggest, Les?' Trist had great confidence in Read. He was professional and didn't crap on like a lot of other assessors did. He had a good network of contacts and his reports were precise and easy to read, made better by his keen sense of humour.

'At this stage, Les,' Read replied, 'we can't do much except hope for a break. Time is against us of course because anytime now, Clyde Trueman is going to ring you up and ask you when his client will get the insurance money. Let's do this. If that happens, put it all back on me and tell them I haven't submitted my report and you can't do a thing anyway until that happens. We'll just have to stall them off on the chance luck swings our way and I think it will. What do you reckon?' Les Trist was easily convinced.

'All okay with me, Jack. You obviously think that this thing stinks and that's good enough for me. I'll do my bit from this end and we'll see what happens.' Read told Trist that he was going to Flemington.

'Back Eraser in the first race, Jack. He's a first start two-year-old who's pretty smart. He hasn't trialled publicly but I've been told that he has been brilliant on the track. A lot of these boom youngsters often fizzle, so be careful. Watch the market. You could get tens.'

'Thanks very much for that, Les.' Trist had often tipped Read into winners so he noted the horse in his diary. Backing the first winner on the card was the right way to start a day at the races.

10

The man was in another world. He was looking sideways at his naked image in a full-length Victorian cheval mirror. Then he looked down at his hands caressing the curly blond hair of the young nude kneeling in front of him. His cock was being expertly sucked and he was wondering how much longer he could last. It had been going on now for about twenty-five minutes and he was trying to think about anything else but cuming. He started making slow fucking movements in time with the mouth gripping him. David Felton, male prostitute, gently massaged his client's balls, making them tighten. David increased the rating as he felt a change in the taste of the cock. Pay day was getting closer. The man began grunting, noise mixed up with words.

'David, David, oh God, Patricia, Patricia, please help me, please save me, oh fuck.' Finally, Felton could feel the liquid pumping into his mouth. He reached up with his left hand which the man's right hand clasped and squeezed in time with his final contractions. Felton's fingers played with the smooth black onyx and gold signet ring on the third finger of his client's hand. The act over, Felton got off his knees and went to the bathroom to rinse out his mouth. The man trailed slowly behind, trying to hug him.

'David,' he panted, 'that was wonderful, you always are.' Felton looked at the man in the wall mirror.

'Show me how much you appreciate me by leaving a good tip, a better one than that on the end of your dick at the moment.' He giggled as the man self-consciously put his hand down on his slack penis. While his client showered, Felton returned to the other room and took the $300 off the top of the small dressing table. Not bad for less than an hour's work. He looked around him. The small bedsitter flat in South Yarra, in a small side street and off the beaten track, was ideal for his work. He still worked out of an agency but kept the flat for top-shelf clients he pirated when on agency work.

The client he had just serviced was more than top of the shelf, he was top of the town. After the man had kissed him and left, Felton opened the top drawer of the dressing table and removed the hi-tech Pearlcorder mini tape recorder. He slipped out the micro-cassette, put it in an envelope then loaded a new tape into the machine, putting it back in the drawer. Felton felt very pleased with himself. The day was not far off when he would drive out of Bib Stillwell's in a shiny black BMW convertible.

What a great day, Read thought as he headed off to the newsagent to get the *Truth* form guide. The track was sure to be good or even fast and for him that meant honest racing. Backing horses in the mud was a mug's game. Too many things could go wrong. It was about 10.45 am as Read parked outside Sylvia's house. A mangy cat with a rat-tail scuttled out from underneath the car in front of him.

'Hang on, take it easy,' was the response Read got after he had pressed the door buzzer. He stood back and waited.

Read heard Sylvia walking towards the door. There was a pause while she turned the deadlock and then opened the door with a flourish. He let out a long wolf whistle as Sylvia performed a slow pirouette. Her hat and her simple but stylish navy blue outfit and top framed her natural assets.

'Sylvia, you look just great,' Read said slowly, holding open the security screen door.

'No, no, look but don't touch,' Sylvia laughed as she pushed Read away as he tried to kiss her. Read held the car door open and Sylvia slid into the passenger seat, showing Read a good flash of her long, firm legs. Sylvia was on to him.

'Down boy,' she growled.

Before they passed through the turnstiles, Read gave Sylvia her lady's guest ticket for entrance to the members enclosure. As a member of the Australian Jockey Club based at Randwick in Sydney, he enjoyed reciprocal rights with the Victoria Racing Club at Flemington. Read followed Sylvia into the members enclosure and steered her out on to the lawn in front of the grandstand.

'Oh Jack, this is beautiful,' she said, as she took in the gardens and the bowling-green-like lawn. 'I've never been on a racetrack before so this is all new to me.' As Read surveyed all the drop-dead gorgeous girls and women and the men perving on them, he kept his thoughts to himself. *Two things make this world go around – sex and dollars.* Read looked across the track to the totalisator semaphore board and saw that the track rating was good. With her hair swept up under a ritzy, wide-brimmed hat, Sylvia was getting plenty of attention from the men walking by.

'Come on, Sylvia, let's go over to the horse stalls. I want to have a look at a horse I've been tipped in the first race.' As Read told her about Eraser on the way, Sylvia took Read's hand and pulled him closer to her side.

Eraser was being saddled up as they reached his stall. He was a showy chestnut with a shiny liverish tinge to his coat. Enough of his rib was showing – evidence of his fitness. He was on the move and being playful with his strapper who was adjusting the bridle.

'This horse wants to race, Sylvia. Let's go to the betting ring and see what his price is with the bookies.' Read looked at his racebook and saw that Clyde Trueman's horses were in stalls further down the line towards the public car park.

'Show me how to bet, Jack,' Sylvia said, as they moved through the growing crowd towards the rails bookmakers.

'Well, it's pretty simple,' said Read, warming to his task and taking her aside where it was a bit quieter. 'You've got the bookies who give you odds that are fixed at the moment you place your bet. Ten to one means that you put on one dollar to win ten, you get eleven back – your win plus your stake. The tote is different. The odds move up and down just like the bookies but when you place your bet you don't get the odds indicated at that time. The tote might be showing ten to one when you put your money on but at the close of betting it might be four to one and that's all you will get paid. Even so, the tote often pays much more than what the bookies are offering. It depends on where the so-called educated money is going. I'll tell you about place betting later.'

As usual the rails bookies were level pegging with the tote odds. 'No bargains here,' Read grumbled. Sylvia tapped him on the shoulder.

'Jack, that bookie over there has Eraser at seven to one. All the others have him at six.' Sylvia hadn't caught on yet to using the plural when reading off the prices but she was learning fast. Read looked up at the tote board where Eraser was showing nine dollars, which meant about eight to one. With twenty minutes to starting time, he decided to hang off a bit.

'Jack, how much are you going to put on him?' Sylvia asked. Read had confidence in Les Trist's tipping skills and the horse had looked good. He wanted to see if any rush of late money came for it.

'I'm going to back it if I see the price shorten, that'll mean some informed money thinks it can win. I'm prepared to put $200 on it for a win.' As Read spoke, the bookie who had first had Eraser at sevens shortened the price to eleven to two. Read moved.

'Wish me luck,' he called back to Sylvia as he moved into the scrum of punters milling around the rails bookies who were perched above the crowd on their stands. Read managed to secure the eleven to two before the price dropped again to nine to two. The smart money was coming now.

Up in the members grandstand, Sylvia and Read had a good view back up the Straight Six, so-called because it is one of the most famous straight six furlong, or 1200 metre, sprint courses in the world. Starting at the Epsom Road end of the Flemington racetrack complex, the straight track runs in a slight south-westerly direction towards the Maribyrnong River, which is the western boundary of the racecourse. The winning post is opposite the Hill Stand, a general public area.

From the members grandstand vantage point, the view of the winning post is not all that impressive, given that when the horses pass the stand, they still have just under 200 metres to travel to the finishing line. As the horses show their rear ends to the spectators in the members and run away from them down to the post, it takes a good pair of binoculars and an ability to judge angles to call the finish of a close race.

Eraser's race was over five furlongs, or 1000 metres. He was drawn towards the grandstand side of the track. Read was leaning against Sylvia with his binoculars focused on the start.

'They're off!' he said sharply, in sync with the racecaller. Eraser jumped out well and headed towards the grandstand rail while the majority of the field set sail for the flat side rail. Watching the field running towards him as they passed the 800 metre mark, Read was in no position to judge Eraser's position. Of the five horses in the division coming down the grandstand side, Read could see Eraser's colours bobbing, one horse off the rail and just behind the two leaders. Over on the flat side, the favourite was out in front.

'I can't see Eraser, Jack,' said Sylvia, worriedly. Having no binoculars and being inexperienced in matching horses and colours, she was having a difficult time.

'Don't worry, sweetheart, he's there with a chance. They'll be passing the birdcage near the horse stalls in a moment and I'll get a better idea. No wonder the racecallers say the Straight Six is their nightmare.' As he spoke, traversing his glasses from the flat side back to the grandstand side, Read found himself looking head-on at Eraser. The horse had well and truly taken the bit and was galloping strongly. Better still, the jockey had him hard held.

'Here he comes, Sylvia.' Read was yelling now.

'Shush,' said Sylvia, feeling embarrassed. Eraser had bullocked his way to the lead but Read couldn't see if he was in front of the horses battling away on the flat side.

All of a sudden, the horses were racing past the members stand. Read and Sylvia stood up. Eraser was still leading the horses on the grandstand side and seemed to be in front of those on the flat side.

'Go Eraser, go!' Read still had his glasses on the horses and was 'whipping' Eraser with the form guide in his right hand.

'Sit down in front,' came a peeved voice from the back of the crowd.

'Piss off,' said Sylvia to no one in particular. The horses were closing in on the winning post. Eraser was responding well to some heavy whip work and his shoulders and neck were silvery with sweat. His jockey looked over at the opposition on the flat side.

'Keep going, keep going, you little ripper, go on, go on, give the bastards some,' Read yelled. Sylvia gripped Read around the shoulders as they jumped up and down. As the horses flashed over the finishing line, Read turned to Sylvia.

'Jesus, I think he's made it, I think he's just got there.'

The announcer's voice came in distorted waves over the public address system. 'Eraser by a long neck, photo for second and third.' Read and Sylvia hugged each other and spun around.

'You little bloody beauty,' Read yelled, waving his winning ticket in Sylvia's face. They kissed and Sylvia poked her tongue into Read's mouth.

'Jack, I've been soaking wet ever since we got here,' she whispered in his ear. Flushed with excitement from the race, Read was now starting to bar up.

'Whoa girl, easy there, settle down,' He put his hands on Sylvia's waist and pulled her crutch onto his raised right knee and rubbed it for a moment. Mutual lust locked their eyes. Two matrons behind them tut-tutted at their public display. Read snapped himself out of it.

'Come on, Sylvia, you can collect the winnings from the bookie.' As they travelled down the escalator, the course announcer called

'Correct weight'.

Sylvia allowed herself to be towed along by Read as he cut across the betting ring to the pay-out section.

'Jack, slow down a bit,' she called, still holding his hand.

'There you are, Sylvia. See that fat bloke with the big bag hanging around his neck, the bag that has B. Hill printed on it. That's our man. Take this ticket and bring back $1300 please. Make sure that you count the money in front of him before you leave because some bookies' clerks can't count properly.' Read stood back as Sylvia eagerly headed off. She was having fun.

'Do I get a tip?' Sylvia giggled, as she handed Read the new $100 notes.

'Let's go down to the champagne bar and I'll buy you a drink.' Read was feeling good. He had backed the first winner on the card and now had a bank for the rest of the day. He had a beautiful woman on his arm who made him feel horny just with a hand squeeze and the sun was shining. Snapping out of his reverie, Read reminded himself to keep an eye out for Ironbar Miller.

So far there had been no sighting and he hadn't run into Neil Ryan yet, who he assumed would be on the course as part of his duty. After a couple of delightfully cold glasses of Moet each, Sylvia and Read walked back to the horse stalls. Read had dropped $100 on the second race because he had been silly and let Sylvia make a selection based on her birth date. Read had $50 each way on it at thirty-three to one, and it was still running.

Read got Sylvia to stand back in the crowd with him when they got to Clyde Trueman's horse stalls. He didn't want to make contact with either Joylene Mills or her boss. Trueman had eight horses entered for the day and Read could see Joylene with the rest of the crew working their backsides off. Trueman was in there with her, checking the girth strap and adjusting the bit. His jacket was on a hanger on the back wall of the stall. He prided himself on leading from the front and wasn't worried about getting his hands dirty. It went down well with his clients. He owed a lot to his days on a drill rig in outback Queensland. Read looked at Razorback, the four-year-old gelding that Trueman had entered in the main sprint of the day down the Straight Six.

Razorback was on the move in his stall and looked a ball of muscle. Read turned to Sylvia.

'After the next race we'll go into the betting ring and keep an eye on Razorback here, as I think that if the money comes for him, he'll be a big show. Let's go and just look at the next race, we'll give the lucky numbers a miss.' Read was not going to complicate things by telling Sylvia what he had found out about Clyde Trueman.

After watching some ordinary horses make hard work out of running a mile, Sylvia and Read took up a position close to Michael Faulkner, one of the leading rails bookies at Flemington. Read knew enough about the Melbourne bagmen to realise that if the smart and informed money came for a horse, Faulkner would be one of the first targets. Razorback was to be ridden by Brent Adams, Trueman's ace apprentice and feeder of ducks at the Botanic Gardens. The horse opened at ten to one with a few of the more timid bookmakers quoting it at eights.

A thin, snappily dressed man wearing a straw Panama hat and white linen suit sidled up to Faulkner and muttered something out of the side of his mouth. His body language was classic racetrack. Faulkner, standing on his raised perch on the rails, leant down and listened intently. Read watched his fingers tentatively stray towards the knob that controlled the odds for Razorback. Panama hat walked back into the crowd as Faulkner took some cash bets from either side of the rail that separated the members area from the great unwashed. Razorback was still at tens.

'What's happening, Jack?' Sylvia was starting to get impatient.

'Take it easy, girl,' Read replied. 'We can't afford to rush in. It's no good backing this horse if there's no solid support for him. It's hard to explain but a lot of horses go out to race and for all sorts of reasons their connections have no intention of winning. Everyone involved in racing would deny this until they were blue in the face but believe me, it's true. I'll explain in more detail when we're relaxing over a drink back at your place.'

'Don't take anything for granted, Jack.' Sylvia was keeping Read on his toes.

Read moved a little closer to Faulkner's stand. He didn't want to be caught short if a rush came. All of a sudden the crowd moved and Read saw some men on both sides of the rails surge forward. They all had thick wads of $100 notes held aloft like prayer books. Read broke away from Sylvia and with $500 at the ready he headed for Faulkner. He was suddenly consumed by doubt: *what if the money wasn't going on Razorback?* Faulkner had wound the odds down from tens to eight by the time Read had reached him. He was on the right horse alright. Read put $100 each way at eight to one for Sylvia and $150 the same way for himself. As Read took the betting tickets from Faulkner, Razorback's price dropped two more points to six to one. Read handed Sylvia her ticket.

'Here you are, Sylvia, there's a present for you. If Razorback loses we'll still be $500 up on the day. Let's hang around and watch the action for a bit to see if his price drops further.'

In the members betting ring there was another flurry of activity.

'What's going on there,' Sylvia wanted to know, as she watched a small group of men cruising the rails. They appeared to be following a tall, well-dressed man betting on credit. He would walk up to a bookie, whisper something in his ear, make a note in a small diary then move on. Like parasitic sucker fish trailing a shark, he was being tagged by punters making small cash wagers in his wake. His target was Razorback because that horse's odds kept shortening as the man laid his bets.

The best price was now seven to two. As the man got closer and moved past, Read recognised him. Just about everyone in Australia knew Rex Jardine, the controversial Victorian Police and Corrective Services Minister who was always in the news. A trendy leftie and civil libertarian, Jardine was well known in the media for his more-than-liberal views about how prisons should be run. He was always getting death threats from exasperated victims of crime and the redneck brigade. Read took Sylvia's arm.

'Let's go up to the stand and watch this race. I think we're in with a show. The Victorian Police Minister has just had a packet on Razorback.'

Brent Adams walked Razorback into barrier 4 at the 1200 metre start of the Straight Six, assisted by a barrier attendant who closed the padded gate behind him. Adams could feel the horse shivering with energy beneath him. He was three horses off the flat side of the track but jockeys who had ridden in a previous race down the Straight Six had told him that the track on the grandstand side was firmer going, even though the track rating was good. After a spell of hot weather the track was watered and the flat side held water more than the other side.

Getting ready for the start, Brent Adams was working out his strategy for getting Razorback over to the grandstand side. There were a couple of speedy squibs in the race and he didn't want his horse to use up too much energy early in the race. The starter moved across to his stand and called to the jockeys to get ready. As the flashing strobe lights on top of the stalls started blinking, the starter got ready to press the electronic button to open the gates of the barrier. Brent Adams knew that one of the attendants was standing at the back of Razorback's stall, ready to give the horse a hard whack on its rump when the gates flew open. Clyde Trueman would come good with a slab of beer for this service.

Whang! The gates flew open with the jangling of the starting bell. Some jockeys yelled and swore, urging their mounts on. Razorback, a good beginner, jumped out well with Brent Adams sooling him on, angling him towards the grandstand side. About two-thirds of the field had the same game plan. Razorback was keen to race and Adams had to hold him hard until he settled in behind the leading pack. He hoped that the horse would not pull too hard as all his energy would be needed for the rush to the finish line. He had Razorback travelling about five horses from the grandstand rail and he was looking ahead, ready to lunge forward if a gap opened up.

The field raced past the 2800 metre starting point and headed towards the birdcage in front of the horse stalls. A couple of horses in front began to roll and shorten stride – a sure sign they would soon drop back through the field. Mick 'Maggots' Brady, the veteran jockey who looked like a garden gnome, was riding Rebel on Adams' left and he was keeping up with Razorback. Nicknamed 'Maggots' by racegoers because of the colourful accusation that he was always riding a dead'un, Brady started yelling at the top of his voice.

'Fuck off up front, fuck off, get outta the fucking way, you cocksuckers, I'm coming through.' He continued his tirade as he spurred his horse and whipped at its right rear flank. As he did so, he hit Razorback's left front shoulder at the beginning of the stroke, causing that horse to shy away and become unbalanced. Brent Adams felt his horse react to the sting of Brady's whip.

'What the fuck, get out with you!' Adams' falsetto yell stabbed across at Brady as he reefed his horse to the right to get out of the way. Rebel had responded to Brady's riding and bustled past the tiring horses up front as most of the jockeys began another round of yelling and cursing their horses and each other.

Adams could see the lawn area in front of the members stand coming up on his right. The field was fanning out across the track as tiring horses slowed and drifted this way and that. Adams scored the jockey's dream, a rails run. Razorback surged forward, sucking in air like a jet turbine. As the crowd roared, Adams knew he was going to win easily as in a couple of bounds his horse had put two lengths between him and the rest of the field. The horses on the flat side were all making hard work of it. Razorback was making a roaring noise like a baying hound in pursuit. His heart was engorged, pumping oxygenated blood at an incredible rate. As the finishing line rushed towards him, Brent Adams found it hard to hold his horse.

'What a run! This will have to be a course record,' the racecaller yelled excitedly as Razorback swooshed past the winning post.

'Go Razorback, you little fu… beauty.' Read just managed to

stop himself using the in-and-out expletive. The last thing he wanted was to be hauled before the VRC heavies for unseemly behaviour. He could lose his reciprocal rights.

'This has been one of the best punting days I've had for a while, Sylvia. I've had bigger collects but being here with you has really made my day. Let's go down and collect. Your winnings will pay your rent for a few weeks. How about that!' Sylvia squeezed Read's hand and kissed him on the cheek.

Brent Adams was standing up in the stirrups as he tried to pull Razorback up. The reins were cutting into his hands from the strain. From the horse's neck and shoulders, big gobs of sweat – like shaving cream – were blowing back onto his face and chest. The horse was galloping as if it never wanted to stop and Adams was getting worried; he didn't want to excite the interest of the stewards. Clyde Trueman had told him that Razorback was a sure thing a couple of days before the race, so whatever the horse had been dosed with had worked with a vengeance.

Adams finally managed to pull the horse up and turned him around for the trot back to the winning enclosure. But Razorback still wanted to break into a gallop. He was racked by nervous convulsions and twitches that vibrated through to his jockey's knees and inner thighs, tightly pressed against his ribs.

Adams didn't want to know anything about what was going on at the Trueman stables. He just wanted to keep on riding winners, get his photo in the sporting pages and bonk all the juicy young pussy he met at racing club promotional piss-ups. He wasn't going to ask any questions. He would do exactly as he was told. The big man from Sydney had him scared shitless.

Down in the betting ring Read and Sylvia were swept along in the flow of the crowd as they made their way to the settling up area. The orchestrated plunge on Razorback had sucked in the ordinary punters and the horse had started hot favourite at five to two. The bookies looked hunted and panicky as they saw the long queues standing triumphantly at the pay-out stands. A huge roar went up as the correct weight signal came over the PA system. The crowd loved taking the mickey out of the bookies. As the bookies' bags emptied, one group of angry punters looked as if they were going to lynch one frazzled clerk who held his empty bag upside down, telling the snarling mob that he was waiting for more cash to arrive.

'Let's get out of the crowd and wait until things quieten down,' Read said to Sylvia as he ushered her into the member's bar. He ordered two mineral waters. At the other end of the bar there was great excitement where Rex Jardine and his entourage had taken over, celebrating Razorback's record-breaking win. Jardine's wife was holding court with him and enjoying herself. Patricia Jardine had been Patricia Jervis before marriage. She was a pure, Victorian Western District squattocracy blue blood.

Boarding school at St Catherine's, a soft Arts degree at Melbourne University while a resident student at Janet Clarke Hall, and finishing school in France had moulded a woman who was comfortable with receiving the respect of her peers and of those she considered inferior. A well-preserved and attractive matron, she had given Jardine four children, three boys and a girl, who were perfect clones of their parents.

'Let's go,' said Read, towing Sylvia after him.

'What a day,' Read sighed as he flopped onto the lounge, pulling Sylvia on top of him. Sitting on Read's knee, Sylvia was counting her winnings in $50 notes.

'One week's rent, two weeks' rent,' she giggled as she counted. Read started rubbing the back of her neck.

'You won't forget your first day at the races, will you? Just remember, there are losing days as well as winning days.'

In her bedroom, Sylvia had reduced to bra and panties as Read came out of the bathroom.

'Come on, Jack, come and have a shower with me. You've been nice to me, now I'm going to be nice to you.' It was a tight fit in the cramped shower recess. Sylvia put her hands down behind her back, fending off Read who was trying to enter her from the rear.

'No, Jack, you're not going to fuck me here. I want you to do me good in bed.'

Read had fucked Sylvia doggie fashion up to just this side of the point of no return for about twenty minutes when she changed the pace and positions. Read rolled over on the bed and propped himself up on a couple of pillows. Sylvia started going down on him while she aroused herself with a vibrator fitted with a tickler. She was looking up at Read as she kept on bringing him to the brink. Read was spinning out, slobbering and not making much sense.

'Look at me, Sylvia, look at me while I cum.' Sylvia's brown eyes appeared to enlarge as she whimpered, a series of shivers rippling through her body – the vibrator was doing its job. With a dreamy gaze, she drained the groaning Read.

11

Don't you try and threaten me, Mr Fucking Smarty-Pants politician. You just do what I want you to do and everything will be okay. Fuck me around and that up-herself, 'my shit doesn't stink' wife of yours will get copies of all those audiotapes I have of you, you know, the ones of you screaming out her name while you were fucking me up the arse. Can you hear me, can you hear me, arsehole?' David Felton was grinning as he gave himself an Oscar for overacting. He wanted to get right on top of his listener and knock all the fight out of him. The silence on the line told him that he had been successful.

The Honourable Rex Jardine, Minister of the Crown, sat in his big, black leather chair in his ministerial office. He was staring at the phone handpiece as if it was a dollop of nauseating filth. Felton had used his codename as he always did when he called through the departmental switchboard. Jardine's mouth had dried up and his tongue was flopping around in his mouth like a bell clapper. He couldn't make saliva and he felt like vomiting. The voice came screeching out at him again.

'Are you still there, Rex? Are you still there? Did you hear what I said? Fucking well answer me, you prick, or I'll fuck you over right now.' Jardine could barely hear his own voice, rasping and detached as if he was standing outside his body.

'Alright David, alright David, I heard you. I heard you. Look, I can't talk right now as I have to go into a Cabinet meeting. Everything will be alright. You'll get your money, I promise you. We'll organise how to pay you when I see you again.' Felton came bouncing back, his voice full of authority.

'That'll be soon, Rex, like in the next couple of days. We'll meet at my South Yarra flat. Just to get the ball rolling, bring me $20,000 in $100 notes.'

'Oh Jesus,' Jardine said, as his guts started churning again. He needed to go to the lavatory. He managed to pull himself together.

'Right, right, David, I hear you. No problem. I've really got to go now. I'll fix that all up so don't go and do anything silly please. Please be sensible. I don't know why you are doing all this. Got to go.'

Felton smiled as he put down the phone. He had taken the first step to getting behind the wheel of that BMW. Jardine stumbled into his office bathroom and dry retched into the toilet bowl. He needed a shit badly.

As he sat there with his trousers around his ankles, staring at himself in the full-length mirror opposite, Jardine hit the instant rewind on his life. As a boarder at Melbourne Grammar, he had managed to suck cocks under the blankets in the dormitory without being caught. Being a prefect and having plenty of pocket money had been a help. He found that he was also capable of being attracted to girls and the realisation dawned on him during his first year at university that he was bisexual. When in homosexual mode, he could take it or give it, it really didn't matter.

Marriage to Patricia Jervis had provided a convenient cover for Jardine and a fast track into political life. As a bonus, she brought money into the marriage. She was the perfect wife and hostess and was not demanding in the bedroom, which was of no concern one way or the other for her husband. He liked fucking her but couldn't get her to try any kinky stuff. It was a real effort just to get her to ride him and it didn't take her long to fall off and get back into the missionary position.

Patricia buried herself in social and charity work and provided good, solid copy for the social pages. Being invited to one of her functions meant inclusion on the A-list and everything that went with it, a place at the top tables at charity dinners, invites to the best boxes at the MCG and the final step into socialite heaven on earth, an entree to the Jardine marquee during the Melbourne Cup Carnival.

As a pederast Jardine was into older teenage boys and men in their early twenties. Only once had he been tempted to hit on a boy younger than sixteen – in the Philippines when he had been on a political junket. The kid had been sweet meat but it was not long after Jardine returned to Australia that the outcry over foreign paedophiles operating in Asian countries had broken out and fear and panic forced him to promise himself he would not stray again. *Why? why? why?* he asked himself. His life had been one of constant turmoil and guilt, punctuated by agonising episodes of self-hate. Time and time again, he had been on the brink of seeking medical help but could never take that final step. On one occasion he had actually made an appointment but cancelled at the last moment. The danger of being found out provided almost as powerful a high as when he had an orgasm.

He had taken incredible risks. Often in Sydney on government business, many times he would find himself in his hotel room babbling and shivering like a malaria patient as he tried to fight back the waves of lust pounding in his groin. Totally out of control, he would drive his hire car up to the wall in Darlinghurst and join the queue of prowling Jaguars, Beemers and Mercs cruising past the line of young male prostitutes, preening themselves on the bonnets of parked cars or posing almost bas-relief against the time-stained sandstone wall that once surrounded the old Darlinghurst jail. Although Jardine had seen TV specials featuring plenty of footage of what went on at the wall, this was no deterrent.

Inexorably, he was slowly sucked into a Sydney-based pederast network. Its members clung to each other for support, reassurance and the comfort derived of feeling that there was safety in numbers. Jardine had met several high-profile Sydneysiders, including a Supreme Court judge, an orthopaedic surgeon, some businessmen and a state and federal politician, which gave him grounds for some bizarre rationalisation of his own position. Too late, Jardine was to find out that a crooked Sydney detective was working for the upper echelon of the network, providing paid protection and tip offs for its members. There are always two sides to every story. The policeman's Achilles heel was his dealing in confiscated drugs, a fact known by his extracurricular employers. If the ship went down, everyone went with it. The media sharks would fill their guts.

Jesus. Jardine came to with a start and looked at his watch. He had been sitting on the lavatory for nearly thirty minutes, feeling squeamish and washed out. He started to undress. His first priority was to find $20,000 for that blackmailing little bastard David Felton. Felton he could silence with money but the other person who knew about his dreadful secret was something else. Jardine lapsed back into flashback mode as he stood under the warm, cleansing shower and soaped himself.

It had happened at the Caulfield races not that long ago. He had been coming back from the betting ring when he had bumped into a beefy man coming the opposite way.

'Sorry,' Jardine said as he prepared to move aside.

'Oh, good day, Mr Minister, sorry, my fault,' said the other man, raising his right hand in a semi-formal salute. Jardine stopped and looked at the man who briefly and discreetly lifted a police warrant badge out of the top pocket of his jacket and then let it drop back out of sight.

'Chief Inspector Neil Ryan,' said the man putting out his hand. 'I'm in charge of the Racing Squad.'

'How do you do Ryan, nice to meet you,' Jardine replied. 'I trust that you are keeping your eyes on things and making sure that our racing industry is protected from all those bad people wanting to get up to mischief. Look, I've got to go, I have people waiting for me in the committee room. You must excuse me. I'll see you around.' Ryan decided to seize the moment. He had been waiting for a chance to orchestrate a meeting with Jardine for weeks and wasn't going to wait and try all over again at some other time. He moved closer to

Jardine and dropped his voice.

'Judge Penman said to give you his regards.' In that split second, Jardine just managed to stop himself from pissing his pants. He almost screamed. He had to summon up all his self-control before he spoke.

'I, er, I think you've made a mistake. I don't know a Judge Penman. Look, I'm running late, now I really must go.'

Ryan expertly blocked Jardine's path without making it obvious. His voice dropped another notch. His words were like blows from a meat cleaver.

'Oh, I forgot. Mr Ron Sephton and Mr Clive Bloxham QC MP also send their regards and said that they are looking forward to your next trip to Sydney. Look, Jardine, don't try and fuck with me. I'll call you next week at your office and I'll use the name Richardson.'

Ryan raised his voice back to a normal level as he walked away.

'See you later sir, have a nice day and good punting.' Jardine felt as if he had been gut shot. Somehow he managed to make it to the lift to take him up to the safety of the committee room.

'Rex, are you alright?' Patricia Jardine said with concern as she came up to her husband in the committee room, champagne glass in hand. Always the perfect lady, she never drank to excess.

'I'm okay, Pat, what's wrong with me?' Jardine said, starting to get himself together.

'It's just that you look as if the Premier has just sacked you from Cabinet. Here, have a sip, it'll do you good.' Jardine allowed his wife to nursemaid him with the champagne. It tasted good and his mouth was so dry that he drained the glass.

'Thanks, darling, that hit the spot. No, there's nothing wrong at all, maybe I'm just a bad loser, I'll get you a refill.' Jardine had dropped $1000 on the last race so it suited him to play that up. The colour had come back into his cheeks and his head had cleared. He was trying to work out how to deal with this policeman who had just come crashing out of nowhere into his life. For some inexplicable reason he was starting to get horny and it had nothing to do with his wife.

Chief Inspector Neil Ryan sat in the small lounge room of his rented flat in Port Melbourne watching the evening TV news. A quiet day had the TV journos trying to beat up news from nothing. There wasn't even a pet down a drainpipe story to save them. Ryan picked up the remote and zapped the TV off. His eyes settled on the photo of a stern-looking middle-aged man in a NSW police sergeant's uniform. He got up and moved over to the opposite wall to straighten the photo. Bitter memories came bouncing back.

Jim Ryan had followed his family's tradition of sending its sons off to the Police Academy. Jim had been a cop in the days before degrees in law and criminology, and diplomas in public administration. He had slogged his way up the time-serving promotion ladder and, after a few stints at country stations, had ended up in Kings Cross, Sydney. The dispensing of justice in the back alleys and laneways of the Cross was rough, sometimes fair and ignored the proclaimed law. It also came at a cost. Jim Ryan had worked through the years of six-o'clock closing, illegal brothels and SP bookmaking. The big boys in the liquor licensing, gaming and vice squads ran the rackets and were at the top of the pyramid. Men like Jim were the foot soldiers and had to make do with the crumbs that fell from the tables of their superior officers.

A crusading MP had managed to set off yet another anti-police corruption purge, such events having become part of the NSW political landscape. Jim had been caught up in the investigative net along with a few other assorted ranks and the odd sacrificial detective sergeant. The dishonourable discharge made him a broken man. He took his family to Melbourne and drank himself to death. *Shit,* Neil Ryan thought as he wiped a small tear from his eye. He was feeling sorry for himself, as he looked around the untidy flat that screamed bachelor. Ryan was still getting over a messy split with his wife that had been all his fault. He missed his two daughters.

From his first day at the Police Academy, Neil Ryan had promised himself that he would not end up like his father. He had managed to struggle through a diploma in public administration but just didn't have the intellectual horsepower to score a degree like most of his rivals in the scramble for promotion. He knew that he would have to make his own luck and grab the chances when they came. His job with the Racing Squad suited him. He had always followed the horses but had never punted heavily until he had got involved with Clyde Trueman's stable.

The tips that he got were unreal and the way things were going, his bank safety deposit box would shortly be filled with bundles of large denomination bank notes. Ryan finally got the big break that he was waiting for when he went to Sydney for an interstate police conference on the racing industry. He was having a drink at the Birmingham Hotel in Oxford Street, just near the NSW Police Headquarters, when Charlie 'Bumper' O'Reilly walked in.

'Gidday, Shorty,' Detective Sergeant Charlie O'Reilly said, as he shook hands with Ryan and eased himself onto a bar stool.

'Jesus, Charlie, talk about the devil. I was just thinking about you. When did we last cross paths?' O'Reilly waved his hand at the barman.

'Three years ago in Canberra at that criminology seminar when you had a run-in with that long-haired faggot of a lecturer. How's the racing game?' Ryan ordered two schooners of Resch's and pushed one towards O'Reilly. Ryan wiped the froth off his upper lip.

'Charlie, it's good. I get entry to every part of the racecourse and there are lots of freebies and lots of good looking birds all hot to trot. A few shitheads are always floating around, you know, the usual spivs and pickpockets but a good smack around the ears usually moves them on. There's always someone around trying to give horses something to make them go faster or slower but the stewards and vets have that pretty well covered. I just make sure that things run smoothly, that there's no dramas and I keep my bosses happy, you know what the score is, Charlie. What are you into at the moment?'

Charlie O'Reilly was drawing rings in the beer glass condensation on the bar top.

'I've got a fucking ripper of a job at the moment, Shorty, one of those special projects that pops up from time to time. Plenty of overtime, I'm basically my own boss and the pricks I deal with are pretty easy to handle. I won't ask you to waste your time guessing, but get onto this.' O'Reilly took a long draw on his beer and smacked his thin lips.

'Shorty, I'm keeping an eye on Sydney's paedophile and pederast ring. Can you imagine, me riding herd on a gang of arsehole bandits.' O'Reilly lowered his voice and looked around him before going on.

'Shorty, I can tell you this. There's a fucking good drink in it. A fucking good drink.' O'Reilly was using police jargon for a sling or bribe.

'In fact, I was almost going to give you a call the other day, but in this day and age, you never know when the phones might be off.' Again, O'Reilly lapsed into police code for the possibility that the phone line might be tapped, more than likely by police internal affairs officers.

'Look, now that you're here, let's go down to the Chows in Dixon Street for some chew and spew. I want to let you in on something that's really big and could mean a lot for you. Mate, you will shit yourself and you'll owe me plenty.'

The laminex table at the Green Jade looked just like all the other laminex tables in all the other Chinese restaurants. Several plates with the remnants of various dishes battled each other for space. The skeleton of a whole, sweet and sour coral trout, half-covered with some balled up paper serviettes, sat like a shipwreck in a shallow pond of sauce. Spilt grains of rice dotted the table amid obligatory rings of soya sauce and puddles of Chinese tea. The waiter cleared the debris and wiped down the table. Ryan was working over his teeth with a toothpick as O'Reilly started talking.

'Shorty, you'd be fucking totally freaked out if you knew how much arse banditry went on in this town and you just wouldn't believe how many top-shelf citizens are involved.' O'Reilly was warming to his subject.

'I was having a bit of trouble in the Stolen Car Squad with all those inquiries going on and I was looking for a place where I could keep my head down and stay clear of all the shit when all of a sudden they formed this task squad to monitor the rock spiders and the pederasts.' Rock spiders chillingly described paedophiles. O'Reilly went on.

'Well, I licked the right arses, you might say, and managed to get on board and there I am, turning up on the doorstep of some hotshot businessman or doctor or politician. Yeah, Shorty, wait'll you see some of the names. Even a dickhead Victorian would know who they are. There I am, flashing my badge and asking them if I can have a word with them and then I watch them shit themselves when I ask them about the young kids that they've fucked and tell them about the crystal clear video footage that I've got. Two suicides so far and more to come, I reckon. I can tell you, Shorty, all this stuff is huge.'

O'Reilly didn't need to tell Ryan he was being paid off by the people he should have been prosecuting. Once he had discovered that he was dealing with quite a few of the rich and the famous, it took him no time at all to propose a protection scheme whereby he tipped off the group about any impending police action. Everyone fell over themselves to cooperate. O'Reilly was banking more than $20,000 a month. A couple of more years and he could give the job the flick.

The other thing that he didn't tell Ryan about was the drug dealing he and another entrepreneurial cop were involved in. The two men removed cocaine and heroin from the evidence room at police headquarters and replaced it with milk powder and other substances. It was an operation that couldn't last for long but it helped with the cash flow. There was only one little problem. The NSW politician in the paedophile ring had found out that O'Reilly was dealing in drugs and had evidence that would stand up in court. The situation had become a Mexican standoff with O'Reilly finally doing a deal that let the politician off paying any protection at all. O'Reilly had seriously considered murder as an option but finally gave that away as a bad idea.

'I'm very impressed, Charlie,' said Ryan.

'You'll be more than impressed, Shorty, when I give you a piece of paper with some names on it,' replied O'Reilly.

'Meet me at the Birmingham tomorrow at lunchtime.'

Ryan unfolded and smoothed out the single piece of A4 paper that O'Reilly had given him. The two men were drinking light beer. As Ryan scanned the list of typed names, his heart jumped and he experienced a rush of emotion mixed with exultation.

'Christ, Charlie, this list reads like the fucking Queen's Birthday Honours List. Oh Jesus, I can't believe it, it can't be, it can't be.' Ryan's index finger jabbed at a name halfway down the list as he blinked a few times to make sure that he was seeing straight. His finger drummed on the name. Ryan's words whistled out between his teeth.

'Rex Jardine, the Victorian Police Minister, a faggot. I can't believe it, I just can't believe it. Charlie, if this is a joke, you'll be looking for a plastic surgeon.' O'Reilly sat back with a self-satisfied smile and sucked the gold cap on his front tooth.

'See, Shorty, I told you that you'd be impressed. Am I right? Look, it's one hundred percent spot on. I've got crystal clear video surveillance footage of your boss Jardine picking up young male hookers off the wall at Darlinghurst and Oscar Award-winning footage of a faggot's party with him sucking the cock and balls of Jason Robley's seventeen-year-old son. I was able to get a secret mini video-cam installed.' Like most Australians, Ryan knew Jason Robley, the award-winning current affairs TV host.

'Christ, Charlie, this is fucking huge. Who else has this info?'

'Shorty, at this red hot moment just little old you and me, partner.' O'Reilly was pleased with himself and called for two more beers.

'Keep the change,' he told the barman.

Ryan sat there at the bar hardly able to believe his luck. A chance meeting with an interstate colleague had dropped the world in his lap. All of a sudden he could see himself in a superintendent's uniform and all that went with it.

'Charlie,' Ryan said, 'how do I square you away for all this? I'm not loaded, you know. My divorce settlement and maintenance for the kids is going to kick my guts out. I'm stony broke. I've got to work out a way how to use this information and then it might still be hard to get results.' Ryan already knew what he was going to do.

'Don't worry, Shorty,' O'Reilly replied. 'If you get a drink out of it, think of me.'

'Charlie, for starters I'll tip you onto some winners at the track,' Ryan said.

'I mean it. I get some really solid inside mail from a stable in Melbourne and sometimes at good odds, just wait and see. I'll let you know when something is going and put my money on for you, that's how confident I am. I've got to get going. One for the road and I'm off. It's my shout.'

'Mr Richardson for you, Minister.' Rex Jardine's secretary flicked the call through to her boss's phone. Jardine felt squeamish as he picked up the phone.

'Hello.' His voice was flat.

'Good day, Mr Minister, Richardson here. How are you?' Jardine was starting to feel angry all of a sudden. This policeman with a face like a side of beef was getting ready to blackmail him.

'Come on, don't beat around the bush. How much do you want?' Jardine was sitting at his desk, rocking back and forth.

'Take it easy, take it easy,' said Ryan, feeling confident and relaxed. With Jardine in the right frame of mind, Ryan was going to keep him that way.

'We won't discuss our business on the phone so we need to meet somewhere and soon, any suggestions?' There was silence while Jardine tried to get on top of things. He wanted to know quickly where he stood with this latest threat to his very existence.

'Alright, let's get this over and done with. I'll drive my wife's car into work tomorrow, it's an olive green Volvo station wagon. You wait for me outside the North Melbourne railway station at ten in the morning and I'll pick you up and then we'll go and park somewhere.' Ryan cut in.

'What's the rego?'

'Oh yes,' Jardine exclaimed. 'Let me think ... umm, it's JAN165.'

Jardine's children had all completed their morning ritual of rising, breakfasting and departing for their respective schools and universities. Patricia Jardine had gone to Camperdown in the Western District for a few days to see her mother so there was no one to challenge Jardine about not being picked up by the ministerial car. He drove out of his Monomeath Avenue four-car garage and set course for the city.

Ryan saw the green Volvo crawling towards him. The rego plates checked out so he stepped out towards the curb. Jardine leaned over and opened the door. There was no hand shaking. He was trying to assert his authority.

'Come on, let's get this over. Where do you want to go?'

'Take it easy, Mr Minister,' Ryan said, 'I'm running this show and don't you forget that for one single moment. Do what you're told. Turn around and we'll go back down towards the railway line. There's a small industrial complex there, pretty quiet this time of day.' Jardine felt crushed. Ryan's voice had a hard, uncaring edge to it, full of authority and power.

'Pull in here,' ordered Ryan.

Jardine sat in the drivers seat, hands on the wheel, looking straight ahead. His stomach started to churn.

'Now look here, Mr Minister.' Jardine winced. He wished that Ryan would stop calling him 'Mr Minister.' 'I want you to be sure of one thing before I tell you what I want.' Jardine steeled himself, preparing for the worst. 'I don't want money, not one single cent.' Jardine turned and looked at Ryan, his mouth opening and shutting without producing sound. He felt like bursting into tears. Jardine suddenly heard himself talking.

'If you don't want money then what do you bloody well want?' Ryan paused for a moment.

'Before I tell you, let's just set the record straight. I know all about you and your mates in Sydney. I've seen video surveillance film with you as one of the stars, especially with Jason Robley's son.' Jardine twitched and gripped the steering wheel tighter.

'All I want, Mr Minister,' Ryan said, 'is promotion – promotion – nothing more, nothing less and you can deliver. I want you to very carefully and quietly promote my cause with the commissioner and any of the other top brass. You have to do it carefully so that you don't arouse any suspicion. You must know how to do these sorts of things. If you can't, then you'll have a very big problem indeed. Understand?' As he exhaled a long sigh of relief, Jardine felt drained. He couldn't believe that he was getting off so lightly. He started to warm towards Ryan, almost as he would to a newly found friend.

'Look here, Mr Ryan, sorry, Chief Inspector.'

'Neil. Neil,' Ryan cut in. 'Just call me Neil.'

'Right, Neil,' said Jardine, getting used to the informality.

'Look, I can't see any problem with implementing your strategy. As you say, it's most important that I do nothing that will excite curiosity. As you know, I'm a regular racegoer and there would be nothing out of the ordinary in my saying that I knew you and regarded your work highly, you know, that sort of thing. I know exactly what to do. After all, I am a politician.'

Both men smiled for the first time during the conversation. The tension eased. 'Leave it to me,' Jardine said. 'I must say that I am extremely grateful for your lenient treatment. I was expecting the worst, of course. I'll do my very best to help you, believe me.' Jardine was so relieved that he didn't mind grovelling. 'Okay then, that's that,' Ryan said. 'Drop me off back at North Melbourne station and I'll train it back to the city. I'll be in touch.' Ryan saluted as he got out of Jardine's car and walked into the station. He felt very, very pleased with himself.

***

12

David Felton carried an Australia Post express post satchel into the South Yarra Post Office. He had decided to buy himself some insurance. Inside the satchel were copied micro-cassettes of his sessions with Police Minister Rex Jardine that he was mailing to Shane Hepworth in Sydney. He and Hepworth had worked for the same gay escort agency in Sydney and on many occasions had worked together when a client had wanted a threesome. As Felton passed the satchel across the counter to the postal clerk, he smiled. There was a BMW inside it.

Twenty thousand dollars, twenty thousand dollars, Rex Jardine groaned to himself as he sat in his study at home. He was racking his brains working out how to organise the blackmail money for David Felton. Jardine continued the conversation with himself. *The dirty, rotten little swine. How could he do this to me? I pay him top dollar, make a fuss of him, buy him presents and he turns around and does this to me. Christ, why is all this happening?*

'Coffee's ready, Rex.' Jardine heard his wife's voice drifting through from the drawing room. He put some files back in the top drawer of the antique, Victorian, colonial cedar desk and got up. He would have to sell some BHP shares out of one of his family trusts of which he was the sole trustee. He cursed David Felton again. BHP had dived in the market so he would lose on that score as well.

'Is that sexy Rexy? Is that Rexy with the eight-inch rod?' Jardine moaned in a whisper as David Felton's voice came sing-songing into his ear.

'David, stop that bloody childish nonsense. Look, I'm very busy here. I've got people running in and out of here all the time. For God's sake, it is a ministerial office, you know. I've got your money so let's organise a time and I'll bring it to you.' Felton giggled.

'You're a good boy, Rexy. You're such a good boy. This Friday at my place in South Yarra. Eight-thirty and bring your cock with you.' Felton tittered and hung up. Jardine tried to get his mind back on to the speech on home detention that he was preparing for the Victorian Union of Civil Liberties.

As Jardine drove through the evening traffic towards South Yarra, he assembled a mental balance sheet of his current finances. Two boys in their final year at Melbourne Grammar, another son at Melbourne University studying Commerce/Law and a daughter at Monash doing Medicine – it all made for some hefty monthly bills even though they were all living at home. As soon as they started flatting, the bills would get bigger. And then there was his wife who thought it far too vulgar to talk about money but could fritter it away, quickly and efficiently. She had access to family money but it was legally tied up and controlled.

The real spendthrift was the malevolent demon inside him, the one with the permanent hard-on, the demon that kept on exploding and demanding more and more. Jardine's ministerial salary and electorate allowance were constantly plundered by payments to male prostitutes. Some weeks he had paid out nearly $1000 and now Felton was going to blackmail him and, like all blackmailers, he would not know when to stop.

'Come in, Rex,' Felton said softly as Jardine went to knock on the slightly opened door. 'Lock the door behind you and show me the present you've brought for your loving David.' A dimmed bedside lamp lit the room. Felton was stretched out on the double bed, naked except for a white silk G-string. His solarium-tanned skin had been oiled and there was musk in the air wafting up from the smouldering incense sticks. Jardine cleared his throat. His mouth was dry and he could feel his pulse quicken and, against his will, his cock harden.

'It's here, David, $20,000 all in hundreds.' Jardine placed the thick envelope on the dressing table.

'You're so good to me, Rex,' Felton said. 'I trust you implicitly so I won't even bother counting it.'

'Please, David, how long are you going to keep on doing this,' Jardine said. 'I'm not made of money, you know. You've got to be reasonable, please.' Felton put his hands behind his head, confident and assured.

'As soon as I have enough for the BMW convertible I want. Twenty thousand a month for the next three months and we'll call it quits. I'm being very reasonable, don't you think? Now come here, sexy Rexy, and I'll give you a freebie.' Felton rolled over on to his stomach and raised his buttocks. He turned his head and looked back at Jardine, his blue eyes urging Jardine on. Jardine was consumed all at once by anger at his predicament and burning lust. The demon had snapped its chain and was raging out of control. He undressed quickly and moved in. Felton pointed to a pyrex bowl of hot water on the bedside table that had a tube of K-Y gel standing in it. Jardine whimpered as he lubricated himself. Then as he entered Felton he made himself a mad, impossible promise. He would have himself chemically castrated.

Read was perving on the girl on the bike in front of him. He had pulled up at the lights at the intersection of Canning and Lygon streets, Carlton. The girl was standing up, balancing on the pedals and see-sawing the front wheel right and left as she waited for the green. She was in her early twenties and had a sculptured, athletic body. Her cornflour blonde hair was ponytailed through a blue baseball cap. She knew that she was a stunner. Her tight, navy blue lycra shorts concealed paradise. *She's got a bum on her like two hard-boiled eggs under a silk handkerchief,* Read thought. He beeped his horn in lusty approval as the lights said 'go.' The girl pushed off, giving Read two stiff fingers. He was on his way to the Werribee Veterinary School to see veterinary pathologist, Professor Steve Flower, who had been referred to him by Mike Rowlands of Sydney University.

Read wanted to get up to speed on the current crop of stop and go drugs being used in horse racing.

'Mike Rowlands rang to say that you'd be coming to see me, Jack.' Read followed Flower down the corridor that had doors leading off to offices and a couple of laboratories.

'Here we are,' Flower said as he ushered Read into an office crammed with books and horsey paraphernalia. An almost life-size coloured anatomical chart of a horse claimed the wall behind Flower's office chair. A horse's heart suspended in a laboratory jar of formalin held pride of place on a shelf. Flower took off his laboratory coat and hung it on a peg.

'Well, what do you want to know?' Read sat down opposite Flower.

'Steve, I'm here to pick your brains on the menu of drugs available to nobblers of racehorses these days.'

'Oh yeah, then how much time have you got to spare, Jack?' Flower asked ironically.

'Fuck!' Neil Ryan was furious. He was sitting in his car with Rex Jardine in a quiet side street in East Melbourne. 'How long has all this shit been going on for?' As Jardine told Ryan about being blackmailed by David Felton, the big policeman's guts churned and he became angrier. He could see his plans for personal advancement going up in smoke all because of this pathetic faggot sitting next to him. The hard, barely controlled edge of his voice made Jardine wince.

'Mr Minister, blackmailers are greedy bastards and they just never know when to stop. After this prick gets his BMW he'll suddenly decide that he wants something else: a world trip, a fishing boat, stereo equipment, an Amex card – you name it, he'll think of it. See what I mean, you fuckwit.' The sudden abuse jolted Jardine and he looked at Ryan with the eyes of a beaten man.

'I'm sorry, Mr Minister, I'm sorry but can't you see the mess you've got yourself into?' Ryan said, as he patted Jardine on the shoulder. He kicked himself for being silly and slagging Jardine. He didn't want to kill the goose that still might manage to lay.

'Look, give me all the details on this David Felton and I'll get the tapes off him and frighten him back to Sydney. After I've finished with him, he won't come near you again, believe me.' Ryan went into 'read my lips' mode.

'You'll just have to be very careful.' Ryan dropped his voice and spoke with concern.

'We don't want this sort of thing happening again, do we?' Jardine turned to Ryan and nodded like a scolded child while Ryan jotted down some telephone numbers and the address of Felton's South Yarra flat. Jardine opened the passenger door and walked away without looking back. As he drove off, Ryan already knew how he was going to deal with Felton.

Felton ended the call on his mobile phone, drew back on the joint to the point of becoming dizzy, puffed out a big, curling smoke ring and felt immensely satisfied with himself. Now Jardine was recommending clients to him. What a bonus. With a bit of luck he would meet more men willing to contribute to the David Felton provident fund. *They might have to be encouraged a little bit,* Felton mused to himself. This latest client sounded like a macho man who walked on both sides of the fence, most probably married with kids. He was obviously a close contact of Jardine's and Felton had made an appointment with him for the coming Saturday evening at ten at his South Yarra flat. Felton would tape this person right from the first contact. As the New Guinea Gold swept into his bloodstream, Felton started thinking about a first-class, all-expenses paid world trip.

'Just a bit harder, Jack. Up a little higher. Yes, right there. Just keep doing it there. Oh yes, that feels so relaxing.' Read was massaging Sylvia's neck as they lay in bed, his right thumb and fingers kneading the muscles, running up and down the vertebrae from the middle of her upper back to the base of her skull.

'If you were a cat you'd be purring,' Read said, as he gently increased the pressure.

'Oh yes, yes,' Sylvia mumbled into the bed. She was lying on her stomach and had a pillow under her breasts to help keep her weight off them. Her skin was still damp from recent exertion. Read had ridden her hard from behind for a long time.

'You're not bad, Dad,' she said with a smile. She was getting fond of the older man. He made her feel comfortable and he was a good listener. She was also tuned in to his sense of humour that took the mickey out of people and brought them back to earth. Read put more baby oil on his hands and returned to his task, pushing his fingertips into Sylvia's hairline and then letting them crawl up onto her scalp. She gave a little shudder of pleasure.

'You've got another ten minutes of this, sweetheart, and then I'll have to go,' Read said.

'You don't start work until this afternoon but I've got an appointment this morning.' Sylvia rolled onto her back and pulled Read's head down to hers. She put her tongue in his mouth and her hand between his legs. She had a cheeky smile on her face.

'Do me again, Jack, and this time put a little bit more effort into it, will you,' she said. It was an order.

13

Read pulled up outside Snowy Baker's gym and sauna in Footscray. He followed the airborne trail of Sloan's Liniment, sweat and Tiger Balm into the lopsided building. Inside, it was another world. Faded boxing promotional posters plastered the walls and black-and-white photos of champions past hung at odd angles. A part-Aboriginal youth was belting the stuffing out of a heavy punching bag. His spindly legs told Read that when the going got tough in the final rounds, he wouldn't make the distance. Some young tattooed white kids were trying to spar, while a kickboxing Jean-Claude Van Damme look-a-like with jelled hair, taking himself very seriously, performed for a mixed gaggle of bikie types and skinheads.

Besides a vintage model sauna room, the gym featured two antique sweat boxes in which the victim sat, head protruding from a hole in the top. These boxes were the favourites of quite a few jockeys, and Read had been told that he would find the crack jockey, Ray Hicks, at the gym on Friday mornings, honing his weight for race day. As Read made his way past the sauna room he came to the alcove where the two sweat boxes were. One was empty but there was Ray Hicks in the other, a towel wrapped around his lower face and neck, acting as a seal to keep the steam from escaping.

'Gidday Ray,' Read said, as he came abreast of Hicks. The jockey wrinkled his brow and looked at Read enquiringly. Sweat was running over his forehead, disappearing into the towel.

'Jack Read, Ray,' said Read, waving his inquiry agent's licence half-heartedly in Hick's general direction. Hicks didn't seem all that impressed. He moved the split lid of the sweat box and opening the front, stepped out. As he swung into view, Read could see why Ray Hicks was called Dangles and what kept Edith Trueman interested. The jockey was hung like the stallions he rode and he was uncut. The steam had wrinkled and shrunk it but Read still felt rather inadequate.

'What's the go,' said Hicks as he walked over to the wall and took a large towel off a peg. His skin moved over his muscles like a sheet of clear plastic. He carried barely an ounce of fat. Read felt more relaxed now that Hicks had the towel around his waist. Neither of them attempted to shake hands.

'Ray, I'm the assessor doing those insurance claims on Dapper Dan and Gold Crest. I'm just tying up a few loose ends and won't take up too much of your time. I know you're a busy man with a tight schedule. You were riding Dapper Dan the morning he was killed. What went wrong? You were lucky that you weren't hurt.'

Ray Hicks looked hard at Read. He was very controlled and Read gained the impression that he was trying not to lose his temper.

'What's all this about? That claim's been paid out, according to Clyde Trueman, so what's the drama, mate?'

'Look, Ray,' Read backed off. 'The insurance company is just doing a review of recent claims to see if it needs to change its policy guidelines in the thoroughbred industry. You know what those bean counters are like. They have to dream up things to do to keep themselves in a job. People like me are just the spokes in the wheel. I still reckon that you were bloody lucky when that horse ran through the rail.' Hicks looked a little less cranky.

'Yeah, I suppose so. I reckon you can say I was lucky. I've had the odd race fall but I've always managed to walk away in one piece. That Dapper Dan was spooked by a bird, a big mad magpie flapping all over the place. He was always jumpy at the best of times, always sweating up when you didn't want him to. That bird sent him off and the next thing I know, he's gone one way and I've gone the other. There's nothing else to say. The rail speared him like a shish kebab.'

While he was talking, Hicks was drying himself off. As the

jockey pulled on his Y-fronts, Read decided to put him to the test.

'Thanks, Ray, it was nice meeting you. I'll get out of your hair. I see that you're riding the card tomorrow at Caulfield. Good luck. Hope you get up on every one. Oh, by the way, what's the go with that Miller bloke from Sydney who visits Trueman's stables from time to time?' As he spoke, Read tuned his antennae for Hicks' reaction. The jockey was good under pressure. He managed to clamp down on expressing any signs of recognition and went on dressing. He pretended not to hear Read's question.

'Yeah, see you later,' he said as he turned his back on Read.

'Hello, who is it?' said Felton as the security intercom in his flat came alight and beeped.

'Is that you, David? It's Don here, Rex Jardine's friend here to see you, remember?'

'Oh Don, David here. How nice of you to be so punctual. Sure, come right up. Second floor, unit 4.' Felton pressed the button that opened the ground floor security door. He opened the top drawer of the dressing table and checked the tape recorder. It was all systems go. Felton glanced at himself in the mirror on the wardrobe door, *Aren't I gorgeous in my silk nightshirt and nothing underneath.* He had smoothed his skin with rose-scented jojoba oil.

It was just a quiet knock on the door. As Felton removed the security chain, a lot of things happened at once. He barely had time to glimpse a large man smiling at him before the heel of the man's hand hitting him squarely where the end of his nose joined his upper lip. The heavy blow drove his septal cartilage back into his nasal cavity. Eyes streaming tears and blood gushing from his nose, Felton staggered backwards onto his bed, with not an ounce of fight left in him.

'Oh Jesus, oh Jesus, fuck, fuck, what have you done to me?' he sobbed as he struggled to refocus his blurred vision. All he could see was the shape of his assailant standing over him. Neil Ryan looked down at the figure on the bed.

'Now, now David,' he said, 'just take it easy. Here, take this.'

Ryan handed Felton a warm face washer from the nearby en suite. Felton gently pressed it to his swollen nose and puffed eyes. As he looked up at Ryan, his vision started to clear. There were two men in the room.

'Oh God, I want to be sick,' he said, lurching into the small bathroom. He knelt in front of the toilet bowl and vomited up the pizza that had been his evening meal along with blood that had run down his throat. His head started to spin again as he splashed warm water onto his face and gargled to clean out his mouth. 'Why have you done this to me,' he said again and again, as he staggered back into the bedroom.

'Sit down and shut up, fuck face,' Ryan said, as he pushed Felton back onto the bed. 'Look sonny, let's get right down to the business in hand. You have some audiotapes involving a certain person. You know who I mean so don't try and bullshit me. You are going to give them to us, then you are going to pack up some clothes and then we are going to drop you off at the interstate bus terminal at Spencer Street Railway Station and then you are going to fuck off back to Sydney where you belong. Come back to Melbourne or try and contact that certain person again and I'll kill you, do you understand?'

As Felton stared stupidly into space, Ryan thrust his right hand into Felton's crutch and gripped him hard with a twisting motion at the base of his scrotum. The searing pain cleared Felton's head and he tried to scream but Ryan clamped his left hand over Felton's shattered nose and mouth. It was all too much. Felton's urinary tract sphincter relaxed its grip and he pissed himself. Ryan pulled away, shaking urine off his hand.

'You dirty little cunt,' he barked.

'Have you got any more of these stashed away?' Ryan demanded, as he counted the micro-cassettes he had taken from the top drawer of the dressing table along with Felton's address book.

'This will make interesting reading,' he said, putting it in his jacket pocket. The fronts of the drawers of the Indonesian-made dressing table were fret worked, allowing the tape recorder to pick up plenty of sound.

'No, there's no more, you've got the lot,' Felton mumbled, dejected, still holding the blood-stained washer to his face. He was now sitting, forlorn, on the edge of the bed. From the moment the two men had burst into the flat, the second man had remained silent. He was lean, of medium height and would not stand out in a crowd.

Detective Senior Constable Phil Burns had known Ryan since his first day in the job. The big man had been his first sergeant and had saved him from being dishonourably discharged when he had turned up one day, drunk on duty. Whenever he had something dirty to do, Ryan could always rely on Burns to help out.

'Alright now,' said Ryan, 'pack up your gear and let's get out of here.' Felton threw some belongings into a large travel bag and put on a tracksuit and runners. Flanked by the two policemen, he was walked to a Nissan Patrol parked in the street. Ryan had decided to take a risk and use his personal car for this job but had still taken out some insurance. The registration plates would lead any enquirers to a Holden Commodore that had disappeared without trace three years back.

'Sit in the front, David,' Ryan ordered, as he got into the rear passenger seat, leaving the driving to Burns. As the Nissan drove off, Ryan exhaled slowly. He had scanned the side street and was satisfied that no stickybeaks had witnessed their departure. Burns drove the Nissan the route Ryan had told him to take – right into Park Street, South Yarra, north across Domain Road and into Birdwood Avenue that wound through the Royal Botanic Gardens towards the city. With all the trees fully leaved and the sparse street lighting, driving along that stretch of road late at night was like being in a quiet, shady tunnel.

When he had got into the car, Felton had failed to notice that his seat was missing its removable head rest. He suddenly wondered why the car had not kept going down to St Kilda Road.

'Where are we going?' As he was about to continue speaking,

David Felton died in an instant – no drama, no fuss. Ryan had placed the barrel of the captive bolt pistol on the nape of Felton's neck and pulled the trigger. With a sharp crack, the .22 Long Rifle blank detonated, its expanding gases driving the piston which in turn drove a retractable, ten millimetre diameter, high-tensile steel shaft deep into Felton's neck, tearing through his spinal column and severing his internal carotid artery. He sagged forward and slipped down in his seat until the seat belt halted his progress. Dark, port-red arterial blood welled up out of his neck wound and ran down his back beneath his tracksuit top.

Burns looked straight ahead and drove carefully within the speed limit and obeyed all the road rules. Ryan had told him that the job would be dirty and he was not surprised by the shot when it came. He was there to do a job, not to ask questions. He wound down his window to blow the cordite fumes out of the car.

'Whew, leave the window down, Phil,' Ryan said. 'First he pisses on my hand and now he shits himself.'

As death closed down Felton's major nerve centres, his external and internal anal sphincters relaxed and his rectum evacuated its contents. His bladder drained off what was left in it after the episode back at the flat. Ryan hoped that the dead man's underpants and tracksuit would contain the mess. A good scrub with hot water and Pine O Cleen later would fix things up. Ryan wrapped the pistol in its oily rag and put it back in the small travel bag on the back seat floor. The weapon was a relic of the old abattoir days when captive bolt pistols were used to kill cattle for slaughter. Ryan shifted across and sat behind Burns with the breeze blowing in his face.

'Alright, Phil, you know where to go. Nice and easy now, steady as she goes.' Burns nodded, tuned the radio into an FM music station and started tapping the steering wheel along to the golden oldies.

The Nissan travelled along Footscray Road, over the Maribyrnong River and turned left into Whitehall Street.

'Next left, Phil, and douse your lights.' Ryan pointed ahead where the watery light of a street lamp beckoned. The street was more like a laneway that led down to that part of the Maribyrnong River where local fishing boats were moored.

'Pull in here and I'll open up.' Ryan alighted from the vehicle in front of a large roll-a-door that had a judas gate set off to one side of it.

Neil Ryan's brother-in-law was a Greek Australian who operated a small fish-processing business. A real ocker, he and Ryan were still good mates despite his sister's marital split with the policeman. Ryan opened the judas gate and hit the switch that rolled up the door. The darkness of a moonless sky comforted Ryan. The Nissan rolled slowly through the opening as the door closed behind it. Ryan switched on a single-tube fluorescent that bounced feeble light off a long stainless steel bench used for opening oysters and cleaning fish.

'Back up to here, Phil,' Ryan said, pointing to the bench. He dropped the tailgate of the Nissan and lifted out a forty-four gallon drum with a clip-on lid. The drum had holes all over it that Ryan had punched with a solid roofing punch. He then pulled out a pack of large, heavy duty, orange garden rubbish bags and threw them down next to the drum.

'Jesus, these mothers are heavy when they're all in the one container,' Ryan grunted as he dragged a big hessian bag over the tailgate and let it drop to the floor with a thud.

'Alright, now for our catch of the night. Give me a hand to get our mate out of the car and onto the bench. Hang on while I get the seat belt off him.' They lifted Felton out of the seat and laid him out on the bench. Ryan stepped back to the car.

'Fuck,' he exclaimed, wrinkling up his nose as he looked at the brownish-red smudge where Felton had been sitting.

'Get those aprons and gloves on and let's get started, Phil.' Ryan walked over to the wall and unhooked a heavy, dark green plastic, neck-to-ankle apron. He took elbow-length matching gloves that had been washed and stored in a nylon tub. Selecting a long, razor-sharp filleting knife, worn flexible and thin by use, from a tray of assorted knives, he quickly cut Felton's clothes away, gingerly handling the jocks and the tracksuit pants on the blade of the knife and then dropping them into the drum. Remembering the soiled front seat of the Nissan, Ryan used Felton's singlet and some bleach that he found in a cupboard to clean up. The bite of the bleach sharpened his senses and chased the other odours away. Turning on a plastic hose, Ryan washed the flour-white body of David Felton, the wash off running pink at first, then clear, through the drain holes in the benchtop onto the graded floor then into a drain outlet that took the waste illegally into the nearby river. The EPA wouldn't be happy but the scavenging river prawns and fish would.

With Burns assisting, Ryan pulled Felton onto his side, arms flopping at weird angles. In the feeble and staccato light caused by a faulty fluorescent tube starter, Felton looked like a slink, a stillborn calf, vulnerable and defenceless. His tongue dangled from his mouth and his cheeks were now shapeless folds of grainy, putty-coloured flesh. The morbid flush, that purple plimsoll line of death had not had time to become established, nor had rigor mortis set in. Ryan chose a shorter bladed knife and with one deft stroke, slit Felton open from his breastbone to his pelvis. Burns grimaced.

Carefully cutting the perineal membrane without damaging what it protected, Ryan eviscerated Felton's major organs, spilling them out onto the benchtop. Reaching up into the chest cavity, he expertly spun the knife, freeing the lungs, heart and spleen from their attachments. Burns winced as he watched the vital parts being dragged into view, almost as if they were a grotesque extension of Ryan's gory hand. Ryan started issuing instructions.

'Get one of those plastic rubbish bags, Phil, to put his guts in. Tie it off and then drop it in the drum. Get some sash window weights out of that bag on the floor and load a few of them into the drum too. We want to make sure our friend stays on the bottom.' As Burns did as he was told, Ryan hosed the cadaver down again. With a dexterity that spoke of countless pig and kangaroo hunting trips, Ryan dismembered Felton's gutted corpse while Burns placed the parts in plastic bags and alternated them in the drum with more sash weights.

'Clip the lid down and bring that manual forklift over and we'll load up. I'll give this place a good hose down and then we'll split.'

Using the forklift, the two men loaded the drum into the back of the Nissan. With Ryan acting as traffic controller in the laneway, the Nissan crept out of the processing plant. As Ryan climbed into the drivers seat he breathed a long sigh of relief. Not a soul in sight and the job almost over. He started talking, more to himself than for Burns' benefit.

'I suppose that cunt had copies of those tapes made but I'll just have to take a chance on that. If he did, the person who has them won't really know what to do with them. There's no point in playing coulda, shoulda. We could have made him talk, maybe not. Ah well, it's almost over now. Thanks for the help, Phil.' Burns grunted acknowledgment. Ryan liked men like Burns. They did their job and didn't yap or ask any questions.

Ryan drove the Nissan through an old industrial complex and down to the banks of the Maribyrnong River. The area became a sort of open space lover's lane in the early hours of Saturday morning. There was already a parked car well away in the distance. The dull glow of its internal light gave its position away but after a while the light was switched off and it was impossible to pick up the shape of the car in the darkness. Its two panting and rutting occupants were otherwise engaged. They could have been on another planet.

'We'll just sit here for a while Phil until our eyes adjust to the dark and then I'll roll the drum into the river. There's a deep hole close to the bank on the inside of this bend. One of the boys from Footscray used to fish here regularly for bream and I used to drop in and have a stubbie with him when I was in the area and knew that he was down here.' *Ryan was fucking unbelievable,* Burns thought. *He missed nothing, absolutely nothing. He's got a whole inventory of experiences and contacts that he can draw on whenever he needs to.*

Sweet dreams, Mr Felton, Ryan mused as he rolled the drum into the river, giving it one last strong push. The drum wallowed on the surface, half-submerged as the air was pushed out of the holes

122

by the incoming water, then it slowly sank into twenty feet of water, settling with a sooty puff into the thick, sticky silt on the river bed, an accumulation of decades of ignorant industrial pollution. A fine stream of bubbles continued to rise to the surface. *Just like a bag of berley,* Ryan thought. The river prawns and eels would have a feast in the weeks to come when they invaded the plastic-wrapped baits. Ryan took the opportunity to change the plates on the Nissan. As he drove off, he was whistling. He had taken an incredible risk by killing Felton and disposing of him in the way that he had. The whole enterprise could have gone terribly wrong at any time but so far, so good. Now he had Rex Jardine exactly where he wanted him. The politician would view Ryan as his saviour and the pressure was now on him well and truly to deliver and repay the favour. Ryan thought that he would cut an impressive figure in a superintendent's uniform.

'Here you are, Phil, here's some fruit for the sideboard, something for your trouble,' Ryan said, as he handed Burns fifty new $100 notes.

14

Clyde Trueman sounded his ebullient self but Read detected an underlying edge of concern.

'Ah, hello there, Jack, I'm just calling to find out when the claim on Gold Crest will be paid out. The Prendergasts have been on my back so I'm just passing the buck, as it were. You know what owners are like.' Read thought that by now, it was almost certain that Trueman had been alerted by Hicks the jockey and Griffiths the vet about all the nosey parker questions Read was asking that didn't have much to do with the Gold Crest claim. Read tried to placate the trainer.

'Look, I can appreciate your concern, Clyde, but I'm just the ham in the sandwich here. Centaur is reviewing all its claim procedures as we speak. Before I go on, it goes without saying that nothing I say relates to you or your clients but as you well know we've just come out of a recession and during tough times, insurance companies become the target of every desperate businessman trying to cut their losses. We all know about Jewish stocktakes.' Read was referring to arsons where insured businesses with trading problems were conveniently burned to the ground.

'A lot of owners have killed off their non-performing horses and have then claimed on their insurance for accidental death. I'm doing my very best for the Prendergasts and I'll give Centaur another call before lunch. To take the pressure off you I'll also speak to the Prendergasts and reassure them. Don't worry, Clyde. I want to get all this cleared up and get back to Sydney, believe me. I've got a dog that misses me and a panel beater who wants to get paid. See you.'

'Go ahead,' Read said into his mobile phone. A woman's voice came pinging back.

'Is that Jack Read? It's Joylene Mills again, Jack, can you hear me?'

'Yes, Joylene, reading you loud and clear. I'm on a tram so it's a bit noisy. What can I do for you?' There was a pause and then Joylene continued.

'Jack, I need to see you again about what we were talking about before. Can you meet me at the same place in Kensington?' Read sensed that a break might be coming his way.

'Sure, sure, Joylene, no problems. When?'

'Jack, how about straight away if that's okay with you. I've got this afternoon off.' Read had nothing planned and he wanted to hear what the strapper had to say, sooner, rather than later.

'I'm on my way, love. I'll train it across to Kensington from Flinders Street. I'll be there in about half an hour. Looking forward to seeing you again. Cheers.' Read liked using public transport wherever he was. It was relaxing, letting someone else battle through the traffic and it was a chance to watch the passing parade, especially from trams. *A shame that the unions had stuffed things up along the way,* he thought. The trams and trains in Melbourne looked as if they were running on time. Maybe the unions had woken up to themselves.

As the train clickety-clacked on its way to Kensington station, Read looked around the carriage. *Why was eating and drinking allowed on public transport?* he thought. The stained flooring and seat coverings bore the scars of spilt liquids and countless barrages by meat pie and potato chip shrapnel that had defied many steam cleanings. A lot of people sat with their feet propped up on the seats opposite them. Read wondered how they treated their own furniture and what sort of hovels they were heading home to.

Two Asian youths eating Hungry Jack's chips were sitting on the floor in the doorway nearest Read. Passengers who had boarded at North Melbourne had meekly stepped over the obstacle. As the train slowed coming into Kensington, Read became an Ugly Australian.

'Can't you two clowns read English?' he said, pointing to the sign that warned against standing in the doorways. Read's body language said that he was going to use the two youths in his way as a human gangplank. Still sitting and grinning, they wriggled out of his way and gave him clear passage.

'Ignorant fuckwits,' Read snarled, as he strode off.

'That nasty-looking man from Sydney has been back at the stables again,' Joylene said as she stirred her coffee.

'He came here just after breakfast time last Tuesday, about eight. He was in Clyde's house for about half an hour then he left. He looked pretty cranky too.'

'That's our Ironbar for you. Happy little chappy,' replied Read.

'Be careful of that one, Joylene, he's not called Ironbar for nothing.' She wrinkled her nose as Read gave her a potted history of Ironbar Miller, leaving out a lot of the scary stuff. He didn't want to frighten her off altogether. She continued her briefing.

'Well, it wasn't long after … after Ironbar,' Mills used the name almost gingerly, 'after he left Clyde's place that Griffiths the vet turned up and went inside to see Clyde. He was there for about half an hour too and then he took off. When Clyde came down to the stables he wasn't too happy. It usually takes a lot to bother him but somebody had given him bad news that morning. So there.'

Read ordered Joylene another coffee and a glass of mineral water for himself. He had no doubt that his sniffing around had stirred things up but Ironbar really worried him. The thug was a killer. What had started off like a routine claims investigation was starting to get very messy.

'Joylene, you've been a terrific help, believe me, but be very careful and don't go and do anything silly, please.' Read spoke with genuine concern as he rose from the table and patted Joylene's shoulder.

'Don't worry, Jack, I won't,' Joylene replied. 'Now that I know what that Ironbar person's like, I'll be well and truly keeping my eyes open and my mouth shut. I just keep on thinking about the horses and what these people might be doing to them.' Joylene led Read out of the café.

'Want a lift anywhere, Jack?' she said.

'Thanks, Joylene, but I'm alright,' Read replied, 'I'll walk back down to the station and catch a rattler back into town. Be good.'

As Read took his seat in the train, he was thinking about Joylene. She was a good sort and a genuine horse lover and Read didn't want to see her get into any trouble or be harmed in any way. He wished that his partner John Steele was working with him and then he wouldn't have to be looking over his shoulder all the time. The train pulled in to Flinders Street Station. Walking down the front steps of the station entrance, Read brushed off a fit-looking beggar who asked for 'a note to buy a meal with' and then told Read to 'get fucked, you capitalist scum' when he got the knockback. *Who would have thought you'd ever see beggars on the streets in Australia?* pondered Read as he walked up Swanston Street.

Looking at his watch, he headed up Bourke Street and on impulse, walked into a movie theatre. After getting sick and tired of watching an oiled and pumped-up Sylvester Stallone trying to be a big man, Read walked out into the early evening. He caught a tram going up Swanston Street. He had decided that he would walk back to Welsh's house from the tram stop opposite Melbourne University.

Read knew that something was terribly wrong from the moment he opened the front screen door at Welsh's house. The main front door was half open and he could hear gurgling and groaning coming from the back of the small house. Read's adrenaline started squirting into his system.

He silently cursed Welsh's stupidity. *How many times have I told him about leaving the front door and the screen door unlocked and open with all the addicts and desperates that hang around the council flats down the street? Now some bastard's got in and done him over.*

Read overcame his panic and switched to full alert. *Jesus, the shithead might still be in the house,* Read realised. He stepped warily into the front room study that always looked as if it had been ransacked. Nothing. He turned a rickety Victorian chair upside down and wrenched off one of its legs. Now armed, in a fashion, he crept down the short hallway and standing back and to one side, flung open the door to Welsh's bedroom. Again nothing.

'Peter, Peter, are you there?' Read's voice bounced back at him, flat and thin. He took the last few steps through the kitchen and looked to his left. The illegal, tacked-on bathroom with its jungle of indoor plants was clear. Then Read saw the large, shiny, rising suns of blood on the light brown vinyl flooring. *Jesus, Jesus, let him be okay please, please.* Chair leg raised at the ready, Read took a deep breath and moved the last few steps to the doorway leading into the small back room.

Peter Welsh was lying on the floor with his shoulders propped up against a low day bed. His head was slumped on his right shoulder and his eyes were open and staring. His nostrils had been torn away from his face and his nose had been pushed away to one side. He was blowing bubbles of blood through his mashed lips with a wheezing sound. A bloodied telephone handpiece was lying on his lap. Read picked up the phone and called emergency services. He tried to be precise and hold back his panic.

'Attempted murder at 176 Canning Street, Carlton, one adult male victim with bad oral and facial injuries and possible internal ones, requiring intensive care. Assailant or assailants have left the scene. Please hurry.'

'Peter, what the fuck happened,' said Read, as he turned Welsh on his side and got his mouth pointing to the floor and cleared his airway. He didn't want Welsh drowning in his own blood. As if on cue, Welsh gagged and then vomited up large, stringy clots of congealed blood onto the carpet. Turning his head, his eyes bored into Read's. His message was clear and chilling. *It's all your fucking fault, Jack.* Welsh used crude sign language. *I can't speak. My jaw is broken, I can't breathe and I'm in terrible pain. Why oh fucking why has this happened to me?* Read was devastated as he tried to comfort

Welsh. The heehaw, heehaw of sirens told him that help had arrived.

'Police here, anybody home?' Read could hear the front security screen door squeak open and shut a couple of times. The next moment Read sensed someone behind him.

'Police here,' the raised voice said. 'Don't move. Don't turn around. Put your hands on top of your head where we can see them. Now stand up and turn around slowly, very slowly.'

Read did exactly as he was told. The Victorian Police had a reputation for shooting first and asking questions later. A uniformed senior constable had his service revolver trained on Read, holding the handgun in the classic two-handed grip. Another constable stood behind his partner but still in the kitchen area and off to one side, giving him clear vision of Read.

'I'm one of the good guys, fellas,' Read said, 'and with your permission I'm going to slowly get my wallet out of my hip pocket with my right hand and show you some ID,' The policeman tensed and nodded for Read to proceed. As Read kept his left hand raised and was producing his bona fides, two ambulance officers bustled into the room and started attending to Welsh. Clearing his airway and checking him out for fractures and any spinal or neck injuries, the ambos got Welsh ready for the stretcher trip out to the ambulance. Read and the two watchful policemen moved out of the way into the kitchen and discussed the attack on Welsh.

Read told them why he was in Melbourne and staying with Welsh. He didn't mention anything about the intrigue surrounding Clyde Trueman's stables and the involvement of Ironbar Miller.

'Looks like a druggie saw the open door and did a hit and run and your mate copped it,' said the senior connie. 'Mr Welsh must have left the front door open as you say his habit was. It's unlikely that a druggie would knock on the door and then violently attack when the door opened. More likely he entered through the open door and was then challenged at some stage by your mate. He must have had a weapon with him. Also there's no evidence of blood in the hallway which seems to confirm that Mr Welsh was surprised when he was in the kitchen or coming out of the bathroom. From the injuries, a decent sort of weapon has been used and there's nothing left lying around here from what we can see. We'll check outside shortly.' The sudden start-up of the ambulance siren told Read that Welsh was on his way to St Vincent's Hospital.

Read knew exactly what had happened to Welsh but he couldn't afford to tell the police as there just wasn't enough hard evidence. There were too many loose ends to tie up and too much risk attached for people close to him, like Sylvia and Joylene, if things went off half-cocked. When the police forensic people had finished dusting for fingerprints and looking for other evidence, they packed up their gear and left. Read locked the front door behind them and propped a chair under the el cheapo Taiwanese dead latch.

He started to clean Welsh's blood off the kitchen floor and the back room carpet. He was pumped up and knew that he would have no chance of sleeping properly. As he rinsed out a blood-stained towel he silently replayed his version of the evening's events. *Ironbar is on to me and someone has covered his backside, the classic tail following the tail. He knows that I'm living here. He decided to fix me up and made his run. He must have laughed when he arrived and found the front door open. Not that it mattered much. Poor old Welsh wouldn't have known what hit him. Thank Christ he's alive. Ironbar didn't catch up with me but he decided to leave his calling card. The fucking rotten bastard.* Read gritted his teeth and wrung out the towel as if it was Ironbar's neck. *If only it was that easy.*

'So there you have it, Shorty. I'm really in the shit now. Welsh is at St Vincent's and I want you to come with me and hear from him first hand what happened.' Read had brought Neil Ryan up to date and hoped that the big policeman would support him.

'Alright, Jack,' Ryan replied. 'All understood. I'll come and pick you up at Canning Street after lunch and we'll go and see your mate. In the meantime I'll get Larry Hill to organise some protective surveillance, just in case there's another visit by your friend Ironbar. You're pretty sure that it's him, are you?'

130

'Thanks, Shorty and yes, I am sure,' Read said with conviction. He was relieved that at least in the short term, he could go to and from Canning Street without being on tenterhooks all the time. Even so, it was going to be a terrible way to live.

Welsh was propped up in bed and had surgical plastic tubes plugged into half a dozen different places in his upper torso. His face was a mess and his waxy features were mottled by purplish bruising. The area around his nose and mouth were a zigzag of stitches and it hurt Read to look at him. Even Ryan was impressed. He grimaced as he spoke.

'Jesus, he's been worked over, hasn't he?' he said with morbid professional interest. Welsh wobbled his head in the affirmative and made feeble sign language with his right hand. His wired up jaw allowed him to make only muted grunts. His eyes glistened with tears of frustration.

'I'm off to find a whiteboard,' Read said.

Welsh made heavy weather of telling his story on the whiteboard. Read held it up for Welsh and then turned it from time to time so that Ryan could see what was going on. Welsh gurgled as he wrote.

I was out in the kitchen cooking some fish when I heard the front door open. I thought it was you, Jack. The next thing I knew was this big ugly bastard standing in the doorway staring at me. Welsh's description was Ironbar to a tee. *He just stood there tapping the palm of his hand with this rolled-up newspaper in his other hand. I asked him what he was up to and told him to get out of the house but he just kept on asking why I was being smart and following him around. I told him that I didn't know what he was talking about and then he started hitting me. Jesus, Jack, I thought he was going to kill me. He laid into me so hard and loved what he was doing. Who is this bastard and what's going on, for Christ's sake? When I get out of here, am I going to be safe again in my own fucking house? Jesus, I'm so sick and in such pain.*

Read was confused. He had originally thought that Ironbar was on to him but Welsh's version of events denied this. It looked as if whoever Ironbar had organised to watch his tail had stuffed up badly by not giving Ironbar a clear ID of the residents of 176 Canning Street. *Not for long,* Read thought. *Even now, Ironbar must have worked out that he had done over the wrong man. A few words with Griffiths the vet or Hicks the jockey would let him know of his mistake and he would be planning a second run on Welsh's house in no time.*

Ryan moved to the bedside. 'Mr Welsh,' he said. 'Are you prepared to stand up in court and point Ironbar out as your assailant if I arrest and charge him?' Welsh became agitated and shook his head. He beckoned for the whiteboard.

No fucking way, he scrawled. *What do you think I am, a complete fucking idiot? Jack, you've got to sort all this out by the time I'm ready to come home. I'll be in here for about three weeks, maybe more. Badly fractured jaw, smashed teeth, broken ribs and a split spleen where that ape kicked me. It's a wonder I didn't bleed to death internally. When I get out, you'll have to leave, Jack. Sorry, I want my quiet, boring life back. I just want to live in peace.*

Exhausted, Welsh slumped back in his bed.

'It's alright, Peter,' Read said, putting his hand on Welsh's forearm reassuringly.

'All understood. Never for a moment did I think that things would end up like this, believe me. I'll have this case I'm working on finalised before you leave hospital and be out of your hair well and truly, don't worry about that. Just rest and get better. Is there anything that you want?' Welsh waved Read and Ryan away. He just wanted them to leave him alone.

'Well, what can you do about all that?' Read asked Ryan as they walked out of St Vincent's Hospital. 'Nothing much, Jack,' Ryan replied.

'Your mate is shit scared and I don't blame him. He's lucky to be alive and he knows that. There's no way in the world he will testify so I'm not even going to waste my time opening a file on the matter. The boys from Carlton will keep it on their books for a few days and then it'll disappear into the too-hard basket. You said that you wanted to get your Range Rover off the streets?'

'Yeah, Shorty, I'm not using it at the moment and it's a dead giveaway parked near Welsh's place.'

'No sweat, Jack, I can arrange for it to be stored down at the police garage and workshop in Collingwood. The boys might even service it and wash it for you. How's that?'

'Shorty, that's great and thank you very, very much but tell your blokes to go easy. The paint's the only thing holding that car together.' The two men laughed as they parted company.

15

Read's first port of call was the car hire office in North Melbourne where he changed cars yet again. Now that he knew Ironbar would be breathing down his neck, he wanted to be as elusive as possible. Next stop was a Dick Smith's electronics shop where he bought a couple of pressure mats, a buzzer, some fine, twin-core electrical wire and some nicad batteries. Back at Welsh's house he laid the first pressure mat just inside the front door, under the threadbare carpet runner, where anyone coming through the door would step on it. He then laid the second mat under the carpet, nearly at the end of the hallway. He used duct tape to run the wires from the mats along the skirting boards out to the back room where he was camping. Wiring up the nicads to the buzzer, Read had built himself an early warning system. With the Colt Woodsman .22 automatic pistol at his bedside, he was ready for Ironbar's next move. *I hope, he thought.*

The phone in the front room started ringing.

'Jack, Larry Hill here. How's things? Shorty told me about your mate. Not good, eh?' Read liked the way Hill spoke. Clear, to the point and no bullshit.

'Gidday Larry, great to hear from you.' Read had warmed to the wiry undercover cop at their first meeting. *Hill was a man you'd want on your side if the shit hit the fan,* Read thought. 'Yeah, Larry. No good that's for sure. Peter Welsh and I go back a long way and all because of me he's nearly been murdered.' Read briefed Hill about Ironbar, being careful not to tell him too much and not mentioning a word about Sylvia and the involvement of Joylene Mills. He desperately wished that he could unload himself to Hill but he was being sucked down into the quicksand of paranoia and couldn't help himself. He couldn't afford to trust anyone. For all he knew, Hill could be just another bent cop.

'Yeah, Jack,' Hill said. 'All understood. I'll get one of my lads to sit off your place and hang off you when you go out. We might pick up some shithead following you. You've got my mobile number, haven't you? I never switch it off.' Read was relieved.

'Yeah, Larry, I certainly have. Look, I really appreciate what you're doing. We must get together for a drink when we both have time. I hope that all this shit will be sorted out soon. Catch up with you.' The conversation with Hill had made Read feel a bit better. Despite his doubts, he had a gut feeling that Hill was a straight cop. He hoped so.

It was mid-afternoon and the bars at the Lemon Tree were quiet. Read walked in and sat at the end of the lounge bar while Sylvia was setting up for the evening rush.

'Well, how are you, stranger? Love them and leave them, eh?' she said with a half-smile as she walked towards Read. He leaned forward and lowered his voice.

'Sylvia, sorry I haven't been in close contact but I've been flat out and things have turned nasty, believe me.' Read had decided to open up and give Sylvia an edited version of events, stressing his concern for her safety. 'So you see, sweetie, I'm in the shit big time and I'm terrified that the bastards who want to sort me out might decide to harm you to get at me. You understand, don't you?'

Sylvia bit her bottom lip as she polished a glass and listened to Read. She knew that he was being deadly serious. 'Sure, Jack, sure. I believe every word of what you're saying. It's hard for me to comprehend that this is really happening, you know. Oh, you know what I mean.' Read understood Sylvia's frustration and he tried to reassure her.

'Please, just be careful. Always lock your front security screen door and keep an eye open for anyone hanging around in the street or parked in a car. Watch for any cars that may appear to be following you. If that happens, always write down the rego number and then ring me immediately on my mobile, any time of the day or night. With a bit of luck, this mess will be cleared up in a couple of weeks. Sylvia, I'm busting my guts to spend time with you but I'd never forgive myself if you got hurt. Do you understand?' Sylvia stopped what she was doing and stared at him for a moment, then shook her head and smiled.

'Yes, Jack, I believe you. Don't worry. You'd better go, Jack. I don't want my boss complaining about having all my boyfriends coming to chat me up at work. Go on, off you go.' Walking back to Welsh's house from the Lemon Tree, Read felt a little better having alerted Sylvia. She had her head screwed on right and he knew that she had taken notice of him. Feeling a little paranoid, Read walked past Welsh's house on the opposite side of the road, looking and waiting for some time, to make sure that he was not being followed. Before opening the front door, Read checked that the small piece of duct tape that he had placed over the bottom of the door closure was still in place.

'You sound a bit rattled, old boy.' John Steele, Read's partner was being whimsical.

'It's not the time for being smart-arsed, John,' Read reminded him. 'I wasn't counting on getting involved in all this heavy stuff when I started work on what looked like just another straight forward livestock claim. Now my mate Peter Welsh is in hospital all smashed up and I can't spend time with a very attractive young lady I've met down here because I'm shit scared that she might get caught up in the whole disaster along with a few other people.' Read was thinking primarily about Joylene Mills.

'Okay, okay,' Steele replied. 'Take it easy. There you are, I'm my usual serious self once again.' He could tell that the usually flippant Read was worried. He had just finished a good workout at the gym. A noisy but healthy breakfast with his old surfie mates on the Corso

136

at Manly seemed a far cry from Melbourne and the predicament his partner had found himself in.

'Jack, from this distance I think that you've got in deeper than you should have. It's the easy way out but maybe you should just close the file and report to Centaur, telling them that there's simply not enough evidence to deny the Gold Crest claim and that seems to be the case anyway, the way you are calling things. Then you can pack up and come back to Sydney. Once you've left Melbourne, this Ironbar character will drop off, won't he?' Read found himself agreeing with Steele.

'Yeah, John, you're most probably right. There's no point in getting crippled or killed for a few lousy dollars. I've got no doubt at all that I'm on to something big but in this day and age, what with crooked cops, crooked pollies and all the big money flying around, you can't trust anyone. I'll get onto Les Trist at Centaur and tell him I'm closing the file. With a bit of luck I'll be back in Sydney by the weekend. Tell Sandman and Carrots that it's their shout. See you and thanks for the advice. Cheers.' Read was starting to feel better already. Once Clyde Trueman was told that the claim on Gold Crest was going to be paid out, the pressure would be off. *Then the fucking bastards can carry on with all their devious schemes to their hearts' content,* Read thought as he made ready for an early night.

'Jack, this is Joylene Mills again. You must be starting to get sick and tired of hearing from me but I've got to see you again. This time I think I've got something that might help you sort out what is going on at the stables.' Read was no longer as eager as he had been, now that he had decided to drop off the Gold Crest case but he didn't want to let on to Joylene.

'Joylene, great to hear from you anytime. What's happened? Where are you calling from?' There was an edge of excitement to the young strapper's voice.

'Jack, I'm calling from a public phone. I've found one of those little glass containers, you know, those glass things that contain stuff that is injected, c'mon, you know what I mean.' Read cut in.

'Ampoules, ampoules, Joylene. They've got a neck on them that is snapped off and a hypodermic syringe is used to draw off the contents. They come in different sizes. Doctors and vets use heaps of them. Where did you find it?'

'Yes, yes Jack, that describes it, that's what it is,' Joylene answered. 'Where did I find it? In Gold Crest's stall,' *Oh no, here we go again,* Read thought. His voice became urgent.

'Look, Joylene, first be extremely careful handling that ampoule. Don't under any circumstances get any of what's inside it on your skin. Do you understand? Please listen and take notice of me. Put it in a plastic bag or something like that and seal it up and then catch a taxi and bring it to me. I'll pay for the cab both ways. What time suits you?' As Read ended the call on his mobile, he was pondering Joylene's find. *Don't get too excited. The Gold Crest claim is going to be settled and anyway, so what if she's found an ampoule in his old stall? It's odds on that it contained a legal drug. Every stable seems to have empty ampoules lying around in odd places.*

Read watched from the other side of the street as the taxi dropped Joylene off outside Mitty's in Queen Street. Mills stood outside the shop for a while, window shopping and then went inside. Read held back waiting to see if anyone had followed the strapper. Satisfied that the coast was clear he crossed the street and into Mitty's. As the shop catered for the horse racing fraternity, the walls were covered with photographs, prints and paintings of four-legged heroes. Joylene was looking at a display of caps and tee shirts.

'You'd look good in one of those, Joylene,' Read said, pointing to a Vo Rogue T-shirt.

'Oh, hi Jack.' Joylene looked around and lowered her voice. 'I'm pretty sure that no one followed me. I've got that thing in my bag. I put it in one of those small glad bags.' Read took the small package from Joylene and put it in his pocket. She told Read how she had found the ampoule. 'The horse that moved into Gold Crest's old stall is a bit wild. He kicked in one of the boards lining the stall so I had to get a handyman in to repair the damage and when I was

15

showing him what he had to fix up, I saw that glass thing sitting on top of some bedding straw that was packed in behind the boards. It must have fallen down from the top. There's a gap in the piece of wood that runs around the top of the stall.'

'You're a real hero, Joylene,' Read said. 'I'll get someone I know to check what was in the ampoule and then I'll let you know. In the meantime just keep on doing your job and don't get into any trouble. Here's some money for the taxi. I'll stay here for a while and browse around. There's a book I want to buy.'

'See you, Jack,' Joylene said, suddenly standing on tiptoes to kiss Read on the cheek. *She's a good little sort,* Read thought, as he watched Joylene walk out of the shop.

'Well, Jack, that was elephant juice in that ampoule,' Steve Flower, the veterinary pathologist said. 'Etorphine hydrochloride. That should give you plenty to think about. The stuff's dynamite.'

'Tell me more, Steve,' Read said. He had heard the drug mentioned a few times in racing circles as being one of the latest weapons in the armoury of the race fixers. It was supposed to turn hacks into Phar Laps.

'It's a complicated story,' Flower replied, going to the bookshelf behind him and pulling a couple of books out. 'Etorphine is called elephant juice because of its use back in the early 1960s to immobilise big game animals like elephants, hippos and rhinos in the field for capture and conservation. It's truly an amazing drug that's a semisynthetic opiate derivative that has 10,000 times the analgesic potency of morphine. Yes, Jack, I know what you are going to ask, why does a drug that puts big animals to sleep make racehorses go so fast that they can drop dead from exhaustion?

It's got everything to do with dosage, Jack, everything to do with dosage. D-o-s-a-g-e. Dosage is absolutely critical. A relatively small dose of about four or five milligrams given intramuscularly with, for instance, a dart gun can drop a really big bull elephant but a drop, a single drop of the right dosage of etorphine injected intravenously into a horse will turn an average galloper into a racing machine that will run until it drops from sheer exhaustion.' Read asked the obvious question.

'What's the right dosage, Steve?'

'Alright, Jack, let me see if I can impress on you how low the dosage rate for horses can be. Take one of those hypodermic syringes that drug addicts use. Draw it full of etorphine, then squirt the whole lot out onto the ground, making sure that you don't get any on your skin. Now refill that same syringe with water and just one drop out of it will constitute a single dose for a horse, have you got that? A chemist mate of mine says one drop of etorphine put in a swimming pool, then take one drop out. That's a little dramatic but it gives you an idea of what we're looking at. The other thing to remember, Jack, is that this stuff is lethal on humans. It's murder. The amount needed to kill a human is from thirty to one hundred and twenty micrograms. Not milligrams – micrograms. Think of a microgram, Jack, as one hundredth of a drop. A hundred micrograms is a drop. Are you starting to get the drift?'

Read must have looked suitably impressed as Flower, now warmed up, was running at full throttle. 'Back in the early 1970s, a veterinary surgeon and a vet's assistant accidentally killed themselves with elephant juice and for a while the drug was withdrawn from the market. There's a reversing agent or antidote, you might call it, for etorphine. It's called diprenorphine and it's advisable to have some handy if one is using etorphine. Detection of the drug is difficult at present but some equipment will be coming in from the States shortly that will rectify that situation.'

'You don't look too happy, Jack,' Flower said, as he carefully placed the ampoule together with an ID tag into a plastic evidence bag. Read had been hoping that the test would reveal some harmless, legal substance that would be the final clincher for wrapping up the Gold Crest claim and getting him back to Sydney but Flower's analysis had put paid to that. *What do I do now?* he thought. *I just can't walk away from this now that it's almost certain that Gold Crest was being hit with elephant juice and I'd lay money that Dapper*

140

Dan's death was no accident. London to a brick on, the Sydney mob and Ironbar Miller had used their past links with Clyde Trueman to set up a horse doping ring in Melbourne, using Trueman's stables as a base and Griffiths the vet as their technical man. Ray 'Dangles' Hicks, the jockey, was in it up to his balls for sure and true to form, there would be cops on the take, bent bookies, crooked magistrates and politicians lurking around in the background just like those days in Sydney when George Freeman and Murray Farquhar ruled the roost. Read felt flat and helpless. When he was in New Guinea he had been the boss and had always had the whip hand and called all the shots. Now it was Ironbar who was in the box seat. Read tried to stop feeling depressed and turned to Flower.

'Steve, can you do me a favour? Please hold that ampoule and your report here in your office for safe keeping. More than likely, it'll be needed as evidence and I've got no security where I'm staying.'

'Not a problem, Jack,' Flower said, as he took the ampoule over to a locked steel cabinet.

16

John Steele sat back and watched the surf coming in on North Steyne beach as he listened to Read telling him about the not-all-that surprising developments in the Gold Crest case.

'Just move around a little, Jack. That mobile phone of yours is cutting in and out, yeah, that's better. It's a hard one, for sure, I agree. Now that you've got reasonable proof that this elephant juice drug is being used, it makes it a bit more difficult to walk away from the case. Mind you, my advice is still to do that. We aren't the cops, we don't have the resources to get involved in all this heavy criminal stuff and where does it get us in the end? Nowhere. Mate, I'm not going to call you chicken if you turn up at the Steyne on Sunday morning. There'll be a nice frosty schooner sitting on the bar waiting for you. Cheers.'

Read was sitting on a bench in the Exhibition Gardens where he always took his early morning walk. His call to Steele hadn't been very productive. His partner was ultra-conservative and counted the pennies. He was one of those people who believed that there were pockets in a shroud. A friendly Labrador off its leash paused to sniff at Read's shoes before it chased off after its jogging owner. *What do I do now?* Read thought. *I have enough evidence to raise serious doubts about the Gold Crest claim but that will involve exposing Joylene Mills as the person who found the ampoule. It would be impossible for her to continue working at the Trueman stables and then there is the Ironbar factor. Anyway, a good lawyer would have the whole shebang thrown out of court in no time. No, Steele is right.*

This job is all minuses and no pluses. Sydney, here we come. Back to Welsh's for a shower, then breakfast and the morning papers in Lygon Street.

Read's cappuccino clattered down onto the pavement, the toughened glass saucer spinning away on its edge until it bounced to a halt against the tyre of a parked car. The cup lay on its side as the foamy stream slowly stretched out in thin fingers over the bitumen. Read was looking stupidly at a page of the Melbourne *Herald Sun* and the story that had caused him to jerk involuntarily, spilling his coffee, which attracted the bemused attention of other sidewalk breakfasters. He had almost missed the barely three-inch column story buried on page seventeen. *Female strapper incinerated.* Read's eyes smarted as the printed words ticker-taped before him. The last time he had cried had been when his only and younger brother had died at the age of thirty-eight. Joylene Mills had been reduced to ashes when her car had left the road on a lonely stretch between Geelong and Bacchus Marsh, rolled and burned. A passing farmer had raised the alarm.

The only occupant of the car involved in the single vehicle accident was Joylene Mills, strapper, of Ascot Vale. Due to the intense heat, identification was only possible by referral to dental records. Ms Mills was employed by top Melbourne horse trainer, Clyde Trueman. Read sat in a daze, staring at the paper on the table in front of him, as a waiter retrieved the cup and saucer and mopped up the mess on the footpath outside the coffee shop. The waiter was silent. The last thing he wanted to start the day with was a confrontation with a man who looked like trouble.

Read wiped a tear away from the side of his nose and looked furtively around him. He was prickling with embarrassment. His mind was racing. *Joylene, Joylene. You poor little bugger. You never harmed anyone. You loved working with your horses and now look what's happened to you.* Read walked inside and paid his bill.

'Forget the coffee, sir,' the waiter said. Without speaking, Read turned and strode off, the paper tucked under his arm.

'Shitty, aren't we,' the waiter said in a mincing tone to no one in particular.

From the article in the *Herald Sun* and the Telecom 013 information service, Read was soon speaking to the farmer who had alerted the police to the blazing car in the gully near his property. Sid Jamieson was laconic and down to earth.

'No, I didn't see any other cars on the road. Mind you, at that time of night, it's bloody quiet. Mainly used by locals, you know. It was the dark phase of the moon and pitch black. Turns out it was a woman in the car. Poor bugger didn't stand a chance. When I got there, it was burning like a bonfire. Damn lucky we'd burned a firebreak in that gully a couple of weeks ago or else we'd have had a good grass fire on our hands. I couldn't get near the car. Too hot and I thought the tank might explode. Just hope that she died quick, you know. Must be a terrible way to die. She must have been going too fast and couldn't take the corner. She could have had too much to drink, I suppose. Are you working for an insurance company?' Read's mouth was dry and he didn't feel like talking anymore.

'Yeah, thanks for your help, Sid. I'll be up your way tomorrow to have a look at the accident scene. I might drop in on you. Cheers.'

Read looked down into the gully where Joylene had gone up in flames. The roadway was one of those narrow, off-the-beaten track strips of bitumen with a bad case of acne, all little craters and eruptions. For two cars to pass each other, one gave way and pulled over onto the gravel shoulder. The road was obviously not high priority on the local council's major works program. Read could see where Joylene's car had been winched back up to the road.

He had been told that the wreck was being held at the Bacchus Marsh police station where it would stay until after an inquest was held, when it would be picked up by Sims Scrap Metal. *And then Joylene's little Mazda would return to Japan in an ingot of metal,* Read mused, as he walked slowly along the side of the road, using his feet like a metal detector looking for nothing in particular. He had turned around and was walking back along the path that he thought

Joylene's car would have taken as it crashed into the gully, when he saw it. A light breeze was blowing and something caught Read's eye. The rosary beads were hooked up on the leafy branches of a raggedy native bush and a puff of wind had lifted the leaves concealing them. As soon as Read unhooked the beads, he knew what he was holding. Stirring the beads in the palm of his left hand with his right index finger, Read choked up at the sight of them. The last time he had seen them was when Joylene had them. He put the beads in his shirt pocket and walked slowly back to his car.

As he drove back to Melbourne, Read speculated on how Joylene had met her death. *There had to be at least two people and another car involved. Someone with local knowledge knew that stretch of road. Joylene more than likely knew her killers. They must have thought that she was dead when her car went into the gully but she wasn't because somehow or other she had managed to throw her rosary beads out of the car. The car would have been on fire at the time. Jesus, that must have been an effort. The absolute terror that must have gripped her. Joylene, people can't do these things and get away with it. I'll get the bastards, I promise you. I won't let you down.* Read remembered another grisly and fiery murder in another place. Joylene's death was a carbon copy of the murder of the Sydney trainer, Ted Barnes. The modus operandi was the same and both murders had the same common denominator – Ironbar. As the skyline of Melbourne poked its head out of the summer smog, Read patted the beads in his shirt pocket. Joylene had sent him a message from the grave.

Cleaning the Colt Woodsman .22 automatic pistol made Read feel a little bit better. It didn't exactly make him feel ten feet tall but it helped with his peace of mind. Read used the handgun for target practice to keep his eye in. In New Guinea, he had kept the locals amused by plinking empty beer cans that the kids had thrown in the Sepik River for him. He sprayed some CRC over the parts, wiped off the excess and reassembled the weapon, using the shorter of the two barrels. The chequered walnut grips filled his hand well. The magazine, located in the butt was loaded with Long Rifle hollow-point bullets. A small, factory-drilled hole in the end of the lead projectile helps it become a mini-hand grenade.

Hitting a close range target at 1100 feet per second, the bullet makes a short entry hole but as it meets resistance, the hollow point allows it to expand and mushroom out, breaking up, the fragments spinning and whirling. The effect on flesh and organs is spectacular. Its energy sapped by milliseconds of creating havoc and the process of disintegration, the bullet or what is left of it, rarely exits. In the hands of marksmen who knew their anatomy, Long Rifle hollow-point .22 bullets have brought down big game. Read worked the slide mechanism a few times and nodded with approval. Deliberately drawing in his breath, he raised the pistol and aimed it at an imaginary target. His hand was steady and he was proud of his control. He felt better and not so scared, now that he had decided what to do.

'Now come on, Jack. You can't do that. I'm really offended, I can tell you and I can just imagine what the Prendergasts are going to be saying, believe me.' Clyde Trueman was moving a solid silver Phar Lap paperweight up and down across his desk blotter pad. The wattles under the trainer's neck flushed as his indignation racked up his blood pressure a couple of notches.

'Look, I'm sorry, Clyde,' Read said. 'I really am but there's been a development in the Gold Crest case but before I go on, that was terrible, absolutely terrible about Joylene Mills. What the bloody hell happened?' Silence and then Trueman cleared his throat. Read was listening carefully, his antenna tuned, waiting for Trueman's response.

'Yes, shocking, just shocking. The whole stable's in shock. The funeral's on Friday so we'll all be wearing black armbands at the track on Saturday. Joylene was a damn fine strapper, believe me. You know, the police said that there was hardly anything left of her, what with the fire and all.'

Yeah, and you know more than you're letting on, Clyde baby, Read thought, as he listened to the trainer rabbit on before he jerked him back to the real reason for the call.

'I'm putting you on notice, Clyde, that I have evidence that Gold Crest's death could have been caused by the administering of illegal substances. That's the technical gobbledegook. In language that you and I understand, Clyde, the horse was being pumped up with something to make it think that it had a rocket up its arse. On that basis, the claim will be denied. I can't say any more at present but you'll get it in writing in a couple of days with copies to the Prendergasts as well. You know what this means.'

Trueman cut in. 'Yes, Jack, I know exactly what it means. It means that I'll be calling on all my clients to change their insurers immediately. That's what it will mean.'

'Let me finish, Clyde,' Read jumped in, determined to curb Trueman's indignant swaggering. 'Just remember that if this story gets out and around the traps, your stables will be on the nose with the racing clubs and with your other owners and what about intending clients? Remember, Clyde, perceptions can do more damage than facts, just ask the politicians. Owners don't want their expensive horseflesh used as fucking guinea pigs by some doper. I'll say it slowly again. What all this means, Clyde, is that this will end up with the lawyers and if shit happens, it'll end up in the courts. I don't want to end up blueing with you. There's nothing to be gained by that for either of us. I've got to do my job, you've got to do yours. Catch up with you.'

Clyde Trueman slammed his phone down at the same time he crashed the silver paperweight down on the desk.

'What's all that noise in there, Clyde? What's going on?' *Shit,* Trueman thought, as he heard his wife walking towards his office.

Larry Hill handed the folder to Read.

'Here's that file from the morgue that you wanted to look at, Jack. Have a look at it but you can't keep it. I've got to take it back to my contact by five this afternoon.' He sipped his orange juice as Read scanned the post-mortem report on Joylene Mills. The bar at the Pumphouse Hotel in Fitzroy was quiet and Read and Hill had taken their drinks to a small table near a window looking out onto

Nicholson Street. A tram ran past, raising swirls of dust from the fine sand directed where its braking wheels made contact with the tracks.

The post-mortem report made Read grit his teeth. What was left of Joylene Mills told how she had died – badly beaten about the head and left arm fractured. Her injuries had been inflicted before her car went into the gully. Read sucked in his breath as he turned over a glossy, colour photograph of a thing on a dissection table.

What he assumed to be Joylene's head and upper torso was a shapeless, charred lump, all glazed and crusted. Her lower legs had been burnt off. He closed the file and finished his beer that had suddenly tasted flat and sour. *Here I am, alive and well,* Read thought, *drinking beer while what's left of poor old Joylene is sitting inside a plastic bag in a coolroom down at the morgue.* At that moment Read was seized by a surge of emotion. It was the survival instinct. It felt good to be alive. He got his mind back to the business in hand. The coronial inquiry would return a finding of murder by a person or persons unknown if there were no charges laid beforehand.

'Thanks, Larry,' Read said, pushing the file across the table to Hill.

'I just wanted to check a few things out, morbid interest I suppose, as much as anything else. There'll be a murder investigation for sure and that should stir things up, especially at Clyde Trueman's stables. What else is happening?'

'Nothing much, Jack,' Hill replied. 'Your mate Ironbar must be on a decent earn as he spends a lot of time moving between Melbourne and Sydney, sometimes twice a week. He's a busy boy, believe me. How's your mate Peter doing?'

'Oh, he's doing okay but the poor bastard's still as windy as all hell,' Read said. 'Can you blame him? And all my fault too, when it comes to the bottom line. He's going to be in hospital a little longer than they thought. They've found a hairline fracture at the base of his skull and there's a few complications. I try and drop in to see him every other day, usually in the evenings. Larry, what do you make of Rex Jardine, your minister?' Larry Hill swirled what was left of his orange juice.

'Between you and me, Jack, he gives me the shits. He's more concerned about the crooks than us, and the bleeding hearts and civil libertarians can get his ear anytime they like. What do you expect of this government? I know that the commissioner and Jardine have had some almighty blues. They hate each other's guts. There's a big push on by the poofters, the girls as well as the boys, to work their way into certain areas of the job. It's becoming a real power struggle. They're always sending a deputation to Jardine's office about one thing or another. He's a man of many parts. He's quite a punter at the track, you know. Shorty Ryan would know all about that, seeing that he spends most of his time there.' Hill grinned.

'The racetrack's Shorty's office. You should know that. It's pretty good eh, you get paid good dollars to do what you like doing best. That doesn't happen to many of us, Jack.' Read grinned as he stood up.

'Thanks again, Larry, for your help with that file and for keeping an eye on Welsh's house. Is that arrangement still on?'

'Yeah, Jack,' Hill gave the thumbs up sign. 'I've got one of my eager young connies on the job. He's fallen in love with working undercover and then there's the odd bit of overtime for him. It all adds up. See you around. And keep out of trouble.'

17

Shane Hepworth curled his fingers and looked down at his bitten nails. The last time he had heard from David Felton was weeks ago when the audiotapes had turned up in the mail. He hadn't even bothered to play them, throwing them into a drawer. The person on the other end of the telephone was no help at all.

'No, darl, we just stopped hearing from David. One day he was here, the next day he was gone. We're still holding some money for him, a few hundred dollars. Haven't seen him for weeks. Some of his clients have been calling in wanting to book him too. You never know.' The transvestite receptionist at the Golden Boys Escort Service became conspiratorial.

'You never know, darl, our David may have fallen in love and run away with a sugar daddy.' The high-pitched giggle coming down the line made Hepworth wince. He wasn't in the mood for all that sort of crap.

'Sorry, what did you say your name was?' Hepworth asked, trying to get the conversation back on track. The transvestite sounded miffed.

'I didn't say, darl, but since you must know, it's Fleur. Now I've forgotten what yours is. Oh, I'm so forgetful. Isn't that dreadful of me? All these gorgeous men I have to deal with.' *Oh, for God's sake, put a plug in it,* Hepworth thought. He tried to be forceful.

'Fleur, if you speak to David Felton, tell him his mate Shane in Sydney wants to speak to him urgently, very urgently. You could be right. He could have gone away for a trip with a client but it's not like him to do something like that without letting someone know. There's always a first time for everything, I suppose. Now Fleur, could you please take my number and keep it in a safe place.' He slowly recited his phone number.

'Please repeat to me, Fleur, thanks a lot.' As he put the phone down, Hepworth started chewing his fingernails again. They were down to the quick and one of them started to bleed. *It's not like David to walk away and leave his money at the agency,* Hepworth thought and then smiled, *he's such a tight arse – in more ways than one.* Felton and Hepworth had been casual lovers but Felton was always chasing dollars, and free love wasn't his whack. Hepworth walked over to the chest of drawers and took out the package of audiotapes. *The vibes aren't good. Something bad has happened to David.*

'Yes, Mr Minister,' Ryan said firmly, 'that matter has been fixed up. No, there were no problems. He understood your position very clearly and realised that he'd been very silly. He's packed up and returned to Sydney and I told him that you would never contact him again and that he was never to contact you. He understood that. In fact, he was very cooperative and sensible about it. Like a lot of these people he'll soon find new victims but we're not worried about that, are we? The important thing is that what could have become an absolute disaster for you and me has been neutralised.'

Ryan wanted to create the perception that he and the politician were co-conspirators with common goals and he knew that he was being successful. He could hear Rex Jardine exhaling slowly with relief. 'Chief Inspector, er, Neil, that's very good news. You've done very well indeed. Congratulations. I'm so pleased that you've managed to get such a good result so quickly and in such an uncomplicated manner.' Jardine was feeling pleased with himself as he wiped the film of sweat from his upper lip. He had been on edge for days, waiting for Ryan to call. Ryan let some silence elapse before he started talking again. He knew that he was dealing with a man who could easily fall off the edge again. He lowered his voice and spoke slowly.

'Listen carefully, Mr Minister. I've managed to put out this brushfire but don't go off and start getting cocky again, if you get what I mean.' Jardine pursed his lips at the double entendre. Ryan pressed on.

'I've got a job to do and I want to be able to do it without having to wipe your fucking arse for you all the time. Do you understand? Save your cock for your wife. I'm not joking. If you fuck up again, the tapes I took from our mate will end up with your wife and the Premier. Do you get me?' Jardine's mouth started working as he waved away his secretary who had walked into the office.

'Yes, yes, Mr Richardson, I've taken note of all that and I'll act on your advice straight away. I have to dictate a letter now, so I'd better get going. Thank you again. Goodbye.' A wave of mixed emotions swept over Jardine, relief that David Felton was no longer going to blackmail him but concern that the big policeman had merely exchanged places with him. Jardine dug the nails of his right hand into the palm of his left, bruising the flesh.

Neil Ryan was a hard-bitten and ruthless man who would stop at nothing. Jardine stared ahead in a trance as an image of David Felton passed before him. *Ryan would only have frightened David off. He wouldn't have hurt him.* Jardine snapped out of it and clenched his thighs together and swallowed hard. He couldn't let himself go to the brink again. He had to keep himself under control.

The pre-dawn sun was battling to get its eyebrows above the tumble of low cloud covering Melbourne. Read sat alone in the members stand at Flemington, a solitary dot on the landscape of empty seats. It was cool but the hint of a warmer day was in the air. Read was wearing a jacket and his binoculars hung from his neck. The early morning training session was in full swing and rising up from the track below him, still shrouded in wisps of mist, Read heard the mingling of the snorts and whinnies, some of them synchronised with the sound of hooves cutting into the dirt and grass. Floating over the top came the human sounds, trackwork riders and jockeys talking and singing out and then the voices with more authority, trainers giving riding instructions for different horses.

'Now, Mister Collins, we might be able to make you into a jockey yet. Take him along quietly for the first 1000 metres, then let him wind up bit by bit and then let him know he's working over the last two hundred. Don't use the whip. Now off you go.'

'Right, Boss.' The rider's voice trailed off as he cantered his mount off down the track.

Read focused his binoculars on the trainers at their various vantage points. In the strengthening light, Clyde Trueman was easy to pick out with his mustard-coloured corduroy jacket and matching Kangol cap. A couple of riders with arms folded were standing next to Trueman, waiting for the strappers to bring their mounts over. Talking to Trueman was Jim Griffiths, the vet. *I wish I was invisible and standing next to them,* Read hoped.

Read hadn't come to Flemington to clock the horses. He had come to get the details and rego number of Griffiths' Land Rover Discovery, which were now in the notebook in his jacket pocket. Read checked his watch and stood up. He was timing things well. He would make very sure that he was not being followed and then set sail for Collingwood. He was hungry for breakfast and for Sylvia.

'Hi,' Sylvia said as she hugged Read and let him in. Read snibbed the security door, locked the front door and followed her to the bathroom.

'I've parked my car a couple of blocks away. The walk did me good. It's great to see you, Sylvia, it really is. I've been thinking about you a lot. It's been more than a week since I've seen you. I'm being serious.'

As Sylvia prepared to clean her teeth, she said in between gurgles and gargles, 'That's nice if you mean it and you're not just worried about your cock, Jack. Go up to the bedroom. It's too early for breakfast and I want to have a bit of a sleep in if it's alright with you.' Read grinned and did as he was told. He was in bed by the time Sylvia came in. Her hair was down and she was wearing an oversized T-shirt. She smelt of toothpaste and moisturiser.

'Move over, Jack, and let me get into my own bed. If you want to stay here, be quiet and massage my back.'

She pulled up the shirt and rolled onto her stomach. Read brushed her long hair to one side and did as he was told.

'Um, that's nice. No, over to the left a bit, down, a bit more, ah, that's it, right there.' Sylvia closed her eyes and luxuriated in Read's expert touch. He knew just how much pressure to use and she wondered how many other women he had massaged his way to sexual success.

'Jack, how's this case of yours going? Is it still dangerous? Go on, don't be mean. Tell me.' Read wasn't going to fall into the trap of weakening and telling Sylvia more than she should be told.

'Sweetheart, things should be all cleared up soon but I still want you to be careful with your security. When it's all over it'll be a big night out on the town and all will be revealed. Now my arm's getting tired so roll over.'

Read's hand moved down between Sylvia's legs and started a more arousing massage. She parted her legs to make his job easier.

'I knew it wouldn't take long for you to get down there,' Sylvia said. 'Don't stop.'

18

Jesus, why do I get myself into situations like this? Read thought, as he drove into the beer barn carpark. He had driven to Thomastown in Melbourne's north to meet a contact Larry Hill had organised for him. Even before he opened the door of his car, the waves of sound from the rock band blasted over him. Heavy, buzzing vibrations of percussion instruments pumped through huge speakers sounded like the onset of a Hollywood earthquake. While trying to cope with the noise, Read joined the scrum impatiently waiting to pass the scrutiny of the praetorian guard of no-neck bouncers defending the entrance. Mixed up with the male bouncers were their female counterparts, the door bitches. It was hard to tell the boys from the girls. Read had not come to the venue to have his eardrums ruptured. He was going to conspire to commit a crime.

When a bouncer who had overdosed on steroids demanded he put out his wrist for stamping, Read felt indignant and stupid. He looked down at the smudged purple skull and crossbones which had the date on it. Before he allowed himself to be swept along by the eager crowd, he scanned the ID numbers worn by the black-tracksuited security patrol. Larry Hill had told him to make contact with number thirty-six. *Not out here, must be inside,* Read thought, as he was drawn into the maelstrom. Looking around, he could easily see that he was well and truly out of his league. The crowd was a mix of youngies and bikies, the two groups protecting their own territory as if by prior treaty. A second look reassured Read a little. Quite a few of the bikies looked older than him. Beer barn was a conservative description.

The vast area was a conglomeration of island bars, each with a separate theme. Spunky and frantic young men and women, dressed to match, pirouetted expertly through the melee, balancing trays of drinks. Bouncers were everywhere, monitoring the crowd and picking up empty glasses. With strobe and multicoloured disco lights knifing across each other in a kaleidoscopic battle, it took a while for Read to adjust to his new surroundings. A sweat-drenched disc jockey, who looked as if he had sampled a cocktail of drugs on offer from the cruising dealers, was imprisoned in his glass cage, waiting for the band to take a break. Read bought a pot of light and moved around on the fringe of the crowd, looking for number thirty-six. A couple of bikies brushed past Read and he was forced to give ground. *No sense in getting into a blue here,* he thought.

'Are you being looked after, buddy?' Read felt a light tug at his right elbow and turned. A young sharp-faced bloke tricked out in all the right gear was looking at him. He could have been Greek or Lebanese. His body language said 'dealer.' 'Oh, I'm sorry. I thought you were someone else. Sorry, mate,' the man said as he blended back into the crowd. Read smiled. *He thought I was an undercover cop. I could have been a crooked one.* Read chided himself. *The dealer probably knows all the crooked ones.*

Then he saw him. Number thirty-six was standing back off the crowd talking to one of the patrons. He was well built, rocking ever so slightly back and forth on the balls of his feet. Read reckoned that he was in his mid-thirties. As the man talking to number thirty-six walked off, Read moved in putting out his hand, trying not to yell to make himself heard.

'Gidday, mate. Noddy told me to come and see you. He said you'd be able to help me out.' As the man started to speak, Read wished he could lip-read.

'How are you? You're Jack,' thirty-six said, as they shook hands. He didn't give his name and Read wasn't going to press him for it. If this was how the game was played, he wasn't going to rock the boat. 'Follow me,' the bouncer said, heading for the far side of the building. Read found himself out in the delivery area behind the kitchen. The low hum of the exhaust fans was a welcome relief from the bedlam he had left behind.

'What's the job, Jack?' *He doesn't waste words,* Read thought, as he took the folded envelope from his pocket.

'The rego and address details are all here,' Read said.

'The owner of the car is a vet and there'll be all sorts of drugs in it. Most of them will be in those large, smart-looking plastic fishing tackle boxes, you know those big ones, Yankee, they are, Plano is one popular brand. You know what I mean. Anyway, I want the car broken into. Make it look like a druggie has done the job. Take everything that looks like drugs. Look in the glove box and under the seats. That's it.'

'That'll be one thousand in advance,' thirty-six said, zipping Read's envelope into his tracksuit top pocket. Read handed over ten, folded $100 notes just as he had been told to do. Thirty-six took the money without counting it and put it with the envelope.

'Thanks,' he said. 'I'll call you on your mobile from a public phone when the job is done and arrange a drop. Don't call me, I'll call you. Let's split.' Read didn't even bother saying goodbye, now that he had got used to dealing with Larry Hill's taciturn contact who could have been a cop moonlighting as a bouncer. He found that he had to retrace his steps and re-enter the blast furnace of sound. The band was on a break and the hophead DJ was in his element, giving a fairly good imitation of a doped out, whirling dervish.

Read was working his way to the front of the hotel when he lost his bearings and found himself surrounded by Comanchero bikies in one of the side bars. They had formed a circle and it was obvious that they were waiting for something to happen. It was happening – they were rapidly siphoning off the hotel's stocks of Jack Daniels and many of them had that super-alert and hyperactive look that told Read that they had been giving the speed a fair old nudge as well. The verbal diarrhoea was flowing thick and fast.

'The shout's on me, buddy.' A bikie at least five feet six tall and six feet wide pressed a pot of Jack Daniels and Coke into Read's hand. He smiled grimly and accepted the drink, sure that a refusal would offend.

'Hey, Cube, you motherfucker. What about me?' another bikie yelled out at Read's new drinking mate.

'Listen, fartface, go fuck your grandmother,' Cube said, turning to Read again. Read beat him to it.

'Jack's the name,' he said, raising his glass.

'What's the go here?' Cube skolled his Jack Daniels and let out a yell that would have won an international yodelling competition. He wiped his wet, loose mouth, camouflaged by a ginger fuzz of beard and moustache.

'A couple of bros wiped themselves out on the Calder Highway and we're having a wake for them. Hang about. There'll be a show on in a jiff.' A brave waiter fought his way through the pack with a tray of jugs of Jack Daniels. *It'd take brave or just plain stupid bouncers to try and control this menagerie,* Read thought. An animal roar told him that the show had started. All eyes were on the stripper as she was ushered through the crush into the cleared circle. Read was hemmed in on all sides and found himself gawking, along with the rest of his new-found companions.

The overweight girl wore blue mechanic's overalls with holes in all the wrong places. She was carrying an open toolbox with a few spanners and screwdrivers sticking up out of it. A few gyrations and her overalls, a patchwork of Velcroed pieces that pulled apart, were on the floor. Her heavy, drooping breasts, one longer than the other, featured large Swastika tattoos amongst a field of moles. The mob roared into a higher gear as the girl slowly turned, waggling her cellulite-pocked buttocks. On each cheek she had tattooed a large ship's propeller and above, across her lower back, the words 'twin screws, keep clear.'

Read grinned as Cube slapped him on the back. In a trice, the girl was on the floor on her back, raising her spread legs. She had a tattooed map of Tasmania in the obvious place with Devonport up near her navel, which was pierced by a large gold ring. Hobart was hidden in the jungle below. She put her hands down to her hairy crutch, displaying herself.

'Fuck me dead,' Cube exploded. 'She's got a cunt on her like a pig with its throat cut.' Not to be outdone, another bikie submitted his contribution.

'She's got piss flaps like a spaniel's ears,' he yelled, bursting into forced laughter at his own joke. The crowd roared back. The girl reached into the toolbox and with a dramatic flourish, produced a huge, black dildo. It stood up like a Black Power salute. Soon the bikies' slow rhythmic stamping sent vibrations up Read's legs to the point where he could feel himself starting to bounce. Lubricating herself with K-Y gel, the girl worked the dildo into herself. All hell broke loose. Read felt claustrophobic, stuck in the middle of the meatloaf of sweating bodies. Then someone close to him let go with a terrible fart, the stench burning its way into his sinuses. He gagged as he tried to hold his breath. Sticking his elbows out, he tried to work his way out of the crush. Cube looked around and re-established eye contact with Read.

'Hey, buddy, stay with it. She'll fuck a few of the bros shortly and then there'll be a gangbang out in the carpark. I'll save you a place in the queue.' He threw his head back, chortling, exposing rotten teeth stumps. Read managed a weak grin as he finally burst clear. He almost ran out into the carpark, deep-breathing to clear his lungs, the ruckus and yackety-yak from the bikies tumbling after him. As he drove off like a prison escapee, all he could think about was getting home and standing under a long, hot shower.

Shane Hepworth put down the telephone and sat on the edge of the two-seater lounge, thinking. He and David had often sat there, arms around each other, sharing a bong. He had just made another useless call to the Melbourne escort agency that now regarded him as a nuisance caller. The fact was that David had simply disappeared off the face of the earth. Hepworth was in a bind. After the weeks of silence, he was resigned to acknowledging that something dreadful had happened but he was terrified of getting involved. Reporting David to the police as a missing person would do exactly just that. He adjusted the headphones as he continued to listen to David talking about the sexual preferences of Rex Jardine, Minister of the Crown. Felton detailed dates, times and places and described with anatomical precision the physical landmarks on Jardine's body, including a boomerang-shaped birthmark on his penis. Then followed several tapes of sessions between Jardine and the male prostitute. Because the tapes were clear and explicit, Hepworth was able to pick up a lot of the intimate sounds. Jardine was a very demanding client. Hepworth started to feel horny. *David, you really do have the gift of being able to turn people on,* he thought, as he rubbed his crotch.

He didn't know much about politics but like many people in Australia, he had seen Jardine on TV. He looked and sounded straight, which was obviously good for him in his position. Some of the gay magazines had done features on him, applauding him for his liberal stand on prison reform, Aboriginal land rights and other civil liberties issues. He was always turning up at all the right opening nights and charity dos and was a constant guest on TV current affairs shows and talkback radio. If only the public knew all about their hero. Felton had caught himself a very big fish indeed. Hepworth put the tapes back in their envelope and wondered what he was going to do with them. *Maybe I should just chuck them out with the rubbish,* he thought, then changed his mind. *No, David deserves better than that.*

The evening TV news made Hepworth's mind up about what to do with the Felton tapes. He was watching *A Current Affair* with its talking head Jason Robley, when he saw anti-corruption crusader, Barry O'Shea QC being interviewed. O'Shea had been appointed head of a new untouchable unit, designed to flush out corruption at all levels in government. He had already brought down some top-ranking NSW police and a couple of politicians, surviving a murder attempt along the way. Hepworth felt as if Barry O'Shea was speaking directly to him.

'You see, Jason, the time has come when ordinary people have to take back control from those who have abused the trust that the people put in them in the first place. Police and politicians especially must realise that they are answerable and accountable to all those ordinary Australians out there who want their society back on an even keel again. Believe me, I won't rest until every crooked cop and rotten politician is where they belong, behind bars.' Jason Robley asked the question that Hepworth wanted to ask.

'Mr O'Shea, you're a man who hasn't flinched from taking on the toughest of jobs and you've faced a lot of danger. We all remember how lucky you were to escape being murdered when the bomb planted under your car failed to detonate. What do you say to our viewers out there who may have information about examples of corruption or criminal activity but are frankly too frightened to come forward?' O'Shea leaned forward and looked straight down the camera.

'Jason, thanks for asking that question. My commission does not want to have honest people compromised. It does not want to have their safety jeopardised. For those who have information that could be valuable to us, we offer absolute discretion and confidentiality. I say to these people, Jason, stand up. Stand up for yourself and your families and I will stand with you.' The camera panned back to Robley.

'For those viewers wishing to contact Mr O'Shea's commission, there is a confidential, twenty-four-hour hotline. You'll be speaking to a real person, not a recorded message and you will not be asked to give any personal details. The number to call is up on your screen now. The number is 130130. I repeat, 130130. Thanks again for your time, Mr Barry O'Shea, and our good wishes and support go with you. Well, viewers, there's a man that we can all be proud of. Australia needs more Barry O'Sheas.'

Hepworth went out into the kitchen to make a cup of coffee as Jason Robley introduced the next story about a woman who shared her house with 265 cats.

The Boeing 737 commenced its let-down over Botany Bay and lined up for its landing on runway Thirty-Four Left at Sydney Airport. It was a clear, still morning that backdropped Sydney beautifully and Read wondered what the city would be like without the harbour. *Just another crappy city,* he thought. John Steele had told him that he didn't want to use the telephone, so Read was flying up from Melbourne for the day. Steele was a little paranoid about phones but with all the tapping and scanning that went on, he couldn't be blamed. Steele was waiting for Read at the Qantas domestic arrivals area. He was casual in shorts and sandals and had that gym-fit look about him.

'Good flight?' Steele said, as he shook hands with Read.

'Yeah,' Read replied. 'Up and down and here we are. What's the go, John?'

'Let's get on the road and I'll fill you in on the way back to Manly,' Steele said, as they headed for the carpark.

'Barry O'Shea and I go back a long way, Jack. We grew up together in Manly and started off surfing together, then he and I were junior clerks in the army before I pulled the pin and went to PNG. He stayed in the army and did his law degree then went out into private practice. Since I've been back in Australia, we're in the gym every morning after a swim and on Saturdays we have our session at the Steyne. He's one hundred percent, believe me. No bullshit and no fucking around. He's made a lot of enemies as a result of this anti-corruption commission he's running but he's tough is our Barry, must be the Irish in him.'

Read had met O'Shea at the Steyne but had not had much to do with him. Balmain and that side of Sydney was Read's stamping ground and in between fishing and shooting trips and hanging about at Maggsie's panel shop, his weekends were well organised. Read sat and listened to Steele as they drove over the Harbour Bridge. He was wondering what information O'Shea had that would relate to his problems in Melbourne.

Steele drove the Toyota carefully, passing abusive judgment on the drivers around him.

'Jesus, can you believe what that dopey bitch in front is doing?' he said. The Mercedes was doing more than eighty kilometres an hour as the woman driver adjusted combs in her hair – with both hands. A blast from Steele's horn jerked her back to reality and she put her hands back on the steering wheel.

'We're going to meet with Barry at my place at lunchtime and you can listen to what he's got. Some micro-audiotapes turned up and if they're for real, they're dynamite.'

Coming down Sydney Road into Manly, Read could see that there was not much surf up but the beach was still crowded. Steele was always complaining about the wackers from the western suburbs bringing their bad manners to his patch.

'A lot of them make the trek looking for drugs,' he said.

Steele made the introductions.

'Yes, I've met Jack a couple of times at the Steyne,' Barry O'Shea said, as he shook hands with Read and sat down in Steele's front room that overlooked the wonderful stretch of ocean that comes foaming ashore on Sydney's northern beaches. The two young National Crime Authority bodyguards assigned to O'Shea had taken up their positions down in the street. In sloppy shirts and boardshorts they were just another pair of beach bums. O'Shea continued.

'I suppose John has told you that he and I go back a long way. I've always respected his opinion.' O'Shea grinned. 'He would have made a good prosecutor. In a job like mine, I need independent and objective advice from time to time, to help me keep things in perspective and these tapes are one of those times. You realise, Jack, that this meeting is strictly off the record.' O'Shea indicated the micro-cassette player on the occasional table at the side of his chair. 'I got these tapes from an anonymous informant and they make very interesting listening. The tapes are good quality and John has heard them. He told me that you are currently in Melbourne, working on a case and may know a little bit about the alleged central character in these tapes.'

Read nodded. 'All understood, Barry. I only hope that I can be of some assistance.'

'Alright,' O'Shea said, activating the player. 'Let the show begin.'

O'Shea, Steele and Read sat listening to David Felton's tapes. Their faces registered their response to the perverted and tortured coupling of Rex Jardine and David Felton. They winced at some of the imaginative demands made by Jardine and acceded to by Felton. Read found himself grinning nervously but managed to look suitably serious again. *His poor fucking wife and kids,* he thought. *The world is a crazy place.* When the final tape was played, the three men sat for a while looking at each other. O'Shea spoke first.

'Well, gentlemen, not nice stuff but this sad, warped behaviour has been with us since the beginning of time but if this man on the tapes is Rex Jardine then it is a whole new ball game. On the basis that it is Jardine, then a minister of the crown has compromised himself so comprehensively to the point where he is being or is about to be blackmailed. In his position, the potential for high-level criminality and the perversion of justice is frightening. In the event of his behaviour being publicly revealed, we must consider the inevitable, massive collapse of morale in the Victoria Police and the corrective services. Mind you, this sort of scandal can have a flow-on effect in respect of other states as well. Can you imagine the media feeding frenzy?'

It was O'Shea's show, so Read and Steele let him go on without interruption. 'Now, this is a Victorian matter and, for the moment, out of my jurisdiction up here in NSW. There are NSW connections, of course. The informant claims that he lives in Sydney and this David Felton was apparently born here and until recently was still working in Sydney as a male prostitute before he shifted to Melbourne for a change of scenery. If our informant and the tapes are for real, then this Felton person has gone missing and that is certainly a matter for action, given the circumstances. In the short term, I'm going to sit on this. If I passed this brief on to the Victorian authorities, I could just end up doing all the bad bastards a favour by alerting them if Jardine is our man. These things can be like cancer, you know, spread all over the place. I have no trustworthy personal contacts on the Victorian front. Coincidentally, we have a situation here in NSW where something that could be just as big is on the go. I have to be very careful, as people in high places will do anything to protect their territory. Now, I've had my go, you have yours.'

Steele gave the nod to Read who stood up and paced the floor.

'Look, Rex Jardine is certainly high profile Australia-wide and as you say, Barry, if all this is for real, then if and when it all gets out, it will be explosive stuff. Now, I've got myself in a right old mess with some racehorse claims in Melbourne and it looks like there's all sorts of shit ready to hit the fan, you know, doping, race fixing and the odd bit of bashing and murder just to keep everyone on their toes.' Suitably impressed, O'Shea rolled his eyes. Read went on. 'My links with Jardine are tenuous, to say the least. On my observations of him in the betting ring, it does appear that he gets inside information from the Clyde Trueman stables, they're the ones I'm dealing with on these claims. I know that it isn't much but I'm now convinced that the Trueman camp is on the nose well and truly. It's just another angle.' Now it was Steele's turn.

'All I can do from this distance is to give some advice for whatever it's worth. Jack's the man on the spot. It might be an idea for Barry's people to try and re-establish contact with the informant, that could be difficult, of course. Now that we've listened to these tapes, Jack can do a bit of sniffing around about Jardine when he gets back to Melbourne. Sorry, Jack, I'll rephrase that, researching. He could also see if he can pick up anything on this Felton character.' Steele laughed. 'I can just see you now, Jack, sidling up to all those faggots. They'll think that you're rough trade, for sure.' Read wasn't impressed.

'Yeah, big deal, John. All bullshit aside, it makes sense to suss out Jardine to see how involved he may be with the Trueman camp. Remember that little prick Murray Farquhar, the Chief, mind you, the Chief Stipendiary Magistrate of NSW, passing on the George Freeman tips to all his Labor pollie mates. Just imagine having been put away by that piece of shit and then finding out later how bent he was. Jesus, we should never forget that sort of history. Yeah, point taken about the Felton faggot. I'll try and be nice to all his sensitive, little, arse bandit mates.' O'Shea got to his feet and put the tapes and player back into his briefcase.

'Well, chaps, got to go. Nice to have met you again, Jack. Take it easy down there in Melbourne.' He turned to Steele.

'See you at the gym tomorrow, John. Catch up.'

Steele and Read stood at the window and watched O'Shea and his two minders drive away. The surf was building up as the onshore breeze made its presence felt and the beach was getting busier.

'Here we are,' Read said, taking in the scene, 'looking out on all these people enjoying themselves on such a great day while all this other shit is going on. Was all this happening when we were kids?'

'Most probably,' Steele replied, 'but on a much smaller scale. People seem to be greedier than they were in the sixties and the seventies and then that puffed-up fool Whitlam started pissing in the pockets of all the trendy minority groups. In fact, his government created a lot of them and if that wasn't bad enough, that clown Fraser followed in his footsteps. A lot of fuckwits discovered that they could swap their votes for dollars and away it went. We can blame the pollies but who puts them there? Jack, it's every man for himself now, that's the problem. Look at those crooked cops that we've dealt with. We've become a very selfish society. Well, that's the end of the sermon for the day. Let's go and have a bite and then I'll take you back to the airport.'

'Okay,' Read replied. 'Pity I haven't got time to get back home to Balmain. I wanted to have a few words with Honest Bernie but it doesn't matter, I'll give him a call from Melbourne. Let's go.'

'By the way, Jack, I know you feel obligated to look after your mate Welsh until he's recovered,' said Steele, 'but when you go back to Melbourne you should tidy up any loose ends as quickly as you

166

can and come straight back to Sydney. With all the shit that's been going on down there, it's just not worth risking your life and limb for, mate. Will you do me a favour and consider it?'

'Okay, I'll think about,' Read replied.

19

Read stood up to let the young woman take the window seat. He was aware of an earthy, womanly odour, not corrupted by perfume. It was that clean, fresh-sweat smell. She had no make-up on and wore her long, black hair loose, down her back and over her shoulders. He guessed she was in her late twenties and she had just a hint of hippiness about her. She smiled at him and opened her book. Read couldn't help noticing that it was about astrology. *That fits in,* he thought, as he took in her clothes – a loose, raw silk top, ventilated with embroidered openings, hanging outside a long, almost ankle-length skirt, probably a light linen. *Op shop, I'll bet, as well as the necklace of coloured resin beads.* He looked down at her unvarnished, shortish nails, a couple of which were chipped. *She works with her hands too.* Read flipped through the fishing magazine he had bought at the airport. *Some of the lures that they make these days are works of art. It's a shame to risk losing them. I wonder what the fish think?* The hostie arrived with afternoon tea.

'Thanks,' the woman said, as Read passed the tray on to her. 'Anytime,' Read replied, trying to start up a conversation. As she disposed of a small meatball in her empty fruit juice container, he put her down as a vegetarian. Read tried again.

'Far too nice to be flying,' he said, gesturing at the clear vista of the long-thawed out snowfields being passed on the left of the aircraft.

'Great bushwalking country down there, good trout in those

streams too, the water's cool and bubbling and no pollution. Just like mineral water.'

'Yes, it's beautiful,' she said in a light, girlish voice that Read found instantly sexy. He looks as if he was a spunk when he was younger, she thought. *He looks tough but I think he's kind. He reminds me of Richard.* The woman had lived with Richard for a while in Noosa. He was a lot older than her but he was tanned and fit. He loved fucking her and was so much better than her previous lover, Sean, who was younger than her. He was always rolling the next joint and bludging off her.

Worse still, he sometimes made her wait more than a week before he fucked her and then it was a jump-on and jump-off job, so long as he got his rocks off. A divorcee with a whingeing ex-wife and grown-up children, Richard had run a lawn mowing business that had brought in good money. She had got a job in a health food shop and managed to save. Things were great for a while. He cried when she told him that she was going to leave. The woman turned to Read.

'My name's Ella, what's yours?' she said.

'Jack, Jack Read. I was going to introduce myself, Ella, but didn't want to hassle you. Where are you off to?' Ella looked at Read and smiled.

'Home to Melbourne. I've been up to Coffs Harbour to see my brother and my little niece. It's lovely up there. I lived in Sydney for a while and then moved down to Melbourne. It's quieter than Sydney and I like that. What about you?'

'Pretty boring stuff,' Read replied. 'I live in Sydney and I'm doing some work in Melbourne, insurance. As I said, pretty boring. What line of work are you in, Ella?'

'I'm a dressmaker. I specialise in bridal. It's pretty demanding and some of the clients can be real bitches but they're in the minority, thank goodness. I want to save up and buy a little house in the country in Tasmania and live there with my cat.' She giggled. Read wanted to clear the decks as the plane started its descent into Melbourne. They were over the Eildon Weir.

'What about marriage and children?' She was wearing no appropriate rings. *Of course, these days, that doesn't matter,* Read thought.

'Oh, there's always time for that. I'm on my own at present. I'd love to have a little girl like my niece but I might change my mind and want a little boy. Who knows? Now, Jack, seeing that we're playing tit for tat, I'd say that you're divorced with a family.' She liked his grin.

'Wrong, Ella. Never been down the aisle. Never. Haven't been able to find a woman who'd put up with me. As for children, none that I know of. Next question. How old are you? I'm pretty good at these sorts of guessing games. I won't muck around. I put you in the late twenties.' Ella put her hand to her mouth to suppress her laughter as the pilot hit the dive brakes again, sending low vibrations through the aircraft. She looked at Read inquiringly.

'Are you for real? Seriously?' Read put his hand on Ella's forearm.

'Sure. No, I'm not kidding, really. You just look that young. You've got a very young, fresh voice. I can tell that you don't smoke. Alright, level with me. How old are you?' Ella giggled again.

'Would you believe thirty-seven?'

'I don't believe you,' Read said, as the plane, flaps down, banked and lowered its undercarriage, ready for touchdown at Tullamarine Airport.

Read was getting good vibes so decided to press his luck as he and Ella walked towards the exit.

'Ella, how are you going to get home? Someone picking you up?' She bit her lip and looked expectantly at Read.

'No, I'll have to get a cab. One of my girlfriends was going to come out but something happened at the last moment and she can't make it.' Read jumped into the breach.

'Ella, I'm staying in Carlton. Let me give you a lift home. I'm not running to any timetable, so there's no problem.'

'Are you sure, Jack? I live in St Kilda. It's not too far out of your way, is it?'

'Come on, let's get your bags and get you home,' Read said, as they arrived at the baggage carousel.

Ella lived in a small, rented semi-detached house in a quiet side street off St Kilda Road. Read helped her to her front door with a backpack that had seen better days and a bilum, a large, coloured and woven vegetable-fibre string bag from PNG. The native women carry everything, from their babies to huge loads of firewood and sweet potatoes in the spacious bags hanging on their backs, with the load suspended from their foreheads by the braided handles. Bilums had become de rigueur with inner-city alternative lifestylers. As Ella opened her front door, a tabby cat leapt into her arms.

'Oh Tiger, darling. Did you miss mummy? I've missed you,' cooed Ella, offering the cat to Read for a pat.

'Hello pussy,' Read said, not very enthusiastically, giving the cat a cursory touch on its head. He wasn't a cat person. *When they're not out murdering the local bird life, they're getting under your feet waiting for a tin of that stinking food to be opened. At least some dogs work for a living.* Tiger was still getting the full treatment from his mistress.

'Isn't he beautiful, Jack? Just look at him. I used to ring him up every night when I was away. The girl next door has done a wonderful job looking after him.' Tiger was lapping up all the attention. He feinted at Read with his paw and had his claws unsheathed. Read gave him a stern look. *The little bastard's defending his territory.* Read was still standing in the doorway.

'Ella, I'd better be going and leave you with your unpacking and your little mate. What do you say to having dinner with me one night? There's a nice little Italian place down near the markets that I go to whenever I'm in Melbourne. You'd like it.'

'Why not?' replied Ella, walking into a room and returning with her card. Tiptoeing, Ella kissed Read on the cheek.

'You're a nice man, Jack.' Read looked at himself in the rear view mirror as he drove away. *No, I'm not, I'm a real cunt.*

Read had met Honest Bernie when he had moved into Balmain. He had needed a small but difficult plastering job done and had been told that he would find his man down at the Welcome Hotel. Read and the son of Maltese migrants had clicked over their first two schooners of Reschs and it didn't take Read long to find out that Honest Bernie had other skills. He had been a minor enforcer on the fringe of one of the Sydney mobs and most of his persuasive powers had been used convincing defaulting SP punters to honour their commitments.

The dominance of the TAB had taken most of his work away but he still did a bit of work for some of the illegal casinos. He also knew how to get things at the right price, from white goods to bags of Sydney rock oysters. Read had woken early one morning to find a brand new washing machine and refrigerator, still in their cartons, on his front verandah. He wondered which truck they had fallen off.

'How are you, you big black bastard?'

Honest Bernie chuckled at his colourful salutation that alluded to Read's time in New Guinea. Never having strayed off the bitumen, he had been fascinated by Read's purposely embroidered tales of life in the tropics.

'Bernie, how's things in Balmain? I was in Sydney two days ago and didn't have time to come over. I'm alright but I need your help. I want you to do me a big favour, a big favour. I want you to come down to Melbourne. I don't want to say much more on the phone. I'll explain everything when you get here. Don't worry, I'll pay your fare.'

'Shit,' Bernie exclaimed. 'I've never been to Melbourne in my life. Do you believe that?'

'Yes, I do,' Read replied.

'I'm amazed that you've actually crossed the Sydney Harbour Bridge.'

'I've been to the Gold Coast, Jack,' Bernie said lamely, trying to save some face.

'Jesus, Bernie, I almost forgot. Have you ever been in an aeroplane?'

'Give me a break, Jack. When do you want me to come down?' Read became his serious self for a moment.

'Thursday, the tickets will be waiting for you at the QANTAS counter at Mascot. You don't mind flying economy, do you?' Honest Bernie started to lose his sense of humour.

'The trouble with you, Jack, is that you've spent too much time in the jungle with all those blackfellas. You've forgotten how to treat a white man properly.' Read came straight back.

'You could have fooled me, Bernie. I thought Malta was part of Africa.'

Honest Bernie took the bait as he always did.

'You big shit, Jack, you'll keep. Now try and be fair dinkum and give me an idea of what's on down there, just a little taste to stir up my appetite, c'mon, you big jerk.'

'Okay, Bernie, we're quits, until next time. Seriously though, I don't want to tell you anything more until you and I are face to face. It's a big ask, believe me, and if you knock me back, I'm not going to hold it against you. All I'm going to say is that it's illegal, very illegal. You know that I don't rob banks or TABs so you'll just have to be patient, my friend. Everything still okay at my place?'

Honest Bernie was checking out Read's Balmain house, keeping the letterbox clear of any junk mail and throwaway newspapers, and acting as caretaker, sleeping over usually at weekends.

'Everything's sweet, Jack. No problems. The bloke three doors down from you had his car stolen last week but apart from that, nothing else to report. I'd better get going and see if I've got any good mocker to wear when I get down to that poofy Melbourne town. I'll be wearing a big sign around my neck with my name on it. See you, big fella.' Honest Bernie put down the telephone and turned the TV volume up. His wife was out in the kitchen putting a leg of lamb in the oven. He started to cough as he lit up another cigarette.

'Now you look in your late teens,' Read said, as he stood in the doorway to Ella's house. She was standing there cuddling her cat. Dressed in black slacks, a filmy blouse and Doc Martens boots, with her hair in two plaits, she looked like a well-built school girl. He felt a bit silly as he handed Ella the single rose he had bought on the way over.

'Oh, thank you, aren't you nice? Come in, Jack, and stop being stupid. I'm thirty-seven, remember, so just get used to it. I'm just finishing a phone call. Sit down and make yourself comfortable.' Read did as he was told and took in his surroundings. Sitting in an old sofa with stuffing sticking out, he noticed what looked like an embroidered bed cover hanging from the ceiling, like the canopy in a sheik's tent.

A big wooden bowl of potpourri sat on a primitive, packing-case coffee table and a small forest of incense candles sitting on top of an oriental sideboard were giving off wispy spirals. Sarah Vaughan was doing her thing on an early model CD player. Tiger the cat suddenly appeared in the doorway and when he saw Read, his tail bristled and stood straight up.

'Tiger, Tiger, good pussy,' Read said, feeling ridiculous. Disdainfully turning, showing his pursed arsehole to Read, Tiger strutted back into the other room. Read scowled. *Bonzo would sort you out, you little shit.*

'Alright, let's go,' Ella said, as she picked up a small clutch bag and walked out of the house ahead of Read. Bringing up the rear, he enjoyed her sexy swagger. Read drove around Albert Park Lake and through Port Melbourne to North Melbourne.

Ella was enjoying her meal.

'This is nice. The vegetables are so fresh and crisp and the rice is just right, it's Arborio, which is the rice that you should use for risotto. What's your fish like, Jack?'

'Like it always is Ella, good. I've never had a bad meal here.'

'I'm glad you brought me here,' Ella said.

'I eat mainly vegetarian but I like seafood too. I used to eat meat but I've got to the point where I can't stand the thought of all that dead meat and butchery.' Read didn't want to start an argument but he thought the fish might have something to say about being dragged out of the sea, much against their will, and then having their guts slit open. Farmed salmon in Tasmania and spring lamb frolicking in high-country pasture all ended up the same way. The restaurant was busy and there was plenty of movement out in the street.

Ella was a survivor. She and her brother had grown up in Queensland after an unremarkable childhood. Her parents were still alive but Ella didn't get on with her father. She was close to her brother who, despite being a qualified and skilled cabinetmaker, had opted out for self-imposed exile in the dope-rich hinterland behind Coffs Harbour. *What hope did his little girl have?*

Read thought. *Living like some sort of heroic white kanaka might be a great adventure and a novelty for the first few months but when the rainy season is in full swing, it's not much fun paddling through the mud with a kerosene lamp in the dead of night to have a shit in a flooded-out pit lavatory.* Read sat on a coffee while Ella dealt with a home-made tiramisu. She had clear skin that didn't need make-up and a seductive innocent giggle that turned Read on. He liked the honesty of her obvious sexuality. Read took the more direct route down St Kilda Road on the return trip back to Ella's place.

Read was standing in Ella's kitchen when without warning, she put her arms around his neck, kissed him on the mouth and jumping up, wrapped her legs around his waist.

'I decided that I'd fuck you when we met on the plane,' she said before pushing her tongue into his mouth.

'Now I believe in the power of prayer,' Read chuckled as he sat Ella on the baltic pine kitchen table and gently kneaded his right hand into her crutch. Ella slowly exhaled and her voice dropped a couple of levels.

'Oh, that's good, that's so nice.' She moved her pelvis forward to increase the pressure on her clitoris and felt the wetness moving into her panties. Read worked her right breast out of her bra with his left hand and played with its nipple that became proud at once. Ella's voice became husky like a smoker's.

'Let's go into the lounge room, Jack, it'll be more comfortable there.' Without saying anything, Read locked the door behind him, leaving Tiger on the other side. *I don't want you perving on us, you little shit*, Read thought, as hands on her waist, he followed Ella through to the front of the house. Moving to the front bay window, she made sure the drapes were closed off. Switching off the lights with the exception of a small art deco table lamp, she lit up a pineapple-sized and shaped scented candle that threw out flickering shadows. Sitting on the sofa she started taking her boots off. Fascinated, Read started undressing slowly while looking at Ella, who still undressing, looked right back at him. Her skin was firm and white, and her breasts had hardly dropped at all.

'I'm really wet, Jack. Taste me.' Read had wasted no time in barring up and he held himself as he knelt in front of Ella and took her fingers in his mouth. He was heavily into oral and had no problem. Ella tasted like egg white with just a suggestion of acidity. He remembered reading somewhere about the comparative pHs of the vagina and lowering his head, went down for more.

'Don't you cum, Jack, don't you cum, don't you dare cum,' Ella half-groaned, half-grunted with stern urgency, as she sat astride Read who had exchanged places with her on the sofa. He was doing his best not to give in and tried to think about anything else but what was happening to him. He was supporting Ella with his hands on her breasts, nipples poking between his fingers. She was grinding herself hard and Read was getting a bit uncomfortable. Ella had her eyes closed and a blush was spreading into her cheeks. Her full lips framed her open mouth and she was breathing hard. Read arched his back.

'Come on, beautiful girl. Come on, beautiful girl. Fuck you. Come on, come on.' Ella was almost hyperventilating as she climaxed and slumped down onto Read.

'Jesus, quick,' exclaimed Read as he pushed Ella off him and rolled her over onto her stomach and entered her doggie style. He couldn't hold on any more.

'I'm cuming now, Ella. Oh fuck.' Ella had backed hard into Read and he felt her trembling for the second time. His hands skidded over a film of sweat as he held her to him. She sounded as if she had just run a hard one hundred metres. Read sounded as if he needed an oxygen mask. His heart was banging away like a New Guinea slit gong. He managed to control himself, exhaling slowly to get his breath back and still inside her, rested, as the flickers from the candle jitterbugged around the room.

Read drove home carefully through St Kilda. He could still taste Ella. *You are a lucky bastard,* he thought, *First Sylvia, now Ella. It's just too good to be true but don't knock it. They're both top girls. If only this Ironbar thing can be sorted out, a man can stop looking over his shoulder and there'll always be a good excuse to come down to Melbourne.*

A street prostitute who looked barely in her teens staggered and almost fell in front of his car and as he swerved, Read was glad he was travelling slowly. The girl looked at Read through kaleidoscope eyes. She was off her head with dope. *You fucking mean cunt,* she mouthed as he drove past. *It's a happy little world we live in,* he thought, as he tuned the radio to station 3AW. Keith McGowan, the midnight-to-dawn talkback jock was talking to an audience of insomniacs and other night people about his visit to the Great Wall of China.

20

At Tullamarine Airport, Read's eyes were drawn to the stocky, swarthy plasterer looking around on the upper level, finding his bearings. He was sure that Bernie had a lifetime supply of Brylcreem stashed away somewhere. What was left of his hair was dyed black and looked like liquorice straps plastered to his skull. He had certainly put on his best mocker for Melbourne. A shiny, blue suit of uncertain vintage with razor-sharp trouser creases was upstaged by a bright yellow, decorated tie the size of an old-fashioned surfboard. At ground level, trouser cuffs rested on scuffed, black, patent leather shoes.

Big fella!' Honest Bernie pumped Read's hand as he came off the escalator near the Qantas domestic baggage collection area.

'Where's your name tag, Bernie?' Read grinned, as he indicated the gaggle of hire car drivers holding up placards bearing the names of their passengers.

'Don't give me the shits, Jack,' Bernie said, as he started to light up a cigarette until Read showed him the No Smoking sign.

'That filthy habit will kill you one day, Bernie,' Read said as they left the terminal.

After circling the block and making sure that the coast was clear, Read ushered Bernie into Welsh's house. He had kept his eye open for any of Larry Hill's surveillance team but if they were on the job, they were certainly being low profile.

'The Hilton it is not,' Read said, showing Bernie where he was going to sleep.

'This mate of mine who owns this place is down at St Vincent's Hospital all smashed up. He looks like being there for another couple of weeks.' Read looked at Honest Bernie who was staring in fascination at the collection of books that marched from the floor to the ceiling in irregular rows, contained in a collection of all shapes and sizes of bookshelves.

'It's like that in all the rooms,' Read said. 'My mate's a bit keen on books, you might say. There's some fairly heavy reading in that lot, believe me.'

'Well, Jack, what's the go?' Bernie sat back and blew a smoke ring which Read waved away in annoyance. Read delivered a concise precis of events without going into all the stuff about Rex Jardine and the surveillance provided by Larry Hill's men. Bernie sat up and took real notice when Read started in on Ironbar.

'Whew,' he said. 'So that's what he's been up to. He's been working his way up the ladder for years, you know, keeping on the good side of George Freeman and Lennie McPherson. I hardly have anything to do with that mob these days, Jack, so I can't tell you much more than you already know. I had a drink with Ironbar about three or four years ago at a do for some coppers at Lennie McPherson's place. He's knocked off plenty of people in his time. He's bad news, that's for sure. So you reckon that he fixed up your mate and this girl who worked at the stables?'

'And I'll be next, Bernie,' Read emphasised, getting to his feet. 'I don't mind telling you that I'm shit scared and unless I get my act together, you'll be getting pissed at my wake, if someone even bothers to throw one for me.' Bernie lit up another cigarette, ignoring Read's over-acted scowl.

'Well, Jack, what's the brief?'

'Pretty simple, Bernie,' Read said.

'I'm going to kill Ironbar and I want you to help me.'

Read had to hand it to Honest Bernie. It took a lot to rattle him.

'Oh Jesus, Jack, I thought that you were going to ask me to get

179

involved in something really dangerous. You sit there and have the cheek to tell me you've brought me all the way down to this jumping town … sorry, city, just to tell me that you want me to help you whack Ironbar Miller. C'mon, big fella, you can do better than that.'

The two men laughed. Read spoke first. 'I wish I was joking but you know I'm not. You know the score. You're the only person I thought I could trust for something like this but as I said on the phone, if you're back to Sydney on tomorrow's plane, that's it. No recriminations and if I can work my way out of this mess, I'll still get on the piss with you down at the Welcome, even though you are a wog.'

Honest Bernie tapped the filter end of another cigarette on its packet before lighting up.

'Jack, I don't know how to say this. I haven't got the gift of the gab like you, but you and I get on really well, you know what I mean? Ever since that first time you came down to the Welcome to see me about doing a job at your house, I felt that you were a bloke who was fair dinkum. You can work with your hands as well as your mouth, ah, what am I trying to say? … There's no bullshit about you, that's what I mean.' Bernie was starting to get tongue-tied but Read sat back and said nothing.

'I reckon that we're mates, I hope we are, that's what I reckon, we pick and we stick. So after all this crap I've been going on with, I'm telling you that I'm with you, big fella, on this Ironbar thing.' Bernie sat there for a moment, chewing his bottom lip.

'There's something else, Jack.'

Bernie was sitting in his tee singlet and boxer shorts. He fingered the gold cross around his neck.

'We'd better get this job done quick because I'm fucked, Jack, fucked because of these.' Bernie pointed at his cigarette before he took another long draw. Read sat up and leaned forward. He winced as Bernie let go with a dry cough that hurt to hear.

'I've got lung cancer, Jack.' Read's eyes widened.

'The quack said that it's gone too far to do anything about it. He wants me to try that chemo, that, er ...'

'Chemotherapy,' Read helped out.

'Yeah, that, but fuck that. A bloke down the street's been on it but Jesus, all his hair has fallen out and he says that it makes him as crook as all shit. No way. I'm going to keep on fagging until I drop and you'll be at my funeral, big fella, before I'm at yours. So when do we do what we've got to do?' Read hesitated nervously before he spoke.

'Bernie, that's terrible news, it really is. Are you sure your doctor is on the ball? You should go and get a second opinion.' Read found himself giving all the standard responses.

'Jack,' Bernie replied, 'the quack I've just told you about is the second one I've seen. Don't worry, I was off to see a second one in a flash, you know me, scared shitless. I might end up topping myself, who knows?' Read felt depressed and flat.

'There's nothing more that I can say, Bernie.' He half-smiled.

'I'll promise you one thing. I won't have any more shots at you for smoking. Let's hit the fart-sack. I'll give you the battle plans over breakfast.'

Honest Bernie's dry retching and coughing woke Read before his normal rising time of 5 am. Read's depression had not evaporated and for some inexplicable reason he found himself feeling guilty about two-timing Sylvia with Ella. *Stop being childish,* he told himself. *Sylvia's a free agent and so am I. Ella has needs and she satisfies them without any bullshit. Grow up.* Read took Bernie up to Lygon Street for a subdued breakfast.

'I know where Ironbar stays when he's in Melbourne,' Read told Honest Bernie over coffee.

'There's nobody else staying there as far as I know but we'll have to be careful. We'll have a good look at the place and then work out a plan of attack. When we finish here, we'll hit the road.'

Honest Bernie sat well off the Ascot Vale Road house in Read's car while Read went for a walk. He knew that he was taking a huge risk but he and Bernie had driven past the house a couple of times and there was no car parked in the side driveway. A contact in Telecom in Sydney had given him the phone number for the address and an unanswered call from his mobile told him that the house was almost certainly empty. The garage under the house had a closed roll-a-door and that was another matter. A confident walk into the side driveway, a quick glance through the garage side window and Read breathed a sigh of relief. The empty garage gave him breathing space.

The busy front garden afforded Read plenty of cover and he walked up to the patio at the front door, looking for a way in. There was no sign of an alarm system. The heavy front door had two keyed locks and Read knew that they were deadlocks. *No Hollywood movie, credit card, lock-picking here,* Read thought. He laughed to himself as he lifted the front door mat. *It's not going to be that easy, dickhead.* He was ready to walk around the side of the house when he saw the row of plant pots sitting on their matching saucers, lined up against the front wall. One, two, three, Read started to feel silly as he lifted the plant pots. He lifted the fourth pot.

'Fuck,' he said aloud. There, under the pot was a brass key. Two paces back to the front door and the key activated both locks. Read didn't push the door open. Ironbar may have put something on the inside of the door to warn him of unwanted visitors. Read pocketed the key and could hardly stop himself running back to Bernie and the car.

'Bernie,' Read said, holding up the key. 'It's our lucky day. Move over, mate, we have to find a locksmith, quick.'

'Now we've got to go and do some shopping, Bernie,' Read said, as they drove away from the house after replacing the original front door key in its hiding place. Read had checked the new key and it had opened the door. Double check, double check. He had been caught out before by bodgie-cut duplicate keys.

'I'm glad I came down here, Jack,' Bernie said, lightly punching Read on the left shoulder.

'This is going to keep my mind off other things.' Read's first call was to a Tandy electronics shop where he bought two cheap walkie-talkie units. Second stop was an Aussie Disposals store where he picked up a heavy duty, zip-up sleeping bag and two folding trench shovels. Read paid cash for all his purchases. Credit cards left an indelible trail.

'C'mon, Bernie, I've got what I want. Now I'm going to take you to Little Bourke Street and shout you some chow food.'

'Not really hungry, Jack,' Bernie replied, 'but I'll keep you company. A couple of dim sims will keep me happy. I read the other day that soy sauce can give you cancer, so watch out, big fella.' Read laughed as he drove on. *The poor bugger hasn't lost his sense of humour.*

Like a moth drawn to a light in a darkened room, Read parked outside Ella's house. As he walked towards the front door, he saw Tiger the cat doing sentry duty in the bay window.

'Come in. It's been hot, hasn't it,' Ella said, as she kissed Read on the cheek. She wore a white shirt tied in the front at her waist and shorts that had once been jeans but had been cut very short and intentionally frayed and holed.

'Stop looking at my legs,' Ella said, looking self-consciously at herself. 'They're like sausages tied in the middle.'

'They look alright to me,' Read replied. Ella slipped in a Joan Baez disc into the CD player. *That's a blast from the past,* Read thought, as Ella went through her routine of drawing the front curtains. He started to feel very horny.

They sat on the sofa drinking lassi, a refreshing Indian drink based on yoghurt that Ella had flavoured with honey and rose water. Joan Baez's strident whining was irritating Read but he was prepared to put up with anything to enjoy Ella again. They exchanged a mouthful of yoghurt as he unbuttoned her shorts. She was wasn't wearing panties. Ella helped Read by taking off her shirt and offering him her right breast.

'I've just had a shower, Jack, and I'm as sweet as a nut so don't hold back. You can lick me all over if you like, and I mean all over. Don't be shy. Just use your imagination.' She steered Read's head down between her legs and massaged his scalp as he worked his mouth up and down.

'Keep going, keep going, don't stop,' she said, as she turned over, pushing her bottom into Read's face.

'Oh, that's absolutely beautiful, that's fantastic. Oh, that's so good, that's so good.' As he warmed to his task, Read ran his tongue from one end of Ella to the other, ending up at the top end of the cleft in her buttocks. Moving her bottom end in time with Read's mouth, Ella came close to climax. Read was nearly there too. He eased down and decided that it was time for a breather.

'Just stay there, Jack, I'll be right back,' Ella whispered and went outside to the kitchen.

She came back into the room with a bowl containing strawberries, a cluster of cherries and a couple of bananas. Read looked at the fruit and raised his eyebrows slightly. Ella was smiling as she ran her tongue over her lips. 'Let's play fruit salad, Jack. Come on, be adventurous,' she said, handing Read the bowl, sitting down on the sofa and spreading her legs. *There's a first time for everything,* Read thought. He remembered Steve Matusiak, the alcoholic opal miner who used to regale him with stories about playing interesting games with cherry brandy. Ella started to laugh and Read joined in. Her saucy, schoolgirl voice was a real turn on. Read started with a strawberry, rubbing it on Ella's clitoris and then eating it. Ella helped by holding herself open and then watched him closely.

'You like this, don't you, Jack,' she said.

'Take it easy. We've got lots of time.' Read nodded enthusiastically as he went down on her again. A couple of cherries later, he peeled one of the bananas and with Ella's help, put it inside her. It was a Cavendish, short and fat and still not fully ripe. Ella was getting excited again as Read circled her upstanding clitoris with the end of the banana in between licking it. She looked at Read fiercely as he began to eat the banana.

'Come on, Jack, finish me off,' she said, pulling him into her, chewing hard on his right nipple.

21

The tension was starting to get to Read. Honest Bernie, with his death sentence hanging over him, was in a philosophical mood and his banter helped keep Read's spirits up. For three nights, the two men had surveilled the Ascot Vale Road house from 11 pm until the early hours. It had been unoccupied and there was no sign of Ironbar or any vehicles. Read had exchanged his Jap hire car for a Holden station wagon. It was more comfortable and Bernie was able to lie down in the back. His smoking was driving Read mad but the warm weather allowed all the windows to be wound down. It was almost 1 am when things started to happen.

'Here he is. It's Ironbar,' Read said, as he put his binoculars to his eyes. 'Yes, it's him alright, Bernie. The same car. Bingo. The bastard's back in town.' As Read kept him in focus, Ironbar activated the electronic roll-a-door and drove into the garage. The door rolled down and a short time later, an upstairs light came on. Read snapped out of his malaise and got his brain working. *That's the time to get him. When he comes up the stairs from the garage, when he's at the top of the stairs, that's the time to pop him. Total surprise so that the bastard has no time at all to react. That's the time when it's going to be you or him. It's all up to you.*

'Okay, Bernie, let's get back to Carlton and put our heads down. Keep an eye out for anyone following us. Tomorrow night could be it.'

Rex Jardine was like a junkie doing cold turkey. To keep his mind above his groin he had set himself a gruelling work schedule.

He still made time to go to the races in order to massage all the right egos. Life after politics for Jardine included a position on the VRC committee. With David Felton having been frightened off and chased back to Sydney, he could relax. He had bumped into the big policeman at the Caulfield races and they had swapped small talk.

He had started putting in a good word for Ryan in all the right places and he was sure that the next round of promotions would bring good news for his self-appointed mentor. He still found it hard to believe that he had been let off so lightly. Maybe there was an unpleasant surprise in store for him. After years of sloshing around in the political quagmire, the unexpected had to be expected. He looked through the itinerary his secretary had placed on his desk.

There were the usual run-of-the-mill unveiling of plaques and speeches at service club dinners. A couple of art gallery exhibition openings would make his wife happy and at the end of the week, the media would make a big thing of him setting an example for blood donors in response to a public plea from the Minister for Health. Jardine took the business card out of the folder in the bottom drawer of his desk. For a few moments he looked at the card with Felton's Sydney phone number on it. A sudden impulse drove him to start reaching out for the phone. Gritting his teeth, he crumpled the card and tore it into pieces. He felt proud of himself as he punched the intercom.

'A cup of tea please, Julie, when you're ready.'

'Thanks, fellas. You needn't have done that. You've spoilt my image by washing it and making it look half-respectable. Thanks all the same.' Read put on a mock display of concern as he picked up the Range Rover from the police garage. As well as being washed, the car had been serviced. 'See you, boys.' Read waved as he drove out into the street.

When Read entered the Ascot Vale Road house, his caution was rewarded. Ironbar had placed a small blob of Blu Tack at the bottom of the front door closure, so that only close scrutiny revealed it. *He's done this and then left through the garage,* Read thought, as he went to replace the Blu Tack, realised that he was being stupid and flicked it away. Honest Bernie was in the Range Rover, just nosing out of a side street where he had a clear view of the entrance to the garage that Ironbar would drive into. He was using a walkie-talkie to communicate with Read inside the house.

'How are you, big fella?' Bernie said, in a dramatic, hushed voice.

'All okay here, Bernie. Sitting and waiting for our mate if he turns up. Remember, as soon as you see him driving into the garage, let me know. I'll hear him from here but if there is someone else with him, I'll need as much warning as you can give me. The glasses are okay?' Bernie checked the focus of the Zeiss binoculars.

'Yeah, Jack, no problems.'

'Okay, that's good, Bernie. Yes, they've got a good night vision rating. Alright, I'm on standby.' Read was sitting on a pillow he had taken from one of the bedrooms. He was on the floor just away from the door that led down to the garage. With his mini Maglite held in his teeth, Read checked the action of the Colt Woodsman, pulling back the slide just enough to check that a round was in the chamber ready for firing. He worked the safety, returning it to the off position. To while the time away and to try and stop the flutters of panic in his stomach, he fantasised about having Sylvia and Ella in bed together. *With a big basket of fruit and veges,* he thought, with a wry smile.

'Jack! Jack!' Honest Bernie's urgency crackled into the room.

'He's there. It's him. It's Ironbar. He's on his own. Jack. Jack!' Bernie's voice and the moment was like a hard slap in the face. Read couldn't help himself and farted. *Thank Christ it wasn't liquid, he thought,* as he stood up. At the same time that he heard Bernie's warning, he heard a motor car outside the house.

'Okay, okay, Bernie. I hear you. I hear you. Keep quiet now. Here we go.'

'Good luck, Jack.' Bernie cradled the walkie-talkie on his lap as the garage roll-a-door opened.

The door through which Ironbar would come was a sliding one. Read had rehearsed what he was going to do but now that the moment had arrived, he was struggling to hold himself together. The car's motor ran for a short while before it was switched off and then he could hear Ironbar opening the door and getting out. The clattering roll-a-door made it difficult to hear but Read could feel a slight tremor as Ironbar started up the stairs. Like shooting stars before his eyes, Read started to think of all the things that could go wrong. *What if there was someone with Ironbar, someone that Honest Bernie had failed to pick up in the glasses? What if the Colt jammed? What if it wasn't Ironbar but someone who looked like him? What if Ironbar had heard something and had a gun out and ready? What? What? What?* There was still time to call it all off.

For a mad, mad moment, Read almost packed it in and bolted for the front door. Then something happened that froze him in shock. The lights came on. Read's balls ended up in his throat and he almost screamed. He had not noticed the switch on the other side of the door that lit the room he was standing in and the person on the other side of the door had just hit it. At the moment the lights came on, the sliding door started opening. Like the freeze frame function on a VCR, Ironbar Miller and Jack Read stood facing each other like posed models.

The almost-full bottle of Jack Daniels that Ironbar had drunk slowed his reflexes. Like a damp, sputtering fuse, a message started to travel from his brain to his nerve centres but it was too late. Read was stone cold sober, operating on autopilot and a nervous system flooding with adrenaline. Holding the pillow in his left hand, he thrust it into Ironbar's face simultaneously with the barrel of the Colt automatic. Read started pulling the trigger the moment he felt the muzzle jam into Ironbar. He could hear somebody yelling and realised that it was himself.

Pop! Pop! Pop! Pop! The pillow muffled the zing of the high-velocity .22 cartridges as the ejected cases tinkled onto the polished Tasmanian Ash floorboards. Ironbar didn't get one word out. Inside his skull, his Circle of Willis was torn, and the disintegrating hollow-point bullets ruptured and pureed his brain tissue and blood. Arms flung wide, he crashed backwards down the stairs with Read nearly overbalancing and falling with him. Ironbar lay on his back with his upper torso on the garage floor, his buttocks and legs still supported by the stairs. One leg twitched twice. His right sightless eye was wide open and appeared to be staring at Read. His left eye, obliterated by bullets, was a puddle of blood that welled up and overflowed across his cheekbone and down onto the garage floor.

Still holding the pillow and the pistol, Read was standing at the top of the stairs, hypnotised by Ironbar's corpse. The sharpness of the cordite fumes bit into his nostrils like smelling salts and brought him back to life. Sliding the safety lock of the pistol on, Read switched the lights off and walked back into the top room to get the walkie-talkie. He was breathing hard and his hands were shaking.

'Bernie, Bernie, can you hear me?' Honest Bernie had seen the lights come on and then after a while, go off again. He was sweating and dry in the mouth, afraid to visualise what had taken place over in the house. He had to force himself to keep his voice lowered.

'Yes, Jack, yes big fella, I hear you. I hear you. What's the go? Are you okay?' Read found himself gabbling.

'It's okay, Bernie, it's all okay. It's done, all done. Get your arse over here. Check that it's all clear and then back down into the garage. Just keep the parkers on. I'll open the roll-a-door. Quick.'

Luck was with them – hardly any passing traffic. Bernie reversed Read's Range Rover into the garage without any fuss, then waited for the roll-a-door to close before he got out. Working in the glow cast by the car's interior light and Read's torch, the two men looked at Ironbar like satisfied hunters back from a pig-shooting expedition.

'Ugly prick, isn't he,' Bernie said, nudging the corpse with his shoe. In his crumpled death pose, the Sydney enforcer looked almost pathetic. Read opened the tailgate and took out the sleeping bag and then went through Ironbar's pockets, finding a wallet that had the usual stuff in it along with a couple of business cards that Read pocketed.

'Okay, Bernie. Let's get the fucker into this bag and into the back of the car. I'll fold the back seat down.' Read threw the spent cartridge cases and Ironbar's wallet into the sleeping bag together with the surgical gloves he had been wearing.

'Jesus, he's heavy,' Read grunted, as he and Bernie lifted the zippered up Ironbar into the back of the Range Rover. Read threw an old painter's drop sheet over his cargo.

'There you are. Sleep tight, you shit. Now we're square for Joylene and Welsh.' Bernie looked back at the floor where about three-and-a-half litres of Ironbar's blood was still creeping over the floor, this way and that.

'What about the blood, Jack?' Read closed the tailgate. 'Don't worry, Bernie. The people who own this house will know something terminal has happened to their mate and they won't be crying copper, I can assure you. It's a message for them and I hope they shit themselves. Now let's get the fuck out of here.'

'Where are we going to dump Ironbar?' Bernie said, as Read drove out onto the roadway. 'You told me to bring my toothbrush. Where are we off to, you big bastard?'

'Coober Pedy,' Read said slowly, as he checked his rear vision mirror and headed off out of Melbourne.

Read had worked on the Eight Mile field at Coober Pedy in the days when most of the opal miners lived underground to escape the heat and the flies. The two main buildings that raised their heads above ground on opposite sides of the gravel road that led to Alice Springs were the galvanised iron and fibro structures that housed competing general stores and flew the Ampol and Shell banners. On the night that Read had packed up and left the opal fields, he had shot out the illuminated Shell pecten on top of the petrol bowser with a Colt .45 automatic pistol and dropped a stick of gelignite down the nearby pit latrine.

Like subterranean warriors, the miners did battle with mountains of brittle sandstone to isolate the beautiful, iridescent hydrated silica running in veins at varying depths beneath the surface. The early miners blasted with gelignite, picked and shovelled, then hand-winched the overburden to the surface, progressing over time to motor-powered and compressed air winches. Nowadays, driving or tunnelling is done by machines, and giant blowers driven by large diesel engines suck the mullock up to the surface like space-age vacuum cleaners.

Read pushed the Range Rover along without breaking the speed limit. His plan was to drive non-stop from Melbourne to Coober Pedy, by-passing Adelaide and taking the back roads through Leigh Creek, on to William Creek and then across to Coober Pedy. The return trip would be back on the bitumen all the way past the old Woomera Rocket Range, down to Port Augusta and then through Adelaide. Honest Bernie sat up. He had dozed off for a couple of hours and a rough patch of repaired roadwork had bumped him awake.

'Jesus, Jack, I hope we don't break down on the way. I wouldn't like to be sitting out here in the hot sun and all, with our mate in the back.'

'Go back to sleep,' Read said. 'Another couple of hours and it's your turn at the wheel. The sun was starting to set and the unsealed road lay straight ahead through scrubby country. The road had recently been graded and the shallow corrugations passing under the wheels made the sound of running a stick along roofing iron. Read took another swig of mineral water. Movement caught his eye. A couple of big red kangaroos were coming at him from an angle on his right and he slackened speed to allow them to cut across his bow without incident. The last thing that he wanted was a smashed up radiator in the middle of nowhere with a corpse that was starting to gas up. The thought made him wind his window fully open.

They had left William Creek well behind and were on the last leg of their journey.

'Hey, Jack. Big fella. Wake up. What's that up ahead?' Honest Bernie was at the wheel and shook Read's right shoulder. It took Read a moment to reorientate himself.

'It's been a long time since I've been out here, Bernie, but I think

192

those lights are our first look at Coober Pedy. Pull over. It's time for a piss and I'll have a look at the map.' They got out and walked around, stretching themselves to loosen up after the tension of the hard, constant driving. 'We're taking our friend to the Eight Mile field, Bernie, which, believe it or not, is eight miles north from Coober Pedy on the Alice Springs road. Now the new highway bypasses the field so that suits us. Less stickybeaks around, I hope. Yeah, I can see it. It's quite clear on the map.' As he walked around the car, Read was happy to see that both number plates were sufficiently dirty and not easily decipherable. 'Let's go,' he said, as he got behind the wheel.

Skirting around the main township of Coober Pedy, which now featured all the above-ground mod cons, including a TAB and restaurants, Read headed north. After a few wrong turns, he managed to find the Eight Mile field. It had been worked over a few times but was now exhausted. Read crawled the Range Rover around a maze of mullock heaps crowning disused shafts. It was the dark phase of the moon and because he had to use the car's headlights, Read was worried about attracting any drifters wandering around the diggings. There were still a lot of Aboriginals on the opal fields and they were likely to pop up anywhere.

'You can be out in this country, Bernie,' Read said, 'having a quiet piss, at three in the morning and I'll lay money that some bugger will spot you.'

It was 10 pm, and twenty hours since he had killed Ironbar. Despite dozing off several times during the trip, Read was feeling weary and wrung out. The pressure was telling. He was heading for the top of the hill on the Eight Mile where the shafts were up to eighty-five feet deep. The deep mining required to get down to opal-bearing levels had frightened off the early miners with their primitive gear. In the late 1950s, a group of Italians, who had walked off the Harts Range mica field when the Indians flooded and destroyed the world market, arrived in Coober Pedy in a convoy of WW2 disposal Blitz Buggy trucks towing heavy diesel-powered compressors. Broke and dispirited, they were heading back to Adelaide but decided to have one last throw of the dice.

They pegged the Eight Mile hill because they had the machinery to handle the depth and their first shaft landed smack bang on top of £25,000 worth of gem-quality opal. In no time at all they were winching forty-four gallon drums of opal to the surface, some of the stones the size of house bricks. The Aborigines squatting on the mullock heaps made good money from picking up opal stones and chips thrown away in haste but spent it all on metho and sly grog. Read had flashbacks of the little kids brushing away flies from their nose candles and the spindly legged lubras being sold off by their fathers and brothers for a bottle of metho or cheap sherry.

Like an underground plague of locusts, the Italians worked out all their deep claims on the Eight Mile and then one morning, like the Arabs and their tents, they were gone.

'We'll have a look around here, Bernie. Just wait a while until our eyes get used to the dark. Keep an eye out for any torchlight or any other movement.' When Read doused the car lights, the two men sat and absorbed the silence. The desert cool had settled over the landscape. After carefully looking around, Read came back to the car.

'There's a nice deep one over there, Bernie. We'll be able to back the car up to the mullock heap but then we'll have to drag our passenger up to the top. Hang on. Let's use our fucking brains.' They pulled Ironbar out of the back of the car and dropped him on the ground.

'Jesus,' Read said. 'He's hard to move. He's still in rigor mortis and he's starting to blow up. Let's get rid of the shit quickly.' Read moved the car to the other side of the heap and used the front-mounted winch to drag Ironbar to the shaft opening.

'Come on, Bernie. Give me a hand to lift up his legs and slide the bastard in. Be careful. We don't want him to jam halfway down. Thank Christ it's a nice big shaft. Let's not fuck this up.' As they let go, they stumbled backwards and their load disappeared down the shaft. A loud bumping noise, silence and then a final thump – the burial service was over.

'Grab this shovel, Bernie,' Read said, 'and we'll drop some mullock down on top of him. I'll knock out some of the old shoring timber and that'll send a little landslide down on top of him. Sweet dreams, arsehole.' Read's voice came bouncing back at him from the depth of the shaft.

Read drove the car away off the hill and parked it about four hundred metres from Ironbar's grave.

'I don't know about you, Bernie, but I'm just a little bit buggered. I reckon that we camp here until dawn and then work our way across country back to the road south, giving Coober Pedy a miss. We don't want to be noticed. There's a couple of blankets in the back. It's going to get quite cool. Shit paper in the glove box and plenty of bottled water. We'll get room service in the morning.'

'I'm glad that it's over, Jack,' Bernie replied, half laughing. 'I was worried that we'd break down on the way or something like that. Sleep tight, big fella.'

As the sun ambled across the desert from the east, the landscape stepped out of the darkness and onto centre stage.

'Jesus, Jack, it looks like we've landed on the moon.' Read came to and rubbed his eyes. He laughed. Honest Bernie was having his first real look at the opal diggings. As far as the eye could see, mullock heaps of all sizes pocked the earth's surface, some grey, some chalky white, others tinged with faded pink. Read got out of the car, stretching and yawning.

'Yeah, Bernie, we could be on the moon for sure. Then again if you half close your eyes, they could be young mushrooms sprouting out of the compost. Look right out there on the horizon. A couple of blowers are working. Here, have a better look through the glasses.' Following Read's directions, Bernie could see puffs of pink dust colouring the early morning blue bag sky. The drift of the breeze kept the sound of the diesel compressors at bay.

'They're starting work early,' Read said. 'That could mean that they're on to opal and don't want to muck around getting it out. It's going to be a scorcher so let's get going. We'll pull up at that truckstop this side of Woomera and have a shower and something to eat. How are you feeling anyway, Bernie?' Read started checking the oil and water. Bernie put the binoculars down and stretched out his arms.

'Okay, Jack. Okay. I'm glad I came, I really am. I'd like to have a closer look at this opal mining caper though but we haven't got time.' Bernie's ratchetty cough interrupted the silence as he opened a fresh packet of cigarettes.

As they drove back into Melbourne, Read felt burnt out and drained. The last thirty-six hours had been the most hectic and traumatic of his life but killing Ironbar had removed the immediate threat of more violence against him, Welsh or others close to him.

He doubted if the Sydney mob would want to start waging a war of retribution on Ironbar's behalf. More than likely, his disappearance would be welcomed by some of his own who were nervous at having a mad dog in their midst. There was always the outside chance that Ironbar's body would be found one day and it would be easily identified as Read had not removed any personal effects. If the worse happened, he doubted if any police investigation would be all that vigorous.

You've got to put all this behind you now. You're alive, Ironbar's dead. You've survived. Look ahead, don't look back, he mused. He looked over at Honest Bernie as they drove past Melton.

'We'll be back home soon, Bernie. I want to go and see my mate Peter Welsh in hospital. I'll drop you off at his place so you can clean up. I'll come back and pick you up and then we'll go and have a pizza somewhere. Bernie, I can't thank you enough. I would have been fucked without you. What else can I say?' Bernie looked straight ahead.

'Look, you big kanaka, I've had the time of my life. I've seen Melbourne, I've been to the opal fields, a rather rushed trip I might say and you've stopped yakking at me about my smoking. What more can I want? Anytime Jack. Anytime you want to knock somebody off, don't hesitate, just give Honest Bernie a call. Come on, now go and see your mate.'

***

22

Edith Trueman gagged and stepped backwards as she opened the front door. Holding her hand to her nose, she edged towards an unusual buzzing noise coming up through the open garage door. She yelped as blowflies zoomed near her face then peeled away. The stench rose from the garage like heat from a chimney. She switched on the garage light and looked down, then stood hyperventilating for a moment. She managed to control herself but not before she wet her pants. The garage floor shimmered – maggots writhed and contracted as they competed for the last of Ironbar's blood. Overhead, squadrons of whirring blowflies pulsed and surged back and forth. Some of the more optimistic ones were unloading their eggs on curled up, infertile scabby residue. Edith almost fell as she backed away.

'Clyde, Clyde. Oh God, what's happened?' she whimpered, as she turned and ran.

Read felt depressed as he waved Honest Bernie into the departure terminal at Tullamarine Airport. The cancer hadn't made its presence visible yet but once it started on its home run unchecked, it would shrivel the nuggety plasterer down to a grotesque, gurgling thing sprouting tubes in a hospice bed. Read didn't want to think about it. Back at Coober Pedy for one crazy moment, he had thought of shooting Honest Bernie, denying him the misery and pain that lay ahead. After they had dumped Ironbar it would have been easy, a couple of shots at the nape of his neck and down a shaft but he couldn't do it. I didn't have the guts, Read said to himself as he walked back to his car.

'Here's a bio on Rex Jardine,' the journo said, as he handed Read a couple of A4 sheets of paper. A mate who worked for the Murdoch organisation in Sydney had referred Read to a journalist on the Melbourne *Herald Sun*. They were sitting in the sun at Southbank, drinking coffee and shooting the breeze about politics. The journo enjoyed having an audience.

'Jardine had an incredible battle to get preselection. I think he set some sort of record for the number of times that he fronted up. His factional enemies reckoned that he was born to be on the other side of the political fence but in the end he finally got across the line. Once he was there he aligned himself with the power brokers and brought quite a lot of corporate money into the party. His wife has been a lot of the power behind the throne. She's amazing with all the charity stuff.'

'Any whiff of scandal about Jardine asked Read?'

'Not that I've heard of. He's a big punter but that's no great secret and there's never ever been any talk of him being into the bookies or anything like that. Then there's his libertarian views but that's par for the course these days from both sides of politics. Jardine gets a lot of support from the gay and multicultural lobbies and the Kooris love him.'

'You mean the Abos,' Read lobbed, trying to get a rise from the journo.

'Well, mate, thanks for your help. See you around,' Read gestured with his arm. 'You've got a great city here.' He got up from the table and shook hands. He was planning his next move. *Nothing much on Jardine worth chasing up at the moment, so it's on to the disappearing faggot David Felton.*

Fitzroy Street, St Kilda. Faggotsville, Lesbiana. Pudenda thrusting against bib and brace crutch. Swollen cocks, foreskins tight and glistening, forcing their way out of skid-marked jocks. Saunas, K-Y gel and amyl nitrite. Street corner sweet meat underage boy and girl whores. Microwaved pasta, bad coffee, bad drugs and pock-marked drag queens. Read thought that the words from

Graeme Davies' book about homosexual culture in postwar Australia hit the mark. He was sitting in his hire car opposite the Chameleon Bar, plucking up enough courage to cross the road and go inside. Barry O'Shea's anti-corruption commission had managed to make contact a second time with Shane Hepworth who had passed on the information that David Felton had hung out at the Chameleon when he was working in Melbourne.

Heads turned as Read walked in and there were a few high-pitched and low-pitched giggles. He looked like a cop and didn't blend in too well with the bar's clientele of homosexuals and transvestites. A forced, soprano voice came clicking over his shoulder.

'Hello, big boy. Lookin' for some nookie?' Read humoured the six-o'clock-shadowed transvestite with a grin and ordered a light beer. The place was dark and smelt of dope and too much cheap perfume and aftershave. The barmaid took Read's money and wiped a place clean for him at the bar. She didn't look queer and was doing a good job. Read waited until she got back to his end of the bar. 'Worked here long?' he asked the girl.

'A couple of years. Are you a cop?' she replied as quick as a flash.

'No,' Read replied, 'but I'd like to ask you a couple of questions, if that's okay with you.' She looked hard at Read.

'Wait until my break and I'll come around and see you in about fifteen minutes.' The transvestite wobbled back to Read on his high heels. He gestured over his shoulders. 'Dahling,' he purred, giggling and putting on the dog. 'The boys and girls over there want to know if you're here to walk on the dark side or if you're a big, greasy pork chop.'

'Look, sweetie.' Read started to reply but the transvestite cut in.

'Dominique's the name, Dahling. Dominique.'

'Oh, I'm sorry, Dominique,' Read apologised. 'No, you go and tell your friends that I'm not a cop and I'm out of things for the time being, you know, it's that time of the month,' Read grinned and winked. The transvestite laughed out loud, throwing his head back, revealing ripe pimples and whiskers popping up through the pancake make-up. He minced back to his friend's table, waving his arms, shimmying and shaking his skinny arse.

'Lisa Benson. Now what do you want to know?' the barmaid said, putting out her hand and moving Read to a vacant table. She was quick off the mark. 'My father owns this place and he's as straight as can be, so am I if you were wondering. I thought that I'd put your mind at rest.' She smiled. 'It's better for business having a straight person behind the bar in a place like this. No dramas or customers falling in love with the bar attendants or vice versa, if you know what I mean. Now, how can I help you?'

'Yeah, that all sounds like good common sense to me,' Read replied. 'Look, I'm doing a favour for a friend of mine in Sydney. It's a bit sad really. His son's a poofter and he's gone missing. He was down here in Melbourne and the word is that he used to come here. His name is David Felton. I was wondering if you knew him.' Lisa thought for a while then nodded recognition.

'Yes, yes. I remember him. David used to come here until quite recently when he suddenly stopped appearing. We all thought that he'd gone back to the action in Sydney. He was a lad, our David.'

'Go on,' Read said. Lisa sipped her lemon squash.

'Well, David was a dreamer. You know that he was on the game?'

'Yeah,' Read said. 'I know he's a male prostitute, so does his father.' Lisa went on.

'David was always going to hit the big time. His big dream was to own a BMW convertible. He used to boast that he had some very powerful and important clients, maybe he did but if he did, he never brought them here.'

'Lisa, do you know where David lived?' Read asked, more in hope than expectation.

'Well, yes. Yes, as a matter of fact I do. I gave him a lift home one evening after closing. Not very far from here. He lived in a unit in South Yarra. I can describe the block of units to you. Hang on a moment, I'll draw a map for you.' As Lisa went behind the bar to get a piece of paper, Read's eyes fell on a beautiful blond girl sitting on the lap of a Neanderthal-looking bull dyke. The young girl was gorgeous. *Some mother's daughter,* Read said to himself, consumed by sudden jealousy. The dyke was wearing sleeveless overalls that had been converted to shorts. She had a head on her that made Mike Tyson look angelic.

Her bulk was half-steroid, half-gym and by the look of her chest, Read bet himself that she'd had a total breast reduction. Covered in tatts, she had gold rings in her eyebrows as well as her nose. When she opened her mouth to speak, she flashed rotting, snaggled teeth. Her ears were a jingle jangle of gold and silver rings and charms, and Read groaned inwardly as she deep tongue-kissed the goddess curled up on her lap. *She'd have muscles in her shit, for sure,* Read thought. 'Here you are,' Lisa said, handing Read a piece of paper.

The agent for the block of units had sent one of his lackeys along to show Felton's unit to Read.

'He did a runner. Didn't pay the rent and pissed off leaving half his gear behind. He'd always paid his rent on time so it's a bit of a mystery why he did what he did. Seemed a nice sort of young bloke too. We've got what's left of his personal effects in a storeroom back at the office. We're leaving a couple of pieces of his furniture here, saves us lugging it around. A new tenant's due to move in next week.' Read had spun him the same cock-and-bull story about Felton being a mate's missing son. 'Bring the keys back to the office when you've finished, mate.'

'Oh, thanks very much,' Read said. 'I won't be long. I'll have a look around here and then I'll be right behind you.'

Read found it when he pulled the oriental-style dressing table away from the wall. The empty, white A4 envelope had not been stamped. It still had invisible tape on the seal. Read whistled as he turned the envelope over and saw the Victorian Government coat of arms. The envelope could have come from any politician's office or government department but it was circumstantial and coincidental evidence linking David Felton with Rex Jardine. Read folded the envelope carefully and put it in his pocket, ticking things over in his mind. *I wonder what was in the envelope? The blackmail may have already begun. And why did Felton skip? Was he taken away against his will?* Read locked the flat and walked back to his car.

'Clyde, Clyde. You've got to go over to the house where Miller was staying. Something terrible has happened there. His car is still there. There's blood down in the garage and there's maggots everywhere. The stench is terrible. Oh God, it's shocking. I've got to go and sit in a hot bath. Please, you've got to do something. Take some bleach or something with you and clean up that disgusting mess and you'll need a heap of air freshener as well. I can't go near that house again until it's all cleaned up. Tell me what's happened, for God's sake.' Clyde Trueman was sitting in his office listening to his wife's voice hitting the high notes. The more wound up she became, the closer she came to hysteria.

'Edith. For Christ's sake, calm down. Sit down and stop raving.' Trueman banged his hand down on his desk, sending his Phar Lap paperweight bouncing. 'Pull yourself together. Let's not go overboard about this thing. I'll go over there tonight and fix everything up. I haven't got the foggiest idea of what's happened to Miller, if in fact anything has happened to him. We're not going to jump to conclusions and run around like chooks with their heads chopped off and I don't want you saying anything about this to anyone. Anyone! Understand? If something has happened we're not going to get involved and that means that there's no question of even thinking about going to the police. Understand? Edith, tell me you understand what I am saying. Come on now, don't worry, I'll fix everything up. You go and have your bath, it'll calm you down.' Edith sat down and looked at her husband.

'Clyde, that Miller gave me the creeps. You know that. I told you that I didn't like him hanging around here but I've always tried not to be a stickybeak. The stables are your business and I've done my best to keep your clients happy. You know that. Now I'm frightened that you've got yourself involved in something that might lose us all this.' She waved her arm around the room at all the trophies and memorabilia. Clyde got up.

'Edith, Edith, give me a break please. I've got a big day at Flemington on Saturday. I'll go over to the house tonight after tea. You get all that cleaning gear out ready for me now. I have to make some phone calls and then I'm going out to check on the horses.'

23

Rex Jardine sat behind his desk in a state of shock. He wanted to go to the lavatory but the nerves in his legs wouldn't accept the frantic messages being transmitted by his cerebellum. A precise and authoritative voice floated around him.

'It's because of the particularly sensitive nature of this case, your public position, your family, that I've taken it on myself to come to you personally and explain what has happened and the procedures that are prescribed by law.' Dr Samuel Bentinck, Director of the Victorian Red Cross Blood Bank, was sitting opposite Jardine, his hands in the praying position under his chin. He was trying not to look uncomfortable.

'You see, Mr Minister, when you attended our blood bank as a prospective donor for that government-promoted initiative, you were treated exactly the same as any other prospective donor. There is a screening process to ensure that all sorts of nasties don't end up in our system. You filled in the same form that all intending donors are given.' Dr Bentinck was rehearsing in his mind how to say what he was going to say next.

'Mr Minister, just wait until I say what I'm going to say and then we'll discuss all the various options available to you.' Bentinck cleared his throat. Jardine dug his fingernails into the padded armrests on his custom-made leather executive chair, trying to stop the rising bile from burning his throat and spilling out of his mouth. Bentinck's speech quickened.

'Mr Minister, screening tests indicate that you are HIV positive.' As the words left him, Bentinck almost slumped back in his chair with relief that he had been able to express himself but he managed to compose himself and sit forward again. Jardine's mouth was working but he was unable to articulate.

'As you must know, Mr Minister, HIV is a reportable condition but the first thing you must do is have a second blood test immediately, to make sure that the original pathology was correct. You must contact your personal physician and brief him. As a courtesy and to ensure your confidentiality, I am prepared to liaise with your physician. Your file is now being handled by me personally and I give you my word that I will do everything possible to help you through what lies immediately ahead. If further pathology confirms the first finding, you must seek counselling as to how to deal with the effect of this on your wife and family.' Bentinck jiggled with embarrassment in his chair. He was running out of things to say. Jardine suddenly came to life with a stumbling run to his office bathroom.

At the sound of harsh retching followed by a bout of nose blowing, Bentinck opened his briefcase and shuffled some papers for no real reason. Jardine wiped his mouth with a paper towel and looked at himself in the mirror. *What am I going to tell Patricia? Oh God, oh God, what am I going to tell Patricia?* Bentinck half-turned to see Jardine framed diagonally in the bathroom doorway. Only the door surround was stopping him from slumping to the floor.

'Mr Minister. Let me help you,' Bentinck said, as he went to Jardine and helped him across the room to a lounge chair.

'Now, easy does it. Sit down here while I get you a glass of water. Let's get your coat off and loosen that tie. There.' Jardine's eyes were like those of a rabbit caught by its back legs in a trap. Bentinck took his pulse and felt his cheeks and forehead. The loss of blood pressure and the clamminess of the skin told the doctor that Jardine was exhibiting all the classical symptoms of shock. He made a short telephone call then went through to the outer office.

'Excuse me, ma'am,' he said to Jardine's secretary. 'The minister has taken a bit of a turn. I've called for an ambulance but there's no need for serious concern, no need for panic. Just stay calm. I'll go with the minister to St Vincent's and then advise his family. I'll contact you later about his condition. You just keep on doing your job. Everything will be alright.' As Jardine was wheeled to the cargo lift by the ambulance men and one of the police guards who was on duty in the ministerial office, he had a vision of a naked David Felton, smiling and looking down on him. As Felton opened his pouting lips, a snake appeared from his mouth and struck at Jardine.

'Give him more oxygen, Gary,' the other ambulance man said, as Jardine groaned and tried to sit up.

'Yes, something real bad's happened over at my other house. No sign of Miller except what's left of a huge bloodstain on the garage floor after one million blowies have had their go at it.' Clyde Trueman rubbed the back of his hand over his mouth and wrinkled his nose.

'Yes, I've cleaned it all up with bleach and detergent but you can still see the outline of the stain on the concrete floor. I'm going to take some caustic soda over there later in the day and see if that does the trick. Miller's car is still in the garage with the keys in it. Okay, okay. When I go back I'll go right over the car with a polishing cloth to get rid of any fingerprints, inside and out, the glass, the dash, the bonnet and boot latches, inside the boot. Everywhere, okay? Did you get that? Did you hear what I said?' Trueman waited as he heard a muffled voice in the background relaying new messages to the person speaking with Trueman.

The man from Sydney always carried out his telephone conversations like that. It was an annoying practice as it involved a lot of repeating and toing and froing. Trueman had to pay him though. He was as cunning as a shithouse rat. 'Yes, I'll get Edith to give the house a good spring cleaning too. No, nobody else will be going near that house until all this mess is cleaned up. What are we going to do with the car? You're going to send someone down to pick it up, no

206

problems. Just let me know when someone is going to turn up. I'll have to open up the house. Listen, this is starting to get a bit heavy. Edith knows nothing and she doesn't ask any questions but Miller scared the shit out of her and then there was that tragic accident when Joylene Mills was killed.

Now the insurance company has jacked up on that claim on Gold Crest and the owners have got their solicitor driving me mad. I'd like it better if things quietened down a bit. Yeah, yeah, I know we've done well and I'm not being ungrateful but if things stuffed up, I could lose my licence and then where would I be then? Up shit creek, you say. Oh, come on, give me a break please. Yeah, everything's okay for Saturday. Ring The Bell is running in the big sprint race down the Straight Six. The vet's been checking him the past couple of weeks and he's tiptop. What do I think he'll start at? You've got to remember that there's more than a couple of good ones in this race. They've come from everywhere for it. We've got some very stiff opposition but with Hicks on our horse and a little help from the vet,' Clyde Trueman laughed.

'We're almost over the line. I reckon that he'll open at tens or better, maybe fifteens. Those last couple of shockers that he put in when we pulled him up will make the books take chances in a race like this one. I've got to go. I can hear Edith coming. I'll ring you later.'

'Here you are, Clyde,' Edith said, as she brought a tray of snacks into the room. On the other side of Melbourne, a technician rewound the tape from the recorder, dated it, entered the details in a logbook witnessed by his colleague and then slipped it into a tagged plastic evidence bag.

Unlike many of her peers, the receptionist spoke clearly and precisely. 'Werribee Veterinary Clinic and Hospital connecting you to Professor Flower.'

'Steve. Jack Read here. How are you? I'm after a big favour if you can see your way clear. I'm not getting you at a busy time am I?'

'No, Jack,' Steve Flower replied. 'How's the investigation

going? I've been watching the newspapers to see if you make the headlines.' Without going into the nitty gritty, Read told Flower about Joylene Mills' death and his suspicions about what was going on at the Clyde Trueman stables. He was careful that he didn't mention Jim Griffiths by name because vets were a cliquey lot.

'Sorry about my levity, Jack. It looks as though things are getting serious. Have you gone to the police yet?'

'Now it's my turn to laugh,' Read said. 'Never trust a cop, well, maybe I'm being a bit too harsh. Let me rephrase that. Be careful what you tell a cop.' The two men laughed.

'Before we go on, Jack,' Flower said, 'let me set you straight on one point. Everyone in the racing game knows that Jim Griffiths does Clyde Trueman's vet work. I've met him a few times but he moves in different circles to me. What I'm saying is that he's not a mate of mine or even an acquaintance, so be rest assured on that count. If he's allowed himself to get involved with doping racehorses, then he doesn't deserve one skerrick of mercy, he has to go down bigtime. So there you are, you know where I stand.' Flower's declaration made Read feel a little easier.

'Thanks, Steve. Mike Rowlands told me that you were a straight shooter, so thanks for clearing that up with me. You can understand how I feel. I drop into Melbourne out of the blue and start asking people all sorts of questions and then a few things happen to push up my paranoia levels. Now the reason for my call. As you know, the VRC vet is Howard Rhodes.'

'Dusty Rhodes,' Flower interrupted. 'Sorry, Jack, keep going.'
'Alright, Steve, what sort of bloke is he? How long has he been in the job and what would his reaction be to a dill like me turning up in his office, making all sorts of allegations about one of Australia's biggest trainers and his vet?'

'Well, Jack, I don't know much about Jim Griffiths but I do know quite a bit about Dusty Rhodes. Your vet mate in Sydney, Mike Rowlands, did his vet course with Dusty who came to Sydney Uni after he had served in Vietnam. They studied together, drank together and played together. Dusty's a real good bloke and very professional. He takes no nonsense from anyone, believe me. He was appointed to the VRC about five years ago when Bill Longlands died. I'll tell you what I'll do, if it's alright with you. I'll refer you to him and leave it at that. I won't mention anything about elephant juice or crooked vets. That's up to you. What do you think about that?' Read's morale was boosted by the support he was receiving from Flower.

'Steve, you're too kind. I really appreciate your offer. I'd appreciate you contacting him as soon as possible as I'm working on bringing everything to a head here. With a bit of luck I want to be back in Sydney next week.'

'I'll be on the phone as soon as we finish, Jack, how's that? By the way, that ampoule is still here, safe and sound.'

'Steve, you're a real white man,' Read said, as he ended the call on his mobile. Moving out into the traffic, Read spun the wheel and turned right at the next opportunity. With a bit of luck, Ella would be home.

Rex Jardine's absence from his office went unnoticed. Parliament was in recess and only a few close friends were aware that the pressure of work and his doctor's orders had led to him spending a week at a health farm at Mt Macedon, just outside Melbourne. As Jardine's government car crested the hill with Melbourne's metropolitan cluster in the distance, his doctor's words came back to him.

'Rex, I'm not going to pull any punches. I'm sure that you wouldn't want me to. Pathology confirms that you are HIV positive.' At this point Jardine had started sobbing but managed to pull himself together as his doctor kept on talking.

'At present you are not, repeat not, suffering fully blown AIDS. We will monitor you constantly and you must strictly follow the diet program I will send you. Medical science has come a long way since the early eighties and almost every couple of months, a new AIDS drug comes onto the market. I am going to start you on a course of AZT immediately while I confer with some specialists in America. Please monitor your weight and report any significant loss. You must check your body daily for any suspicious rashes or other telltale signs. In particular, advise me as a matter of urgency if you get any night sweats or other flu-like symptoms.' Jardine had sat in his doctor's surgery, head bowed like a condemned man waiting for the execution procession to come and take him to the electric chair. The doctor went into a side room and returned with a stainless steel kidney dish.

'Take off your jacket, Rex, and roll up your sleeve. Just a little shot of valium to calm you down.' Jardine didn't even feel the prick of the hypodermic. The doctor's next words were the ones that ground his life down to dust, giving no pity, giving no hope. He had felt as if he was going blind.

'Of course, Rex, there's the question of how we break this to Patricia. You are compelled by law to advise her and if you were to be so foolish as to abrogate your responsibility in this area, the Department of Health and I would be obliged to do so. Of course we can't let things deteriorate to that point, and we won't. Think about it. I'll help you as much as I can but it's crucial that you tell Patricia and not leave it to me.' As the doctor had patted him on the shoulder, Jardine had wished that he'd had the courage to punch the man to the ground and stomp his stupid face to a pulp. Now, as his car drove over the Westgate Bridge, Rex Jardine started thinking about suicide.

Read realised that he had been silly to turn up unannounced the moment Ella opened the door. She had a towel wrapped around her head turban style and was still damp from the shower. She was wearing an old silk dressing gown that didn't seem right for mid-afternoon and she was holding it closed at the top. Her face was flushed and she was angry.

'What are you doing here, Jack? Why don't you ring before you just barge in out of the blue? Can't you respect my privacy?' She kept the door firmly where it was, defending her territory. Read felt like a goose and kicked himself for being so stupid.

'Jack, why don't you go and ring me later, eh?' Read could see Ella looking past him.

'Ella, I'm very sorry,' Read said, with not much conviction.

'I'll get out of your hair.' He was feeling embarrassed and foolish.

'I'll give you a call.' As he turned to go, a beat-up Volkswagen Kombi van pulled up outside the house. It was one of those vans emblazoned with Aboriginal motifs and *Save The Whale and Save The Trees* stickers, the kind that drive around belching oil-soaked exhaust fumes from a clapped-out motor. The driver was in his early thirties, wearing jeans, T-shirt and a blond ponytail. He was cocky and walked past Read into Ella's house like a man on a promise.

'Gidday, man,' he said with a grin. Read cursed himself for acting like a teenage dill. *You fucking idiot,* he fumed to himself as he half-ran back to his car.

24

Flemington racecourse looked a picture, a cliché used by generations of racecallers. The grass on the track and lawns fronting the grandstands looked almost synthetic with their fertiliser-induced greenness, and the flower gardens would have scooped the pool at any horticultural show. Many new rose varieties made their debut at Flemington. The human mares and fillies were already out, promenading their stuff, and in the public areas, people were setting up portable chairs and tables. There was a familiar buzz of expectation in the growing crowd as the main event had been publicised Australia-wide.

By the end of the day's racing, huge sums of money would have been shuffled from one side of the ledger to the other. The winners would party on loudly at the Hyatt and the Hilton, honouring winning trainers and jockeys with Dom Perignon and bundles of cash. The Toorak and South Yarra cappuccino set was still sniggering and gossiping about one well-known owner's wife who rewarded the winning jockeys of her husband's Group 1 winners with the ride of their lives, using their caps, whips and silks as imaginative props. On the other hand, the losers on the day, sullen and quietly angry, would slink away to their homes, cursing the four-legged conveyances and the crooked midgets that rode on their backs.

Read was strolling past the horse stalls as he glanced at his racebook. The main race of the day was the Emirates Conquistador Stakes down the Straight Six sprint course. It was being promoted as the richest, open, 1200 metre race in the world, challenging the status of the Golden Slipper two-year-old sprint run at the Rosehill track in Sydney. *Every man and his dog have turned up for this one,* Read thought, as he strolled on.

Brian Gray had brought Zipper down from Sydney and other interstate stables were well represented. Besides that, a couple of Kiwi entrants had flown in during the week on a hit-and-run mission. It was going to be a hard race to pick. With a fast track, most tipsters expected a record time. Read stood back from the stalls as he drew level with Ring The Bell's box. The usual crew from the Trueman stables was there. The man himself would make his entry close to saddling up time. Read had wanted to bring Sylvia to the races but a last-minute stuff-up meant that she had to cover for another worker at the Lemon Tree who had rung in sick. Read was pissed off with himself. He was still feeling a goose over his performance at Ella's place.

'Hello, Jack, long time no see. Got a winner picked out?' As the hand slapped his back, Read turned in mock fright.

'Jesus, the law. I thought that I was being arrested,' he said, as he shook hands with Neil Ryan.

'How're things with you, Shorty? I've been busy the last week. Keeping all the crooks away from the track, are you? Though from that message I just heard over the PA, you're falling down on the job, mate.' A few minutes earlier, a track official had warned patrons that pickpockets were active in the betting ring. It was a sign of the times. Ryan laughed.

'I thought that you'd be back in Sydney by now, Jack. If you'd gone back without saying goodbye, I would have been very pissed off, believe me. How's your mate who got bashed? Have you run into that crim mate of yours from Sydney, that Ironbar hoon? So far, I haven't seen him at the track today. What about you?'

'Nope,' Read replied, 'no sign of the useless bastard and I hope that I never see him again. Let's not waste our breath talking about that garbage. Yeah, Welsh is almost back on deck. They've taken the wires out of his jaw and he's had to have some pretty extensive and expensive dental surgery. He'll be back home next week. Look, Shorty, I'm just waiting for him to get home and then I'm back off to Sydney – and sanity. I'd like to have a drink with you before I go. I'll always owe you for that quaddie, you know.'

'She's right, mate,' Ryan replied heartily. 'For sure. We'll bump into each other again today. Sing out when you're ready and it'll be my shout. I might even be able to bring Larry Hill along to sip on his orange juice while we hit the piss. What do you reckon? See you.' Read watched the policeman move away into the crowd, doffing his hat to a couple of smartly dressed matrons whose body language suggested they knew him.

Read walked into the members enclosure and through to the betting ring, checking the prices. It was getting close to starting time for the third race and there was plenty of money around. He wasn't in the mood for betting. He had come to watch the big sprint race but wouldn't be having a bet in that either. He scanned the crowd to see if he could spot Police Minister Rex Jardine but there was no sign of him. *You'll keep, my friend,* Read said to himself as he wandered off to the member's bar.

When the main event on the card arrived, Australia's best sprinters and the two New Zealand raiders were entering the saddling enclosure. Read eyed off some of the female strappers who were looking very swish indeed as they led the horses around the ring. Most of them looked as if they worked out in the gym, and the gear they were wearing had that designer-label look, a far cry from the days of gum-chewing, fag-drooping from the mouth, failed ex-jocks with their shonky tips and questionable inside information.

Read put his glasses on the busy scene and picked up Clyde Trueman in a huddle, talking to 'Dangles' Hicks who was riding Ring The Bell. Standing a few paces behind the two men was Jim Griffiths, looking the part in Harris Tweed and R.M.Williams trousers and boots.

'Take the breaks when they come. I don't have to tell you how to suck eggs. The only thing that can stop him today is if you fall off,' Clyde Trueman said, as he legged the jockey up into the saddle, his Bushnell binoculars swinging from the crook of his left arm. He didn't use Hicks' nickname anymore. Not since he found out that Edith was serving it up to him.

The only thing in her favour was that she didn't flaunt the fact around the racing community. He was hoping that she would wake up to herself and stop carrying on like the town bike. A back injury from his oil-drilling days had come back to haunt Clyde with sporadic impotence but he had been told about a new wonder pill being developed overseas that in a few years time would turn men like himself into panting, unstoppable studs. The thought made him smile.

The plunge on Ring The Bell came late and hard and took even the smart bookmakers by surprise. The surprise was the amount of money and the form it came in, cash. There was not that much credit betting. What the bookies didn't know was that most of the cash was drug money in its last stages of laundering. Joe Silver in Sydney used horseracing as one of his washing machines and offered a service to a few of the big Asian and Lebanese drug rings as well as doing his own thing.

With its overwhelming preference for cash, the racetrack has always been a favourite venue for enterprising criminal activity. When he was lording it over the crims and the cops in NSW in the late 1970s, drugs king Robert Trimbole used to give one well-known Sydney rails bookie $100,000 in cash and receive a $90,000 winning betting ticket. Good business all round and no questions asked.

Read stood back and, feeling like a witness at an execution, watched the books buckle. Because of the timing of the plunge, many of them didn't have time to lay off some of the money with the TAB, and quite a few of the weak reeds simply stopped taking big bets on Ring The Bell altogether. The plunge was hitting the interstate tracks as well, so laying off there was out of the question. The surge of activity in the Melbourne betting ring was like a virus, infecting the mug punters who rushed at the bookmakers nearest them. The clerks couldn't handle the rush and as starting time ticked closer, bedlam reigned. On the public side of the rails, a couple of women were knocked down, and on the members' side, ten-dollar punters from the leafier suburbs of Melbourne found themselves swept up in the unseemly assault on the bagmen.

'Look at them with all their fancy airs and graces, they're just like a pack of bloody animals,' a white-haired dignified man whinged as he brushed past Read.

Ring The Bell circled and pig-rooted a few times before he allowed himself to be led into the stalls. Ray Hicks could feel that the horse was well and truly fired up and he took a hard hold of it. He had drawn one barrier position off the flat side rail and looking down the Straight Six course was like sighting down a gun barrel.

A slight tail breeze kept the noise from the crowd at bay and it was strangely quiet at the barrier stalls. The white marquees at trackside, with their fluttering corporate pennants, shimmered in the haze like a modern oasis. Most of their occupants had left their troughs of free food and drink to go outside into the temporary stands to watch the race, giving respite to the army of young and frazzled casual catering staff.

The field of sprinters were race-wise and eager to get on with the job. Only one of the New Zealand horses had to be shoehorned into its barrier stall. The horse, a stubborn gelding, sat back on its haunches impassively and refused to move one way or the other. Six barrier attendants joined battle while the horse's jockey stood by, arms folded. Two men linked their arms around its buttocks while a third twitched its tail. The other three were trying to get some purchase on the horse's elbow joints.

'C'mon, fellas, let's stop mucking around. It's right on starting time. Get the blindfold on him,' the starter ordered, as he supervised the activity behind the stalls. He pointed to a horse still well away from the stalls that was giving its jockey problems.

'K Forrester wants a man there.' An attendant ran over and

took hold of the horse. The starter hurried around to the front of the stalls and towards his stand.

'He's only been in Australia for twenty-four hours and he wants to go on strike,' quipped the Kiwi jockey with a grin as he remounted the troublesome horse that had now decided to cooperate. It was standing quietly locked away. The jockeys set themselves for the start, getting balanced and shifting their weight forward. Satisfied, the starter mounted his stand that was well off to one side and in front of the action. The lights on the top of the stalls flashed.

'All set. Ready now, boys,' the starter called, looking at his assistant who was standing back behind the stalls. The assistant raised his right arm straight up, indicating that horses and jockeys were ready, and at that instant the starter pressed the button on the switch held in his right hand. The heavy-duty twelve-volt battery mounted on the chassis of the mobile barrier stalls sent a pulse of current to the solenoid that tripped the catches at the front of each stall's spring-loaded gate.

With an echoing clang, the gates sprang open and the horses jumped. The New Zealand horse that had given the attendants such a hard time left its stall cleanly and was the first to hit the ground. Like disciplined marksmen in a firing squad marching out of the quadrangle after doing their duty, the starter and his team busied themselves in preparation for the next race start.

As the sprinters split almost equally and headed for either the flat side or the grandstand side of the Straight Six track, the air was filled with the hissing of jockeys and the whack, whack, whacking of their whips as some horses were ridden hard for early position. Ray Hicks had angled Ring The Bell into a forward spot on the flat side rail and the horse was balanced and stretching out well. The pace was hot and Hicks could sense the pressure. It was all around him. Fat wads of cash were down there at the winning post, just waiting for the victors. All the jockeys knew it and it seemed as if the horses did too, as if the greedy urgency was capable of being transmitted from man to beast. There were going to be no dead'uns in this race.

Hicks had a couple of Victorian horses sitting about half a length back off him while over on the grandstand side, Zipper from NSW looked to be leading that division. She's Apples, the tough little four-year-old mare, was a Missile Stakes winner from Sydney and was making her presence felt in the bunch trailing Zipper. Hicks decided to make a bold move at the 400-metre mark out from the winning post to test out the field. It was a bit early for such a strategy but Ring The Bell was cantering easily and wanted to race away. The juice the vet had given him was doing the job.

It was just a matter of timing the last frantic sprint to the line. As Hicks gave his horse some more rein, the Kiwi barrier rogue loomed up three horses wide on his right and matched it with Ring The Bell. It was a challenge that had to be answered. Hicks started raking Ring The Bell with his heels and showed him the whip. The horse took a fresh hold of the bit and leapt ahead. But the Kiwi horse kept coming, boring across the horses on its inside until it was running at Ring The Bell's girth. Hicks ventured a glance across the track and saw that the horses on the grandstand side had dropped back under pressure. It was just him and the Kiwi horse now. He couldn't hear or see any more immediate challengers.

'C'mon, c'mon,' Hicks yelled, as he urged Ring The Bell on. Red lights started flashing in his mind as he sensed danger.

'Fuck! Get off, fuck you, get off,' he screamed in hoarse rage, as the horse on his outside suddenly shortened stride and started laying in on top of him, dragging back on his right leg.

'Get off me, get off me, for fuck's sake, get off me, you sheep fucker!' Hicks yelled at the other jockey as he broke free. The running rail sang like a tuning fork as horse and rider bounced off it. It was time to get out and get away now as he gave Ring The Bell full rein and got his whip going, bouncing in the saddle as he windmilled his right arm.

As he cleared away from the rest of the field, Hicks was riding on a high. He was drenched with sweat from the physical effort and his adrenaline was pumping. He looked across to the grandstand and felt confident and warm as the yelling and cheering washed over him. It seemed as if every man and woman on the track owned a part of Ring The Bell. Hicks knew that he had the race won and was already thinking of his ten per cent winning fee, plus ten per cent sling from the owners, and then there would be the extra sweetener from the man in Sydney and then there would be Edith Trueman going down on him, sucking his balls and talking all that love shit. Yes, life was so good. Then, like a sudden power failure, things started to happen.

As Hicks and Ring The Bell flashed across the winning line three lengths clear, amid the thunder of noise coming at him from all directions, Hicks felt something happening underneath him. It was down inside the horse's thoracic cavity where Hicks was gripping it on the outside with his knees and lower legs. Ring The Bell's heart was tearing itself apart. Tachycardia, the extreme heart beat rate induced by the etorphine, and the horse's massive exertion had ruptured the main aorta that was pumping oxygenated blood out of the left ventricle into his body. It was as if a time bomb had exploded inside Ring The Bell. Litres of foaming, free blood splashed uselessly around the cavity surrounding his heart as his major functions switched off.

Hicks felt the horse going down under him but in those milliseconds he was frozen in time. Knees buckling, Ring The Bell fell in towards the running rail. His nearside radius bone shattered and his lower jaw ploughed into the turf, tearing and peeling back the skin and sending divots of grass flying. Gasps of shock and despair rippled through the crowd like a Mexican wave. From galloping at just over seventy kilometres per hour in one effortlessly synchronised instant to a sickening, gawky crashing halt the next, Ray Hicks had no hope. His wiry, muscled body and finely honed reflexes were of no use to him when he needed them most.

Ring The Bells's 500-kilogram body hitting the ground at that speed launched Hicks into the air like a stuntman shot out of a cannon. As he was hurled over the running rail, a morbid silence descended on the crowd like a thick fog, pierced only by a few raucous, boozy laughs from those who were out of sight of the final dreadful act on one of the world's most famous racecourses.

Ray Hicks, clutching his whip like an aircraft joystick controlling his flight, somersaulted through the air towards a set of steel steps set into the ground beside the dirt training track inside the main track. On his second somersault, Hicks speared into the middle step, his dreams and whip spinning away. Held in place by its chinstrap, his fibreglass skull cap took all the shock generated by his body at terminal velocity as it splattered against the steps.

Like the shell of a soft-boiled egg, the skull cap barely contained the shattered contents of Hicks' head. His displaced first and second cervical vertebrae sheared away his spinal cord. As his lifeless body flopped onto the ground, a pair of seagulls flew away from their perch at the top of the steps.

As the rest of the horses passed the line, the stunned silence of the crowd evaporated. Cries and screams split the air as the horror was revealed. People moved restlessly. Down along the rails near the winning post, shocked racegoers milled around, gazing with morbid fascination at the dead horse and jockey. After a moment of suspended animation, officialdom came back to life and seemed to appear from nowhere. Ambulance crews gathered round with their emergency equipment as the course doctor pronounced Ray Hicks dead. Course workers had erected screens around Ring The Bell as Dusty Rhodes, the VRC vet, and his assistant ran across the track.

'That insurance investigator was right on the ball, I'd say,' Rhodes said as he started issuing instructions. 'I want this horse taken straight down to Werribee. Get on to Steve Flower and tell him that I want every gram of tissue, every millilitre of blood and fluid, analysed to the nth degree and all the results put under lock and key. I'll get a steward to drive a representative from the Trueman stable down to Werribee to witness proceedings and sign out all the paperwork. We could be onto something big here so I don't want any stuff-ups that could come back and bite us on the arse later, understand?' A front-line captain in Vietnam, Rhodes knew how to delegate.

'At first glance we've got the lot here, I'd say, Bill. Can you step over here for a minute please?' Rhodes put his hand on the shoulder of Bill Fleming, the VRC detective, as the two men separated from the huddle who were helping to winch Ring The Bell on to a trailer.

'Bill, I'll send one of the vets with you and I want you to go straight to Clyde Trueman's stables and put the cleaners through the place. We'll use our powers of entry and inspection of licensed premises under the rules of racing. We're looking for drugs, so anything in a bottle, an ampoule, a packet, anything that looks like a drug, grab it. Be very thorough and look in all the likely hiding places, even Clyde's bathroom cabinets, his office, everywhere. The next one's a curly one, Bill.

Jim Griffiths, Trueman's vet over at Ascot Vale, is in this up to his eyeballs. I've already got some evidence against him but it was obtained illegally so we're going to need a conventional search warrant. You'll most probably have to go through the racing squad. I want to hit him quickly before people start getting organised and getting rid of evidence. Griffiths is here on the course. I saw him in the mounting yard with Trueman before the race. The analyst from the VRC lab will have to be in on this one so he can identify any suspicious substances for detailed analysis. Let me know if you run into any problems. Alright, let's get cracking.'

'No problem with Trueman's stables and his residence, Dusty,' the VRC detective said. 'I can enter and search those okay but Griffiths is a different kettle of fish. His vet surgery and his private residence are exactly that, private premises like yours, like mine. You're right. I'll have to liaise with the police racing squad and have them apply to the court for a search warrant. As long as our evidence stacks up, we should be okay. I've got to start pissing in a few pockets. I'll get moving and I'll keep you posted.'

Read lowered his glasses and tried to keep pace with what was happening. The death of Hicks and Ring The Bell had turned everything on its head. Read could imagine the frantic consternation in the Trueman camp. He put his glasses back on the closing stages of the drama down past the winning post. The ambulance had taken Ray Hicks' body off to the morgue to be held in custody by the coroner pending an inquiry, and the trailer with Ring The Bell's broken and leaking carcase swaying on it was leaving the main track at the crossing to take it past the Elms and then out of the course onto Farnsworth Avenue.

Why doesn't the VRC have a proper horse ambulance with an internal winch to handle terrible situations like this? The loony left animal welfare lobby groups will have a field day in the media tomorrow. Pretty frightful PR, Read thought, as he put his glasses back on the group of officials dispersing down on the track. He felt a flush of vindication as he saw Dusty Rhodes directing his troops.

25

On the Wednesday before Ray Hicks rode his last race, the VRC vet had given Read a good hearing, taking notes and asking questions that indicated that he was more than interested. It was obvious that Steve Flower had given him a good rap about Read who administered the king hit when he pushed two full boxes of ampoules of etorphine across Rhodes' desk.

'Whew,' Rhodes exclaimed and let out a low whistle as he examined the boxes. 'There's enough stuff here to knock down every elephant in the world plus all the other large game animals. Where the bloody hell did you get this little lot?' Read stood up and walked around behind his chair, propping himself on it.

'Well, Dusty, it's a long story that doesn't go outside this room but the short version is that you're handling stolen goods. I had Jim Griffiths' car broken into and this is the result. I've got a lot more stuff, most of it legal but there are some other unlabelled ampoules and bottles that need expert appraisal.' The vet looked at Read hard before grinning.

'You don't muck around, do you?' he said, standing up and shaking hands again with Read. 'I really appreciate you bringing me all this information and that,' he said gesturing towards the etorphine. 'I'll keep it here in my safe as I'm sure that you don't want the responsibility of hanging onto it. We'll watch all Trueman's horses on Saturday and make sure that they get pre-race and post-race drug testing. I can turn up at Clyde's stables any time, given my powers under the rules of racing but I'm going to need a court-issued search warrant for Griffiths. Anyway, that's my problem. I'll be seeing you for sure before you return to Sydney.' At the doorway, Read turned back.

'Good meeting you, Dusty. Steve Flower was right.' Rhodes' eyebrows formed a question mark. 'He said that you were a straight shooter,' Read said as he closed the door behind him.

'We should cancel the rest of the meeting. It's the proper and decent thing to do and we should act promptly,' VRC senior committeeman Sir Charles Mortimer said, as he sipped his whisky slowly then dabbed at his lips with his table napkin. For a moment there was silence and a couple of committeemen further down the table looked for a moment as if they were going to support the influential knight. The CEO of the VRC, Tony Briggs QC, rose to his feet, clearing his throat nervously, making a production of looking at the time on his gold Rolex. He poured himself a glass of water from a sterling silver jug and began speaking.

'Gentlemen, the sponsors of the race have spoken to me and their basic sentiments support those expressed by Sir Charles but … but they stressed that if you choose to proceed with the remainder of the card, then they would not attempt to force the point. Then there is also the … the, let us say, the temperament of the crowd to be considered. Just look down for yourselves. We have a crowd of record proportions, everyone enjoying themselves, a carnival atmosphere, it's just like Melbourne Cup day down there. Then there is the most compelling consideration of all, the economic one. The lost income from the TAB will be very substantial indeed. I am sure that you must all share my concern on this point.' The CEO backtracked.

'Gentlemen, we have witnessed a tragedy here today, nobody can deny that. Ray Hicks was our top jockey, now I must stress that the tragedy would have been just as great if he had been an unknown apprentice but you know what I mean.'

As he spoke, Briggs looked straight ahead, being careful not to make eye contact with Sir Charles Mortimer who was glancing around the table trying to see if he had any firm support left. He had none. Any promise of it had evaporated.

'I cannot believe what I am hearing,' Sir Charles said slowly. 'A man, a human being was killed here today in tragic circumstances along with the very fine animal he rode, and this committee and its chief executive officer are assessing this loss of life in accountant's language, as if all this was just some sort of balance sheet to be presented to concerned shareholders.' Sir Charles got to his feet and looked up and down the table.

'Quite frankly, you all disgust me. If I was a lesser person, I would expose you all to the media but that would be breaching committee confidentiality. I never contemplated doing anything like that when I was a cabinet minister and I am certainly not going to start doing it now, so in the short term you will be saved by me adhering to my principles, a quality that none of you seem to share with me, if in fact the word principle features in your vocabularies at all.' The other men at the table tried to pretend that they were somewhere else. 'Good day,' Sir Charles thundered softly, as he left the room without looking back.

Tony Briggs exhaled slowly and quietly. *With that silly old prick Mortimer out of the way, I can sort this mess out right now and we can start putting it all behind us,* he said to himself before speaking again, quickly and with a new authority.

'Right, gentlemen, let's press on. It's been nearly twenty minutes since the accident and the natives are getting restless.' He laughed nervously.

'I've got an announcement ready and it's all systems go. A couple of senior riders were agitating for all the jockeys to withdraw their services for the rest of the day as a mark of respect, I hesitate to use the word strike but the stewards are with them now, convincing them that Hicks would have wanted the show to go on. They'll all be wearing armbands for the rest of the day and all the flags are coming down to half-mast. This is the greatest crisis we have faced in our time together but we will rise above it and be stronger as a result.

Must be off now.' *If I can pull this one off, the bastards will fall over themselves begging me to renew my contract,* Briggs thought, as he half-ran out of the room.

'Ladies and gentlemen.' The course PA carried the announcer's voice loud and clear. The crowd quietened and the bookmakers and their clerks cupped their ears. Read was back in the betting ring, hoping to catch sight of Rex Jardine.

'Ladies and gentlemen, please, an important announcement.' The announcer paused for dramatic effect.

'Using their discretionary powers, the stewards have declared correct weight; repeat, correct weight in the Emirates Conquistador Stakes.' The crowd sighed with relief.

'All races will be put back thirty minutes. As a mark of respect, all flags have been lowered and jockeys will wear black armbands. After careful deliberation and consultation with all parties, including his widow, it was decided that the late Ray Hicks, champion horseman that he was, would have wanted this day's racing to continue. The presentation of trophies for the feature race will be postponed until next Saturday's meeting here at Flemington.

Emirates Airlines, the sponsors, have foreshadowed that in future, the race will be known as the Emirates Ray Hicks Stakes. Thank you for your attention, ladies and gentlemen.' A murmur ran around the course and then, like the lights coming back on after a power failure, it was back to business as betting began for the next race. Up in the VRC committee rooms, Tony Briggs was being congratulated and toasted by his employers with Krug champagne.

Read saw Rex Jardine walking back into the members enclosure. Moving quickly, he drew abreast of the politician who was looking straight ahead.

'Mr Jardine,' Read said, not bothering to lower his voice. 'I was up in Sydney last week and heard you performing on those tapes made by David Felton. My, you do like having fun, don't you? They're going to make good headlines any day now. The media will have a field day with you.' Jardine jerked around and the plain clothes policeman following his Minister moved in quickly when he noted his employer's concern.

'What did you say? What did you say? Who are you? What's your name? Are you a member?' Flecks of spittle flew out of Jardine's mouth, forcing Read to step back. Jardine's grasp at Read's shoulder prompted his police escort to come and stand beside the two men.

'What's this all about?' the policeman said, looking hard at Read.

'Nothing really,' Read replied, removing Jardine's hand from his shoulder.

'I'm a member of the AJC down from Sydney,' he said, showing his guest pass to Jardine and the policeman.

'The Minister must have misunderstood what I said.'

'I asked you what your name was,' Jardine chimed in.

'I want to know your name.'

'Here,' Read said, giving Jardine his business card.

'Must fly. It's been an interesting day, to say the least. Nice meeting you both.' As Read melted back into the crowd, Jardine mouthed something under his breath and sought shelter in the member's bar.

'Bacchus Marsh mourns top jock,' cliched the headlines of the *Herald Sun*, directing the reader to the sports section at the back of the paper. Read turned the paper over and moved his tea out of the way. He was having breakfast in Lygon Street and had a busy day ahead of him. He was going to bring Welsh home from St Vincent's and then he wanted to see Sylvia who was going to take a few days off to go and see her mother in Yass. *Bacchus Marsh, Bacchus Marsh.*

Read read on about Ray Hicks' death and the running of the sensational Emirates Conquistador Stakes, which took up four full pages of text and photographs. As Read scanned the pages, his mind went into rewind. *Bacchus Marsh, Bacchus Marsh. A gully on the bend of a narrow, hardly used road. The place where Ironbar Miller had murdered Joylene Mills. Miller didn't know the area so he needed someone with local knowledge to help him and it would have helped him if Joylene had known that someone. Bacchus Marsh mourns top jock, Ray 'Dangles' Hicks. The local boy made good. Ray Hicks in the Botanic Gardens with Ironbar Miller. Ray Hicks up to his balls in the mob's race fixing when he wasn't up to them in Edith Trueman. Ray Hicks pitching a story and getting Joylene to drive him somewhere and then watching Ironbar smash the life out of her, except one spark of her life kept sputtering, enough to throw her rosary beads out of her car as she went flaming down into the gully.*

Ray Hicks who was now being hero-worshipped in the media and was going to have one of Australia's important races named after him. Read banged his cup down and swore aloud, raising the heads of other breakfasters close to him. He calmed down. *It would all come out. It had to. The VRC vet wasn't a dill. The VRC would need a PR superman to media spin it out of the mountain of shit when all the facts became known. Racing would take a long time to recover. The purge would have to be draconian. The guilty would dob in the guiltier.* Read left the *Herald Sun* on the table and went and paid his bill.

'HIV positive, HIV positive? Stop being stupid, Rex. Just stop being silly, for God's sake. I'm too busy and so are you to carry on with such childishness so grow up. Is this some sort of sick joke?' Patricia Jardine busied herself, putting more ice in her gin and tonic as if that was the end of the matter. In front of the black marble fireplace in his lounge room, Rex Jardine stood stiffly at attention like one of the guards outside Buckingham Palace. He stared straight ahead, unblinking. Dr Sam Bentinck from the Blood Bank had brought the matter to a head the day before, by organising a meeting with himself, Jardine and Dr Walter Medley, the director of Victorian Health Services.

Further blood tests had confirmed that Jardine was HIV positive. The two medicos had been supportive and sensitive to Jardine's position but they had both been hardline when it came to the question of the necessity to advise Patricia Jardine as soon as possible. They had volunteered to be present at any meeting but Jardine could not bring himself to agree to the horrors such a confrontation would present to him and his wife. As a guarantee that he had complied with Bentinck's and Medley's directions, he was to give her Dr Medley's card and she had to call the doctor within twenty-four hours.

Rex Jardine was overdosed on fear and depression. In a mad moment he had dialled David Felton's Sydney contact number but a computerised voice told him that the number had been disconnected. He could not bring himself to even think about telling Ryan. He shivered at the thought.

'Rex, when do you want to eat?' Patricia was back in her role of attentive wife, the conversation of a few moments ago erased. 'Rex, come on.' Her voice hardened. 'Keep this up and I'll lose my temper and where will that get us. Lamb chops, or I have some nice fresh snapper fillets. I'll go and get us another drink.' The gurgling noise made Patricia turn around before she left the room. What she saw made her want to faint.

Rex Jardine had fallen to his knees, sobbing, sucking his breath in and out like a donkey braying. The noise seemed to fill the house and, almost as an aside, Patricia was grateful that none of their children were home. Jardine was holding out his arms like a Bombay street beggar, with a business card extended from the fingers of his right hand. His words seeped through his gulps and gurgles, a long strand of saliva dangling out of his mouth, stretching out and then retracting with each breath.

'Patricia, Patricia. Please forgive me. Forgive me. I've done a terrible thing. I can't believe what I've done. Take this card. Take it and ring Dr Medley tomorrow morning and he'll tell you what has happened to me. Please, please,' he gasped as he fell forward, his right arm still raised, holding the card aloft.

Moving towards her husband, Patricia felt him clutch at her legs like a footballer making a last desperate tackle. She took the card from his outstretched hand and read Dr Medley's name and number.

'Rex, Rex. You haven't been joking, have you? Have you?' Her voice took on a shrill tone as it accelerated up the scale.

'What have you been doing? What have you done, oh dear God, what have you done?' Patricia suddenly jerked convulsively and kicked clear of the arms holding on to her legs. She could feel him dribbling all over her. Grunting and stomping her way clear, her high heels hacking into her husband's arms, she backed away to the doorway, holding her hand over her mouth as if damming back a dry retch. Her voice changed to a weird rasping monotone.

'You only get AIDS if you are a homosexual or a drug addict, or if you got it from a blood transfusion before proper screening began. You're not a drug addict, are you, Rex? No, you're not an addict. No. Are you telling me, husband dear, that you are a bisexual, that you sleep with men? That you fuck men and then come home and fuck me. Tell me, tell me, you filthy twisted pervert. You depraved, rotten animal. The children, my children. Oh God in heaven, what am I going to tell my children?' Patricia picked up her glass and threw it at Rex who was curled up in the foetal position on the floor. The antique Georgian glass ricocheted off him and shattered against the marble fireplace.

'David, oh David, where are you?' Rex groaned and slobbered into the carpet as his wife ran upstairs to the bedroom.

26

'You shouldn't have bothered cleaning the place up, Jack,' Peter Welsh said as he walked back into his house. 'Now I won't be able to find anything, thank you very much.' Welsh had recovered well and was pleased to be home.

'The stay in hospital hasn't done you any harm,' Read said. 'I noticed that there were some honeys of nurses there and by the way, if sometimes bad brings good, your new teeth look great. A decided improvement on the old ones.' Welsh gave a cheesy grin for Read's benefit and tapped his front teeth.

'What's the score, Jack, on that animal that did me over?'

'He's vanished, Peter, he just seems to have vanished. The cops reckon he's gone back to Sydney and possibly back to the Philippines where he used to hang out. I'm sure that you won't be seeing him around here again, ever. Good riddance to the scum. I'll be leaving for Sydney in a couple of days. I have to nip down to Collingwood later this afternoon and then I'm taking you to the Clare Castle for dinner. I've put in a new front door and steel security door and changed the locks. Cleared away all that bamboo and crap at the front of the house too. There's the new keys over on your desk. Be back later.'

'Hi, come in. How's things?' Sylvia gave Read a kiss on the cheek as he walked past her into the house. 'Go into the kitchen, Jack, and make yourself a cup of tea or whatever. I'm just cleaning up the bathroom. Won't be a moment.' Read was a bit unhappy about the prospect of leaving Melbourne. He felt good with Sylvia, whether he was just talking to her or fucking her. He could tell that she really liked him and he wanted to keep in touch with her but with him being back in Sydney, there would be a bit of distance between them. Time would tell. Sylvia walked into the kitchen and sat on Read's lap but the bar stool didn't make a good love seat.

'Well, I've packed up and I'm ready to go to see my mother,' she said as she stood up. 'The bus leaves Spencer Street Station in three hours time and I'd like you to give me a lift please, so to fill in time you can fuck me. That's what you want isn't it, Jack, a goodbye fuck? Come on, you can watch me have fun with my vibrator then it'll be your turn.'

'I'm not saying a word, you're the boss,' Read grinned, as he let Sylvia lead him up to the bedroom.

Read had managed to hold back while Sylvia did her thing with the vibrator, now it was his turn. He was inside her and drawing her to him as he stood up. 'Wrap your legs around me real tight, Sylvia,' Read said, breathing hard. 'Now make like a wheelbarrow.' Sylvia stiffened her arms and started to move forward on the palms of her hands. Her breasts were dragging on the floor and getting in the way. She turned her head but couldn't make eye contact with Read from her position.

'This is hard work, Jack, but it's good. God, you're really getting right inside me, that's so good. Keep going.' After a couple of laps around the futon bed, Read took in the situation and started to laugh. 'Come on, Jack,' Sylvia panted, 'this is serious business.' She gripped Read harder around his middle with her thighs and pushed back hard. Read was still laughing as he started to cum.

'No, no, no!' Patricia Jardine pounded the steering wheel of her Volvo so hard that it almost played a tune as she drove through the local storm that had raced in from the south-east over the rolling pastures checkerboarded with hay bales. Familiar landmarks from her childhood days of driving to and from the homestead saluted her as she passed. She had managed to bring herself to ring the doctor whose card her husband had given her. It had been the most humiliating conversation that she had ever had in her life.

Dr Medley had been very understanding but that had not helped one iota.

'Mrs Jardine,' he had said with genuine concern. 'It would be to your benefit if we met as soon as possible. This is not something that we can just have a brief chat about on the telephone, you understand me? I realise how difficult this must be for you, and my chief concern is for your welfare and to ensure that you are properly counselled. Yes, it is vital that you be tested immediately. I will personally collect blood samples from you in the privacy of your own home at a time convenient to yourself.

Mrs Jardine, please try and stay calm. From my experience with other patients, I know how devastating this must be for you but let's look on the good news side of the equation. Case history is full of examples of people in your position who have tested HIV negative where normal, heterosexual ...' the doctor paused, 'non-anal sex was practised. By far, the greater majority of these cases returned negative results. Now let's be positive. Alright, we're going to make an appointment for me to come and see you at your convenience.'

No, no, no! Patricia Jardine yelled as a drenched hare running at full pelt just made it to the other side of the road in front of the speeding Volvo. *No, no, no. I am not going to be tested like some animal. They are not going to do it to me,* she fumed to herself. It was impossible to think about her husband. She looked at the rain gusting over the landscape, dull patches then clear, racing past her. *It's like my life,* she thought and burst into tears, jerking suddenly back into awareness as the slipstream and blasting air horns of a passing semi-trailer running late for Adelaide swept past her.

Looking into the rear vision mirror, Patricia saw a gaunt, pop-eyed stranger. Frightened, she flicked the mirror away, and gritting her teeth and gripping the wheel as if her hands were grafted to it, drove on. A few kilometres from her home town she pulled in to a garage and bought a disposable cigarette lighter.

The tyres crunched on the quartz-chipped driveway up to the Jervis homestead. The building and its well-kept grounds proclaimed

Establishment and lots of money in the bank due to Frank Jervis' shrewd Melbourne real estate deals when Australia stopped riding on the sheep's back. With Frank now dead for fifteen years, his widow Mavis still lived at the home with a full-time housekeeper and nurse. She still had her marbles but was forced to use a motorised wheelchair.

'Hello, Mummy,' Patricia said as she hugged her mother. 'You look lovely. It's been pouring down on the way up but it looks super here.' Her mother nodded.

'Yes, Pitty-Pat. It was raining here earlier but it's blown over. Look at the beautiful rainbow.' Patricia smiled at the use of her childhood nickname. For a moment, she had almost forgotten the reason for her trip home.

'Mummy, I just want to go for a walk and then I'll come back and sit with you and we'll talk about all sorts of things.' Mavis watched her daughter walk away towards the back verandah.

The stables had always been part of Patricia's life. Her father had converted half the hay loft into a bed-sitter with a shower and lavatory on the ground floor, and the young girl and then young woman had lived there during holidays. Friends had often stayed with her, bringing their sleeping bags, trading whispered stories about their sexual encounters and swapping gossip. She ran her hand along the dark, honeyed patina of the cedar handrail of the steps to the loft. The tack room was still kept in a state of polished and waxed disorder, and photos of Patricia on horseback through the years lined the wall.

She found what she wanted in the workshop next to the stables. The four-litre can was near the ride-on mower and the large plastic container was in the old huon pine wardrobe that her father had put there years ago to store odds and sods. Patricia went back into the stables and undressed, leaving her clothes where they fell on the bluestone paving, just outside the lavatory. Her movements became determined and urgent, and her lips worked over tortured thoughts. She tipped all the petrol into the toilet bowl and then sat on its polished wooden seat. Holding the disposable lighter in her right hand, she started to drink from the plastic container.

Organophosphate pesticide splashed into her stomach, immediately sending its deadly message to her major function control centres. The poison took immediate effect, inducing the medically described 'SLUDGE' reaction – Salivate, Lachrymate, Urinate, Defecate, Gastro Enteritis. The lethal combination of her body's dysfunctions forced Patricia's upper legs to contract, lifting her feet off the ground, and gripping her like giant forceps. The searing pain and anguish flooding her nervous system seemed strangely satisfying. It was cleansing her, scouring out the sickness she was sure she now had in her body and she knew that it would soon be all over and she would find peace. She groaned and then screamed as words frothed and bubbled out of her mouth and dribbled down her chin.

'Clean it out, clean the vile stuff out of me. Oh, Mummy, Mummy! Daddy, Daddy! Please help me. Please.' With her scream rising higher, she lowered the flickering cigarette lighter down between her legs into the toilet bowl.

The local nurseryman, who had the contract to maintain the Jervis homestead's grounds, had just turned off his whipper snipper when he heard it – a sudden whump, like a door slamming. He turned and saw the smoke rising from the stables, followed by the spurt of angry flames. He dropped his whipper snipper and ran towards the fire, yelling at the housekeeper who was in the kitchen preparing afternoon tea.

'Jesus, Jesus, oh Jesus. Mrs Watkins, Mrs Watkins, for God's sake, ring the CFA, the stables are on fire. Help, help!' By the time he had reached the stables, all he could do was raise his hands to his face, shielding himself and backing away from the shimmering heat.

The local press and the police were kind to Patricia Jardine. The Toorak–South Yarra set went into mourning as the bitching and jockeying began to find someone to fill her shoes. The *Herald Sun's* headlines were bread-and-butter stuff.

'Minister's socialite wife killed in tragic, historic stable fire,'

Read sat back and read the story. It was so easy to read between the lines. *She killed herself because she found out about her charming husband.*

VRC headquarters were in uproar. Most of the stewards, including the vets, were in the conference room looking down over Queens Road. Bill Fleming, the VRC detective, had the floor and was warming to his task. What was happening here was a lot more exciting than giving arthritic pickpockets and poorly hung flashers a hard time. He moved to the head of the table, cleared his throat and began with a dramatic voice.

'Gentlemen, Jim Griffiths, Clyde Trueman's vet, has topped himself in his Ascot Vale clinic.' He paused to let the message sink in but it was swept aside by the noisy response in the room.

'Come on, come on,' Dusty Rhodes interjected. 'Give Bill a go.' He nodded to the club detective. 'Go on, Bill.' Fleming cleared his throat again and leant forward, his hands placed on the table in front of him.

'The boys from homicide and the racing squad are over at his clinic right now. The media haven't twigged yet but it won't be long before they do. My sources tell me that Griffiths gave himself a fatal injection of etorphine hydrochloride, more commonly known as elephant juice. The vets will be able to tell you all about that. Apparently he must have changed his mind because he was trying to take an antidote when he carked it. He's left a very detailed note, more a document than a note. The stuff in it is apparently mind-boggling. Names of people, names of trainers, names of jockeys, bookies, horses, dates, places. You name it, Griffiths' farewell letter has it all.'

'Jesus,' Rhodes whistled. 'What a way to go. He would have been trying to get some diprenorphine into himself, that's the reversing agent or antidote for etorphine. Bill, it's imperative that we get our hands on a copy of Griffiths' note as soon as possible. We have to move on this today and we'll –'. Rhodes stopped when he noticed that the chief steward had come into the room.

'Sorry, Dusty, keep on going. My phone's been running hot,' the chief steward said, directing his instructions to Rhodes.

'Sit down with these blokes and establish a task force and be prepared to work around the clock until we get this thing sorted out. I'll get a couple of the best shorthand girls from the typing pool to be by your side with a recorder as well. I want every word, everything documented. I'll keep the flow of information going through to the CEO so that he can keep the committee briefed. I don't have to tell you that the media will be crawling all over us like maggots at any moment. They'll be grabbing anyone they can so be on your guard. Let's pray for some huge international incident that may take some of them off on another trail. Good luck, gentlemen.'

'Alright, chaps. You heard the man. Let us pray,' Rhodes said, as the chief steward left the room.

27

Hi, Jack. Hop in. This is Phil Burns. Phil, meet Jack Read from Sydney. Jack and I keep on meeting up with each other at the track and we've had the odd bit of luck, haven't we, Jack?' Ryan winked at Read. The unmarked police car Ryan was driving had pulled in just around the corner from the Lemon Tree Hotel as he had arranged. Read took the front passenger seat and leant across to shake hands with Burns who was sitting behind Ryan.

'Hi, Phil, how do you get to hang out with the big bloke here?' Burns half-smiled and shrugged his shoulders. *Talkative bugger, aren't you,* Read thought.

Ryan drove off through the traffic, looking and speaking straight ahead.

'Jack, as I said, I've got a bonus for you to take back to Sydney with you. I think that you'll be pleased, it'll give you kudos with the insurance company. By the way, when are you going back?'

'Well, Shorty, the big day's late tomorrow, with a bit of luck. Jesus, it feels like I've been here for years, so many things have happened. I just want to get back and start trying to make a quid again. This job down here has fizzed on me big time, what with all the shit happening at Clyde Trueman's stables. You must be up to speed with all that. We've denied the claims on the two horses that died in Trueman's care but they'll most probably end up in court, though with what's all happening now, the owners might decide to chicken out and withdraw their claims, you know, all the bad publicity etcetera. In that case I'll have had a win. Pretty boring stuff for you blokes, I suppose. Anyway, where are we off to Shorty?' Read looked over towards Ryan as they headed north on the Tullamarine Freeway.

'Jack, remember the time you and I followed your mate Ironbar Miller to that house in Moonee Ponds? Well, during the course of our investigations into other matters, that house came under notice. I suppose you know that the house is owned by Clyde Trueman's family company? Well, I found something very interesting in that house and it's sure to be of interest to you too, so that's why I called you, mate. If we piss in each other's pocket, we'll both come out in front. You never know, one day you'll be able to tip me into something, you know what I mean?' Read shifted in his seat as Ryan took the Moreland Road exit off the freeway.

As they pulled into the Ascot Vale Road house, Read tensed. He started thinking about the last time he had been there with Honest Bernie on that night which now seemed eons ago. He looked down at the calendar on his watch. It had been nine days ago. As he opened his door he looked down the road to his left. Two houses away a house was being renovated. A plumber's van was parked in the driveway and a man in a white boiler suit and peaked cap was unloading some PVC pipe from the roof rack. As Ryan opened the front door and ushered Read inside followed by Burns, Read's nostrils twitched.

The underlying smell of laundry bleach got stronger as the three men walked into the upper room that exited into the garage below. *The Truemans must have cleaned up Ironbar's mess,* Read thought, starting to feel uneasy. Perhaps he had been silly when he noticed that Ryan had been very careful where he placed his fingers and hands when unlocking the front door. The sudden blow to the right side of his collar bone told him he hadn't been silly at all. It all happened so quickly. Grunting with pain, Read went down on one knee, holding his right shoulder with his left hand. He turned and tried to stand up but staggered off balance. He had lost all feeling in his right arm.

'What the fuck,' he said angrily, looking at Ryan standing in front of him, holding his service revolver. Burns was standing a little away from Ryan with his hands on his hips. Ryan was looking exasperated.

'Yeah, what the fuck, Jack. You just couldn't leave well alone, could you? You had to stick your fucking treaclebeak into everything that wasn't your business. I thought I'd do the right thing and sweeten you up with that quadrella, hoping you'd be happy as all shit and fuck off back to Sydney where you belong but no, you have to play the private eye. What a fucking arsehole. Who the fuck do you think you are? Humphrey Bogart?' Read's head was spinning. It was obvious that he wasn't going to leave the house alive and, with his arm flopping around, he knew that he couldn't even make a run for it. He didn't even bother trying to work out Ryan's involvement, all he was thinking about was self-preservation. Some feeling was starting to come back into his arm as Ryan continued speaking.

'Our mate Ironbar, your mate and mine, has gone missing, Jack,' Ryan said.

'Someone's cleaned up a lot of blood off the garage floor. Just get a whiff of the bleach in the air. His car is still down there in the garage and he's not back in Sydney. Where the fuck is he? Something happened to him in this house, didn't it? I don't know if you'd have the ticker to take him out, Jack, maybe, maybe not. Anyway, who cares? Now we're going to go for a drive in Ironbar's car. Maybe I should have said ride, just like in those whodunnit private eye books, eh? We'll put these cuffs on you and then we'll be off.' As Read tensed himself for desperate action, he caught sight of movement behind Ryan and Burns.

'You won't be driving anyone anywhere, Shorty. You'll be coming for a drive with me. Just do what you're supposed to do. Take it nice and quietly and no one will get hurt. You know the drill. Take it easy now.' Read recognised the voice and so did Ryan. As Read recalled later, everything seemed to happen in slow motion. Ryan dropped his shoulders and started to turn to face the person behind him. Bang! Bang!

Two shots, one after the other, sent shock waves bouncing around the room. Read fell to the floor, putting his hands over his ears, wondering if he had been hit. Ryan fell in a heap a metre away and looked all over the place, his arms and legs cocked at strange angles. Read looked up and saw Larry Hill standing, slightly crouched forward, with his revolver in the police-instruction-manual, two-handed grip. He was wearing a white boiler suit.

'Hands on your head and down on the floor, Burns,' Larry Hill barked at the other policeman, as he moved Ryan's gun away with his foot. Without warning, Hill stood over the stretched out Burns and fired a shot into the back of his left thigh. Burns screamed and Read jumped with fright.

'You were a prick from the first day you were in the job, Burns. Now shut up or you'll cop another one. You didn't see that, Jack. He was armed and resisting arrest with violence.' Hill leaned down and pulled Burns' revolver out of his shoulder holster and patted him down to his ankles, avoiding the blood now soaking his trousers.

'You can come up now, Ken.' Read looked around as another man in a white boiler suit came up the garage stairs, holding a twelve-gauge, pump-action riot gun at the port-arms position. Hill helped Read to his feet.

'Take it easy, Jack. Take some deep breaths. You're alright. Everything's okay now. How's your arm?'

`Hill started talking into his two-way radio while the other man handcuffed Burns' hands behind his back and applied a tourniquet to his leg with his own belt.

Read went over to the other side of the room and sat down, shaking and rubbing his right arm. His throat was bone dry and scratchy but he made saliva and swallowed.

'I'll be okay, Larry, as soon as I get my breath. I don't think my collar bone is broken but I'm going to have a decent old bruise, believe me. That cunt knows how to hit. When you've got a few spare moments, fill me in on all this, will you? I can see that you're pretty busy at the moment. I'm just a little bit confused. How long have you been a plumber?' Read said, gesturing at the Prompt Plumbing logo on their boiler suits.

'Internal Affairs, Jack. We've been on to Shorty for eighteen months now. It's very heavy stuff, believe me. I'll try and do my best to keep you out of most of this.' Read looked at Ryan who had not moved but was still breathing.

'What's the go with him?' Leaning over Ryan, Hill felt his pulse and gently touched his eyelids.

'He can blink but I don't think that he can do much else.' Hill's two bullets had ripped into Ryan's torso, creating havoc. As Ryan had started to crouch and turn to confront Hill, the first bullet had taken him high in his upper chest and had travelled on, severing his spinal cord. Shorty Ryan could hear the conversation going on around him. He was still shocked at being gunned down by Hill and couldn't fully comprehend what was going on. He knew one thing; he couldn't move a single muscle.

All at once he started sweating in panic as a great feeling of claustrophobia pressed down on him, freezing him to the floor. He could smell something unpleasant but couldn't feel his urine and faeces spilling out into his pants. Read could hear wailing ambulances pulling up outside as another two 'plumbers' entered the room. Taking a moment to speak to the new arrivals, Hill gestured for Read to follow him outside where already a small crowd of local residents were standing outside on the footpath being advised by one of Hill's men. An unmarked police car pulled in to the kerb.

'Take Mr Read to his home, Ralph,' Hill told the driver.

'What about that arm, Jack? Do you want to go and see a doctor first?'

'No, no, Larry, I'll be okay.' Read opened and closed his right hand. 'Most of the numbness has gone, just a bit of pins and needles left.' Hill opened the front passenger door of the car.

'Jack, I'm flat out here but I need to see you before you go back to Sydney. I'll take you somewhere for breakfast tomorrow morning, okay? I'll be in contact.' Read waved as the car pulled out into the traffic and the driver took directions from him. Read was still trying to get himself together as the car headed back into the city.

'What's wrong, Jack? You don't look too hot. What have you been up to?' Peter Welsh asked, as Read walked into the room, still favouring his right arm.

'No, nothing wrong, Peter. I'm okay, everything's fine,' Read replied, sitting in a chair that had stuffing hanging out of it.

'I've just been saying goodbye to a couple of copper mates.'

Jack Read and Larry Hill were sitting in Read's breakfast haunt in Lygon Street.

'I wouldn't have picked him. To me, Shorty was just a big, tough cop who knew his way around but he frightened the shit out me yesterday, believe me. I owe you, Larry. You saved my pathetic life.' Read had lashed out and like a reprieved inmate on death row, he was enjoying his Hollandaise eggs with smoked salmon while Hill made do with a standard bacon, eggs and tomato.

'Jesus, I'm hungry, Larry. It's that back-from-the-grave feeling, the triumph of escaping death for the time being.' Both men laughed briefly then Hill became serious again.

'Jack, Shorty's fucked well and truly. He's a quadraplegic and rooted for all time. I'm not sorry in the least and it makes my job a little easier. I know Shorty inside out. He'll plead guilty to everything he's charged with, including a couple of murders going back years ago and Burns will do likewise. Also there's more than a good chance Burns will drop his guts about what he and Shorty have been up to. He's a weak animal but having a willing arse-licker around suited Shorty. If all this goes according to plan, I'll be able to keep you right out of things, Jack. I can have you treated like a protected witness and more likely than not, you won't be needed to give evidence. You don't need this sort of publicity in your caper.'

'Yeah, spot on, Larry,' Read said, through a mouthful of toast.

'Keep going. I might end up writing a book about this.' Hill laughed. 'We had Shorty under pretty tight surveillance, and you know what? You were on our books too but for different reasons. But even so, you managed to give us the slip a couple of times. Shorty did too. I'm pretty sure though that he wasn't on to us, I'll ask him when he's stabilised. We had his home phone and his mobile tapped and he made a silly mistake when he started to use the same public phones a lot, so we just tapped them all as well. He called your mobile from one of those public phones yesterday morning. The money got to Shorty, that and the punt. He just loved to punt and he loved the track and all that went with it. Then there was his drive for promotion. He had always wanted to be one of the top men in the job. It wasn't normal ambition. It was more like an obsession with him. Now he'll spend the rest of his days in a prison hospital pissing out of a tube in his cock and having the shit scraped out of his arsehole. If he could physically do it, Shorty would neck himself, for sure.

He had contacts with the Sydney mob but always managed to stay a bit of a loner, you know, the outside man. He played ball with Ironbar Miller because it suited him and he got his feelers into the Trueman stables, that way even so, he still kept his distance. As far as I know, he hardly had anything to do with Trueman on a personal level. He had access to the hot tips about what horses were real goers. He must have cursed you when you drew his attention to Ironbar and even got him to help you tail Miller back to the house in Moonee Ponds.' Read thought back to the day at the Moonee Valley races when Ironbar had been talking to one of Victoria's senior magistrates and Ryan had identified Reg Johnson. To not have done so would have attracted Read's suspicion in the real possibility of Read finding out later who Ironbar's racecourse companion was.

'Shorty must have thought I was the original spanner in the works,' Read said, deciding to be a good listener and nothing more. He wasn't going to tell Hill anything that he didn't know already.

Over cappuccinos, Hill wound up his briefing.

'The Racing Squad is being disbanded and will be reformed after we make sure that there's no more of Shorty's rotten apples lying around. My boss is setting up a mini task force to liaise with the VRC and he's already doing that on a personal basis as we speak, with their chief steward and the veterinary surgeons. It's the biggest operation that I've ever been on Jack, believe me.'

'Good on you, Larry,' Read said. 'I'm no expert on police politics but I am a gambling man and I'll bet now that you'll get promotion out of all this and you deserve it, good luck to you.' Hill looked thoughtful for a moment.

'Thanks, Jack. It'd be nice to think that I will but there'll still be a lot of cops out there who'll think that I'm a dog when all this shit hits the fan.' He shrugged his shoulders.

'Well, we've both got things to do. We'll bump into each other again, for sure. A pity we couldn't have met under more pleasant circumstances.' The two men got to their feet and shook hands. Read had taken a couple of paces when Hill spoke. His voice was low but clear and meant only for Read's ears. Read turned back.

'Jack, I hope that you and your mate from Sydney stashed Ironbar away somewhere safe and sound. It'd be a great pity if he popped up again somewhere to haunt us all, wouldn't it?' Read tried not to look stupid as he stood there watching the undercover policeman's retreating back.

28

See what happens when you give a girl proper notice and don't just barge in on her out of the blue?' Ella said as she closed the front door behind Read, offering her cheek for him to kiss.

'I still feel silly about that, Ella. Let me apologise again. Here's something to make you sweeter than you are.' Read handed Ella a bottle of Tasmanian Leatherwood honey.

'Oh thanks, Jack. I'm not just saying this for your benefit but that's my favourite honey, truly. Do you want a cup of tea?' she said as they walked into the kitchen.

'Thanks. White with one sugar; no, ordinary old tea please, not that herbal stuff.' Ella smiled as she dropped a couple of Lipton teabags into a mug.

'Well, Jack, how's your week been?' Read was tempted to tell Ella what had happened to him since he had last seen her but it was all starting to seem so far-fetched even to himself that he gave up on the idea.

'It's been pretty tame, Ella. I should have been back in Sydney a week ago but there were a couple of things that held me up but I'm leaving tonight, that's why I came over to see you and say goodbye. Sorry, not goodbye but au revoir, as they say.' Read couldn't resist being a stickybeak.

'That bloke with the ponytail who drives the Kombi, the one I met when I turned up here without an appointment, what's his go?'

Ella looked at Read hard then smiled. 'Shane's an old boyfriend of mine. We lived together for three years over in Fitzroy but you know how it is. He wanted to get married but I didn't. Anyway, he went off and got married but it lasted only a year, so there you are. He's a great musician. That time you saw him. He'd come over here to fuck me, is that okay with you, Jack?' Ella smiled again. Read felt flushed and horny. Ella pressed on.

'He's got a great cock, Jack, a really big one and he knows how to use it. It's really hard for me to get on top of him but we manage.' She laughed out loud enjoying Read's discomfort. 'It's alright for you, Jack, to call in on some girl and fuck her but it's not alright for an old boyfriend to call in and have sex with me. God, you're such a chauvinist. You don't like it, do you?'

Read felt a strange mix of lust and jealousy and wanted Ella to keep on baiting him. All the drama of the past few weeks and his narrow escape from being murdered by Ryan was rolling over him. He was alive and needed to be reminded of that. And he desperately wanted Ella.

'Oh Jesus, Ella,' Read said, as he took hold of her, kissed her and pulled up her shirt.'

'What do you think of my new bra?' she said, pushing her tongue back into Read's mouth. Read looked down.

'It's great but I love what's in it,' he replied, lifting one breast free and sucking its nipple. Ella jumped up into his arms.

'Come on, Jack, take me into the front room.' Read had undressed and was sitting on the sofa while Ella went through the drapes ritual. She stepped out of her jeans and briefs and knelt in front of Read. As she went down on him, Read massaged her scalp and started feeling dizzy. Sensing his predicament, Ella stood up and mounted him but she gave him the usual warning.

'Don't you dare cum before I do,' she said sternly, bearing down hard on him. Obeying her command, Read tried to think about other things for as long as he could. As the minutes rolled on, Ella began making shrill little yelps and had closed her eyes. Read gritted his teeth and hung on, pulling down on Ella's shoulders. Then it was all over. Taking herself off Read, Ella gave him a lazy wink and got down on her knees again. She was just in time.

As Read drove back to Carlton to pick up his gear, he was feeling strange. It was like he had been told that he was immortal. The time he had just spent with Ella had made him feel like bursting into song. He laughed aloud as he read the fluorescent bumper sticker on the souped-up Holden sedan sitting in front of him waiting for the green light. 'A Blow Job Is Better Than No Job.' *Some of these buggers who make these things up do have a sense of humour,* he chuckled to himself as the lights changed.

The drive up the Hume Highway had been uneventful, even boring, more so because of the few hours sleep Read had spent at a production-line motel that reeked of lemon-gum room freshener and had lavatory seat protectors that looked like doilies. At last, as he pulled up outside the boarding kennels in Parramatta, he started to feel like he was getting back to normal.

'Good afternoon, Mr Read, he's waiting for you.' The woman who looked like a whippet watched Read walk down the row of mesh cages. Bonzo started yelling as soon as he heard Read's voice, Read stepping back in mock horror as the white bull terrier hurled himself at the gate like a Wallaby prop forward in full flight and then bounced back. The kennels exploded in a cacophony of barking and yelping up and down the scale as the other residents took their cue from Bonzo. On the drive back into Sydney, Bonzo was in total control, sitting up in the front passenger seat with his head out the half-open window, sucking in the slipstream and every so often jumping over to lick Read on the face.

Everything was as it should have been at the Balmain house and Read and Bonzo checked out all the little traps set to warn of any intruders. There was a note from Honest Bernie on the kitchen table. *Look in the usual place, big fella.* Read went out into the small backyard and walked over to Bonzo's kennel where the dog slept in summer. Read put his hand inside and up behind the entrance where a piece of six-inch PVC pipe stopped at one end was fixed like a mini-mailbox. There was a small, hefty parcel in it. Read opened the package on the kitchen table and whistled. There was another note from Bernie wrapped around $13,000 in fifties and hundreds. *Jack, I put that $1000 straight out on Ring The Bell with Max O'Brien. I got fourteens and have kept back $2000 as agreed. I am still alive and smoking and looking forward to seeing you, you big kanaka. All the best. Honest.*

Read went to bed after locking Bonzo outside. He had got Bernie to back Trueman's horse in Sydney as he didn't want to be seen betting on the juiced-up horse in Melbourne. Like a lot of people all around Australia, he had made money from a race that was as rigged as much as any race could ever be. He opened a half-finished book on Jaguar E-Type restoration but soon fell asleep.

After Bonzo had pulled him all the way to the Darling Street ferry wharf and back on their early morning walk, Read took up his usual position on the pavement outside Baker's Café. His absence from the local scene had hardly raised comment.

'Haven't seen you or Bonzo around for the last few weeks,' was all he got from Sue Baker. With Bonzo making do as a footrest under the table, Read started on the papers. It was a Melbourne news day. Tim Clarkson, chief racing writer for the Melbourne *Herald Sun*, had hit the journalistic trifecta – the front, back and inside pages of all Murdoch's Australian papers with exclusive stories about the organised doping of horses at Clyde Trueman's stables and the crisis confronting the VRC.

As Read scanned the pages, every second line seemed to be a headline. *VRC in crisis, VRC CEO Tony Briggs QC resigns, Sir Charles Mortimer heads get-tough reform group on VRC committee, top trainer Clyde Trueman and ace apprentice jockey Brent Adams warned off Australia's racetracks for life. Sir Charles Mortimer calls for the ban on the two men to be widened to include all racetracks in the Commonwealth, calls from Victorian MPs for a Royal Commission into racing, spotlight on bookies' betting sheets for ill-*

fated Emirates Conquistador Stakes, Melbourne rails bookmakers have been ordered to meet with betting supervisor and senior police, bent vet had secret needle.

Dr Jim Griffiths, well-known thoroughbred veterinary surgeon and stable vet for disgraced top-end-of-town trainer, Clyde Trueman, had a specially made miniature hypodermic syringe capable of being hidden in the palm of his hand. Using this device, Griffiths was able to inject the miniscule dose of one drop of etorphine or 'elephant juice' required into a horse's jugular vein. He would do this in the horse stalls at the racetrack on race day when the horse was being saddled up in full view of the public.

Griffiths was experimenting for some time with horses in the Trueman stables in order to establish dosage rates for etorphine and two of them died as a result of this activity. Their owners are now considering their legal options against Trueman and the estate of Griffiths. Griffiths, who committed suicide under dramatic circumstances, left an incriminating suicide note which is the subject of ongoing VRC and police inquiries.

VRC chief vet, 'Dusty' Rhodes, announces new screening equipment being flown in from Switzerland to be used to detect the use of the drug etorphine, commonly known among horse dopers as 'elephant juice.'

Read shook his head. The dominoes were falling over everywhere in the Melbourne racing scene. He found himself whistling *Ten green bottles hanging on the wall.* It would take a long time for things to settle down and return to normal. He was relieved to see that he hadn't been mentioned in dispatches anywhere. Another story caught Read's eye. It was headlined with a large photograph of Larry Hill trying not to give his full face to the camera, and below that, a smaller file photograph of Shorty Ryan.

Undercover police task force snares top cop. Operation Trojan Horse conducted extensive phone tapping and surveillance of Sydney crime figures and targeted certain Victorian police for eighteen months, culminating in the dramatic arrest of the head of the Victorian

Racing Squad, Chief Inspector Neil 'Shorty' Ryan. Informed sources say that Ryan was arrested after a dramatic shoot out at a Moonee Ponds residence. He is currently being held under police guard in the Freemasons Hospital where his condition is reported as being critical but stable. To date, no charges have been laid. Detective Senior Constable Phil Burns is also under police guard at the same hospital with a bullet wound to his leg. During a two-hour press conference at police headquarters, Detective Sergeant Larry Hill stated that Sydney crime boss, Joe Silver, who had assumed control of the Sydney mob after gangster George Freeman's natural death, had moved part of his operation to the Melbourne racing scene.

Hill said that the sudden and mysterious disappearance of Silver's partner and enforcer Lou 'Ironbar' Miller had senior police in Sydney and Melbourne fearing the breakout of a bloody gangland war. Miller was a vicious and ruthless killer and standover man, and it would have taken a determined and committed effort to neutralise him,' Detective Hill said. '

It is now certain that he has met with foul play.' Read smiled at Hill's language. He was ready to fold the paper when he saw Rex Jardine's name jump out at him. The story was the epilogue to all the others. A brief, matter-of-fact report announced that Jardine had resigned from his ministry and from parliament. The journalist mentioned the death of Patricia Jardine had occurred in tragic circumstances and said that tragedy had struck the Jardine family for a second time. Rex Jardine was suffering from a terminal form of leukaemia and was going to America for treatment.

'Well, that's the end of that,' Read said aloud as he got to his feet. 'Come on, Bonzo, home we go. See you, Sue. You're still the best omelette maker I know – after me, of course.

It was Friday afternoon and Read was making his way across the Sydney Harbour Bridge. All around him, drivers were gritting their teeth and snarling, some at each other and others just looking ahead grimly and mouthing all sorts of obscenities. Read had educated himself to switch off and go with the flow. He had checked in with

Steele and things were quiet. There were a lot of summonses to be served and the usual run of household burglary claims but nothing exciting. Sweeping off the bridge, Read found himself alone on the road as he drove into Ultimo.

'Jesus Christ, boys, just when you thought it was safe, guess who's turned up like a bad penny?' The Friday afternoon session at Geoff Maggs' panel shop had just kicked off when Read walked into the workshop. He grinned and made a mock bow.

'Alright, boys, take the piss out of me and then settle down. How have you managed to get along without me?' As they launched another round of mock insults at Read, he walked into the storeroom and got himself a stubbie of light out of the Clifton Pugh beer fridge. Read had taken Geoff Maggs along to a Sotheby's auction when he had been chasing an early Margaret Olley painting and on an impulse fuelled by the amber fluid, Maggs had purchased the early model Westinghouse that Pugh had painted. It stood proudly alone on the storeroom floor and was much photographed and written about. A dust-coated Geoff Maggs appeared and pumped Read's hand.

'Bloody good to see you back, Jack. What have you been up to in Melbourne? I see in the papers that there's been a bit of action down there. You weren't stirring things up down there, were you?' Read shrugged his shoulders.

'Nothing to do with me, Maggsie. I was bored shitless most of the time. I'm glad to be back with all my old pisshead mates, and that includes you. Now where is it?' he said, looking around. Maggs pointed to the far side of the shop.

'We've moved it, Jack, it's ready for the spray booth and the oven. It's over here. Follow me.' Maggs made like a drum roll as he lifted the dust cover off the E-Type. 'There you are, Jack, ready for the big finish. There's not a ripple in it. The seats are away being re-upholstered in Hyde leather and we're waiting for that trim kit that you said was on its way from the States.'

'Jesus, Maggsie, it's looking bloody beautiful,' Read said, standing back like someone in an art gallery admiring a masterpiece.

Running his hand over the primed bonnet he whistled. 'You've done an excellent job, Maggsie. It's like glass, it's going to look great when the British Racing Green is on. That trim kit is here in customs. I'll bring it over next week.' Read turned to the other men who had gathered around the E-Type and gestured with his stubbie. 'What do you reckon, fellas?' Everyone cheered and raised their stubbies and glasses, toasting Read and his car.

'By the way, Maggsie,' Read said, taking an envelope out of his jeans pocket. 'Here's something to keep you smiling. Six grand all in nice new grey nurses. It's all there and there's something else.' Read fished in his shirt pocket and looped Joylene's rosary beads around the rear vision mirror of his car. 'That stays where it is,' he said, fingering the beads. 'What's the go, Jack?' Keith Williams, an NRMA loss assessor asked. 'A gutsy young girl I met in Melbourne gave it to me as a good luck charm, and no smart-arsed comments please,' Read said as he replaced the dust cover on the Jag.

'Off to the track tomorrow, Jack?' Maggs asked. Read paused.

'No, Maggsie, I think that I'll give the gee-gees a miss. I know this sounds corny but I'm going to go fishing. A mate of mine, Michael Mundane, has a fly fishing lodge up at Khancoban in the Snowy country and that's where I'll be for a few days. See you blokes later. I've got a hungry dog to feed.' A chorus of 'See you, Jack,' followed Read as he left the workshop.

As he drove away, Read started to feel strange – spurts of elation interspersed with niggles of depression. *Pull yourself together,* he told himself, *or the next thing you know you'll be seeing a counsellor. On second thoughts, maybe not a bad idea if it's a she and a good sort. A lot of people are dead and you're alive, so enjoy it and stop being a dickhead, just stay away from racehorses for a while.* Read started whistling and he was already practising his fly-casting techniques as he pulled up at the local dry cleaners where he had left a bag of his clothes brought up from Melbourne.

'Here you are, Mr Read,' the girl said as she handed Read his dry cleaning in a big zip-up plastic bag. 'And these were in one of your shirt pockets,' she said with a disdainful wrinkle of her nose as she handed Read the cards he had taken from Ironbar's wallet. 'Thanks,' said Read and headed outside. Sitting in his car, he looked at the cards and realised what the girl was on about. One was a jockey's business card but the other one read 'Shangri La – Young Hot Asian Babes 24/7'. His grin faded when he turned the card over to read 'BIG SYD - READ JOB' and a NSW phone number. *Jesus,* he whistled through his teeth as he sat in his car, his mind racing at what this was all about.

Read drove until he found a public phone and dialled the number on the back of the card. 'Go ahead, Steele here', the voice said. Read froze but calmed himself and quietly hung up.

What the fuck? Read stood beside his car, trying to work out what was going on. The events of the past weeks came spinning past and the number he had dialled Steele on was a different one from the usual. So Steele had another phone that Read knew nothing about. When all the action was taking place, Read was trying to get his head around what the go was with Shorty Ryan, Clyde Trueman and Ironbar Miller, as he always had niggling doubts about someone else pulling the strings. Could it be that his long-time mate Steele was the puppet master – but why? Pulling himself together, Read drove slowly back to his house, running through a list of things to do, starting with upgrading the security on his house and car. As he pulled up, Read wondered how he would handle his next meeting with Steele. *'Fuck, here we go again.'*